Just Two Weeks

Just Two Weeks
A Psychological Suspense

Amanda Sington-Williams

Published in 2014 by Golden Sand Books

Golden Sand Books
www.goldensandbooks.com

ISBN 978-1-8491-4535-0

Printed in the UK by Antony Rowe Ltd

Set in Times New Roman

For Dave, my soul mate.

'What's done cannot be undone'.

William Shakespeare

Part 1
The Holiday

1

A drop of cold water landed on Jo's shoulder. She turned on her side in the unfamiliar bed to avoid the slow torturous drip. Force-cooled air was blowing on her face and she looked around at the white cell-like room, at the rust coloured smear on the ceiling, seeing the sun cut through the slats of the balcony door. Where was she? Then she remembered. In Sri Lanka. On holiday. It suddenly hit her. Mark wasn't here. She was alone.

She reached up and switched the air conditioning off, saw a lotus flower drooping beside her, smelt the musty tropical air taking her back to her childhood in cheap hotels where mould spread across the walls and the bed linen stank of other people's stale sweat. Flinging the sheet off, she went across the room to the balcony, felt the blast of heat. Below were lines of sunbeds, browning bodies. Along the shoreline beach boys prowled, looking out for punters.

The phone rang, making her start.

'Hello?'

No answer.

'*Hello.*'

Someone was there, she was sure, someone breathing softly, someone who couldn't muffle the sound of their swallowing. A click and the phone went dead, leaving only a hiss like wind rushing through trees. Could it have been Mark on a bad line?

Leaning forward on the bed, elbows on thighs, she dialled home, listening to the ring, picturing the phone in the slate cottage. It rang and rang. She dialled again, tried his mobile. But it was switched off. Mark must be at work. She imagined him running around wards, ministering to patients while she sunned herself, spending his money when she had no idea how long it would be before she was earning again. But when they booked the holiday how could they have possibly known how much would change? And what was the use in going over that now? Wasn't it time to get on with her first day here?

Through the open door, she could see a terrace with palm trees and a sparkling swimming pool. She made her way down the steps from her room into that haven of peace and tranquillity. A man was leaning over the swimming pool trailing a net across the ripples as if he were catching fish. Two children were chasing each other round the edge of the pool and the man looked up at Jo, revealing a deep ragged scar right along the inside of his arm gleaming white against his dark skin.

'Good morning, ma'am.'

She smiled at him and tried walking faster, hoping he wouldn't notice her limp, trying to hide the pain in her leg made worse by the long flight.

Feeling the man's eyes on her, she walked across the terrace into the bleak, white dining room, passed red plastic chairs and tables, and headed for the buffet bar. There a straggle of guests queued impatiently, batting empty plates on their thighs like angry children. From the window was a view of the swimming pool – 'I *don't want to be a tourist in a huge hotel. I want to travel, go free and easy'* Mark had said when they'd been looking at the website. Ahead of her, a woman was spooning a small portion of scrambled egg onto a plate. She grinned at Jo. She had a glittery blue nose stud, a tanned, small face. Her hands moved rapidly, scooping up a tomato, a quarter slice of fried bread.

'Hi. You just arrived?'

'Last night. Well, this morning.'

'Yeah? It's great here. You on your own?'

4

'Yeah. You?'

'Me? I always travel alone.' The woman moved along the buffet bar, putting little more on her plate. Western pop drifted from the speakers while Jo, not that hungry either, selected a single roll and butter then followed a waiter to a table laid for two. She asked for coffee, glancing up at the woman with the nose stud who was staring at her. Jo smiled, drank her coffee, revelling in the sensation of caffeine hitting her brain and looked out towards the swimming pool, conscious of a strange knotting sensation in her stomach. What was that about? But she shrugged it off as nerves. It was a while since she had been away on her own.

'Shall I join you?' The woman with the stud was standing over her.

'Sure. I'm Jo. How long you been here?' She wanted another coffee and tried to re-engage the waiter's attention.

'Shall I get you some more coffee? I noticed –' she nodded towards Jo's leg.

'Thanks,' she said, glad that Nose-stud hadn't asked how she'd acquired her limp.

The woman returned, slid the cup and saucer across the table, started on her eggs. She suddenly jerked round to face Jo. 'Hey! Do you fancy going to another beach this morning? This one's OK, but I found a brilliant one the other day. I'm Zara, by the way.' Jo brightened. Already she'd found someone to hang out with. Never mind that Zara might not be her type. Everything was different on holiday, and if it didn't work out she could always make excuses on other days. Or would she find they really got on?

'Twenty minutes. In reception. OK?'

'Sounds great.'

Zara began to walk to the door, stopped, swung and returned to the table. 'You know to carry ID with you, don't you? The police are funny about that sort of thing here.'

'Oh, yeah,' Jo said. 'I carry my passport everywhere when I travel.'

Zara moved her chair nearer, leaned towards Jo. 'And I don't really like saying this –it's an Ok hotel and everything, but –'

'But?'

'Things sometimes go missing from the rooms. Money mostly. Thought I'd warn you.'

'Thanks for the hint. Don't the hotel management know?'

Zara laughed and Jo thought how friendly she was. Not everyone would have bothered to warn a new guest about light-fingered staff. 'They say they'll look into it - meaning *mañana* – you know how things are out here.'

She pushed her chair back again. 'See you in reception. We'll have a great time.'

Sweat trickled down Jo's back. The ceiling fan whirred eccentrically, clicking on each rotation. Zara was late. Fifteen minutes late. There was no one else in reception. Outside, the swimming pool shimmered in the sun and Jo decided she'd give Zara five minutes, no more.

Then at last she saw her strolling across the terrace. She looked stunning in a multi-coloured sarong with a sequined peacock embellished on the front and a pink wide-brimmed hat. Jo immediately felt frumpy with her winter-white limbs.

'Come on then,' Zara said. 'Dying for a beer. I'm taking you to a great private beach.' She sauntered out of reception without waiting.

Jo caught up with her at the swimming pool edge. 'Sorry,' she said. 'Can't walk too fast today. Old war wound.' She laughed and remonstrated herself for saying "war wound". Sounded so hackneyed, but the truth was too complicated to bother with now.

Zara slowed and linked Jo's arm. 'We can take a taxi. It's much better there. You know, more restaurants, more going on. Am I walking too fast?'

'No,' said Jo. 'This is fine.' Her bag felt heavy bumping against her hip.

Zara was wearing flip-flops that made a slapping sound as she walked. A woven beach bag was slung over her shoulders and she said, 'Hi,' to the Sri Lankan attendant Jo had seen before at the pool. Yet again Jo sensed his eyes following her as she walked towards the hotel exit.

There was a line of green auto rickshaws outside the hotel and Zara told a driver the name of the place they were going but Jo didn't catch what she said. They wound through heavy traffic, belching buses, trucks, bikes and other mini-taxis. Dust kicked up from the road as they jerked along. Goats and scrawny dogs shared the side of the road with women, some in saris, some in frilled skirts and blouses, and men mostly in jeans and white T-shirts. Smells of vanilla and cinnamon drifted momentarily from a spice shop. The driver beeped his horn and Jo felt a sinking sensation in her stomach, same as she'd felt at breakfast. But hey, what could possibly happen on a beach?

The rickshaw was travelling at high speed and she clung to the side as they veered in and out of traffic.

Next to her, Zara was leaning forward. She wasn't holding on and Jo felt the inexperienced traveller, the scaredy-cat, unable to sink into the excitement of the holiday. Even as a child, travelling round Asia with her mother, she'd never got used to it, had always hankered after the stability of a normal life.

'Where's this beach?' she yelled above the sound of the engine. Dust blew into her mouth. It was at least half an hour since they'd left. Zara was saying something to the driver. Abruptly he veered right, following close behind another dirty bus. They bounced over a rock-strewn road. Stalls of fruit and vegetables lined the street and shoppers zigzagged across the road carrying their plastic baskets.

The driver suddenly swerved left and they were bumping down a narrow road where yellow beach balls, batik sarongs and painted wooden beads dangled from stalls. The driver stopped behind a line of other auto rickshaws, and said, 'Here. OK?'

'I'll get this,' Jo said.

'You're a star. Thanks for that. I'll get the beers in,' Zara said.

Jo paid the driver, heaved her bag across her shoulder, wondering why she'd brought her heavy book, and followed Zara who was walking fast down the street.

'Hey, Zara,' she called. 'Hang on.'

Her new companion waited while Jo caught up. 'Oh sorry, I forgot. Come on then,' She linked Jo's arm in hers. She was hurrying her, dragging Jo along, her bag pulling on her shoulder as she sweated in the dense heat. The glare from the sun was painful. Zara let go and walked on. By the time Jo had found her sunglasses in her crowded bag, Zara was way ahead of her. She hurried to catch up.

'D'you want me to carry your bag?'

'No. I'm fine, thanks.'

Zara shrugged. 'Up to you.'

'Well, OK. That would be great.'

They reached a beach hotel security gate. There was a man in a navy uniform with buttons that glinted in the sunlight. He nodded to Zara and opened the gate.

'Good morning, ma'am,' he said to Zara. He seemed to know her.

They passed through a gleaming hotel lobby with lit up fountains and sparkling chandeliers. It led directly onto a private beach where the sea rolled gently in, nudging the shore, and sunbathers lay stretched out on their plastic loungers. There was Zara ahead of her, turning round, pointing up the beach to one of the cafés perched on the dunes. All she could hear around her were the sounds of the beach: rollers in the distance, birds clacking overhead, the distant drone of jet skis, surf hitting the sand.

She reached the table where Zara was already sitting with a beer bottle and her pink sun hat on the table in front of her, and took a seat opposite. It was a long beach. Busy and noisy. Jo ordered a Campari and soda with two slices of lemon and, glass in hand, took up a relaxed posture, retying her hair into a knot and fastening it with a clip. Wasn't this what she'd always wanted? All those years of envying her friends who took holidays simply to take it easy and get away from it all, acquire a suntan and read, instead of the constant search for a cheap hotel, travelling around on smelly buses where the passengers got off and peed in the road. Hadn't she had enough of all that as a child?

'This is the life,' Zara said. 'Hey, it's good we're staying at the same hotel. I can show you all the best places. This beach is much better than our own hotel's. It's a bit of a dump there.'

'So where you from? Jo asked.

'I'm a free roller. No family. No ties. Just travel.'

'It's just you have a Lancashire accent. I'm from Manchester.'

'Are you? Right.' With finger and thumb she fidgeted with her nose stud, then lit a cigarette.

Jo said nothing. The sun bore down.

'So you're out here alone on holiday, are you?' Zara said and stretched her legs out.

'I was going to come with Mark, my partner. But –'

'Yeah?'

'He's working. He's a nurse and a drummer, a session drummer, you know. He plays when he can – there's an outbreak of 'flu and they're short of nurses –'

'A nurse? *And* musician. Wow. Fancy having a guy like that for a husband. And you left him behind?'

'What?'

Zara was drinking her beer from the bottle; hard, long takes, eyes drilling into her. 'How come he's at home, when you're out here?' She beckoned to the waiter. He'd been standing nearby, looking out for customers. She ordered a second beer for herself, another Campari for Jo.

'It's not as simple as that and we're not married.'

9

'No? I was married once. Bastard. Never again. Not marriage. I'm not into long term relationships. I prefer good sex without ties, know what I mean?' She slammed the nearly empty beer bottle on the table. 'Fancy leaving a talented guy like that behind. Reckon he's with one of those nurses right now.'

'He's not like that.' Jo was beginning to swelter in the sun as the Campari went to her head.

'That's what *you* think,' Zara grinned, making sure the waiter was watching her, straightening her back, pushing her breasts out. She leaned forward a fraction. 'Going in for a swim. Watch this, huh?' and she handed Jo her bag, untied her sarong, ran down to the sea.

Jo watched her go, feeling frustrated at being condemned to inaction. Why hadn't she remained at the spa hotel? The beach there was perfectly adequate. And why had she come on this holiday anyway? Would it have been better to have cancelled it and cut their losses as Mark had suggested?

Zara returned: striding up the beach shaking her hair, waving. She spent some time fussing with make-up, raking her fingers through her short, dyed blonde hair, then finished her beer.

'That was good,' she said and ordered another. 'Thirsty work, enjoying yourself, huh? Sorry I had a go at you before. I'm a bit hung-over. Look, the bar back at our hotel's not bad. Do you fancy a drink later?'

Jo hesitated. 'Yeah, sure – do you know where the loo is?'

'Back there at the hotel.' Zara pointed along the beach.

'Can you look after my bag? It's quite heavy.'

'Sure.'

It took her a while to reach the hotel. There were several lines of white sun beds where bronzed bodies lay nurturing their melanoma, as Mark would say. Birds dived, picking up discarded tit-bits, and an arguing couple passed her. Jo stumbled, watching the hotel draw nearer with every

10

step. She reached the cool interior, found the toilet and walked into the rose-perfumed room. After she'd used the toilet, she splashed her face, took a couple of tissues from the rose-patterned box, sprayed herself all over with flowery cologne.

As she walked across the lobby, a man in uniform approached her. He boasted a clipped moustache which followed the outline of his upper lip. 'Excuse me ma'am. We have a special dinner tonight –'

'I'm not staying here. Sorry.'

'But you are a guest at our hotel?'

'No, but –' She felt her throat tighten.

'This private beach. For guest use only.'

She began to sweat in the air conditioned air. 'I'm with someone.' Why was this happening now?

'For guest use only,' he repeated, pointing to a sign on the wall.

'Sorry if I'm not supposed to be here. I'll get my stuff and go back to where I am staying. OK?' Would he demand the ID she'd left in her bag? She felt nausea rise in her throat.

His mobile rang and he beckoned for her to go out onto the beach, then turned his back to her and walked away. Why had Zara brought her to a place like this?

As she arrived back at the café she saw Zara lounging in the chair, biting her nails. She'd changed into a black sun dress and had saturated herself in a powerful musky perfume.

'I just got told-off for being here. Why did we come here? .It's my first day. I don't need this.'

'Idiots. I'll go and explain. I need the loo anyway'

'I'd rather just go back.'

But Zara had gone already, hurrying down the beach towards the hotel.

Jo sat and waited, watching the sea.

It was so hot sitting in the glare of the sun. The combination of Campari and the journey yesterday were making her sleepy. She closed her eyes, drifted to the chatter of nearby

11

Germans and faded into a reverie, back to another time when she was beach-combing. It was on a beach in Tangier and her mother had been lying a little way away with a muscular man wearing blue shorts. Her mother was topless, the local men stared without embarrassment. They hadn't been interested in Jo's collection of shells.

A shadow fell across the table and the blocking of sunlight woke her – she was back on this beach with the sound of speedboats roaring across the water. The waiter was collecting the empty glasses; he secured the bill under the ashtray. Jo smiled up at him then resumed looking out to sea. The speedboats were silent for a minute, powered further up the coast. She could hear the distant roll of waves and closer, the surf hitting the sand; closer still, the sound of glasses being washed. She stretched. All she wanted was to go back to her room at the spa hotel. She stared into the middle distance, feeling sleepy again. It had been a long time, too long now since Zara had gone. She glanced along the beach. The waiter moved towards the table, clearly anxious that they should pay and move on.

'I'm waiting for the woman who was there.' She pointed to the empty chair opposite.

She removed her sandal and with the toe of her better leg, drew circles in the sand and thought about Mark, imagining him at work, checking patients, rushing round his ward. Was she too trusting? Some of the nurses *were* very attractive. She glanced at her watch. The waiter had returned.

'She said she was going to the toilet, but it's –'

'You want toilet?' He nodded to the back of the café, picked up the bill, handed it to her.

'You've got one *here*? But I thought –' She grabbed her bag and rushed to where he pointed. Her stomach was knotting and she felt sick. Outside the toilet there was a sink with a bent tap, a cracked mirror. She knocked on the door marked WC, went in.

'*Christ*!' she said while she stood in the concrete room with the cracked toilet bowl and the sound of jet skis buzzing through her brain. She reached into her bag and pulled out her towel. There was nothing else. No purse. No passport. Her book dropped to the floor: *A Memory of Loss* splayed in the dirt. She searched in her bag again, turning it inside out, shaking it violently. *Nothing.* Someone began banging on the door.

'Hang on.'

Squatting on her heels, with her fingers she searched each corner of the dank sour smelling room. How could she have let this happen? Her fingers touched cardboard. She picked it up. A discarded menu. Other than sand and dirt there was nothing else on the floor. She picked up her book from the toilet roll where she'd balanced it, and stuffed it back into her bag, opened the door. Back outside she blinked in the sudden light and wove her way through the tables, aware of everyone following her movements with detached curiosity until she reached the table where she'd sat with Zara. Four pairs of seemingly foreign eyes turned to her expectantly.

'Excuse me,' she said. 'Sorry to bother you, but was anything on the table – you know, when you sat down?' She was feeling giddy and was finding it hard to catch her breath. 'I mean, like a passport?'

One of them interpreted for the others and while Jo waited, her breathing laboured with anxiety, they all got up and moved their chairs back. Jo was down on her hands and knees again searching in the sand, though she knew she was wasting her time.

'*Did* you find anything?' she said again.

'There was nothing here when we came. The table was empty and wiped clean.'

'Are you sure?' Jo said, standing up. Her leg was throbbing.

Someone was tapping Jo insistently on the shoulder. 'Your bill, ma'am.' The waiter shoved a till print-out into her hand.

Sweat was soaking her T-shirt and suddenly she was incredibly thirsty. A sea bird hopped to her feet, pecked at the sand and flew off. 'I'm sorry,' she said. 'I've had everything stolen, all my money, credit cards – and my passport. I was with someone, the woman who was sitting with me. I didn't know her. I only met her this morning. She's staying at the same hotel as me. And she's taken everything.'

'Your bill. You pay,' the waiter said.

'I'll come back and pay it. My money's been stolen. Can't you understand?' Her thirst was becoming unbearable and she could feel a pulse in her temple. Beyond the café the sea rolled in while out of the corner of her eye, she saw a man drag a boat up the beach. He was tanned and lean like Mark. An official looking man had joined them, taller with a smooth baby face wearing a suit. 'Is there a problem?' he said to her.

She tried to explain again. The suited man put his hand up indicating for her to be quiet and, in Singhalese, spoke sharply to the waiter who thrust the bill into the other man's hand and stood sulkily behind the till on the counter.

'I am sorry ma'am. He is new. I am the café manager.' He held his hand out to her and smiled reassuringly. 'What is your room number?'

For a minute, Jo thought she'd been saved. This man understood her dilemma. No sooner had she felt a wave of relief than she realised the mistake the man had made. If she gave him her room number at the spa hotel would the manager let her go, happy to have had the chance to have a go at one of his staff?

He was looking at her, his smile slipping. '*Madam*? We can add the bill to your room number.'

Her tongue was sticking to the roof of her mouth and her throat was sore with dryness. The bill couldn't amount to much. She'd try the reasonable approach, get his sympathy. Maybe that would work.

'I'm sorry. I'm not actually a guest at this hotel.' She was aware of the man frowning, creasing his worry-free brow and reaching into his inside pocket. 'But I am a guest at The Green Spa Hotel, as I said. I have an injury to my leg you see, and I hoped a massage there would help me.' She patted the

14

top of her right leg as if he needed a demonstration of where the pain was. 'I fell from a window.' She was gabbling, her head spinning. 'You'll get your bloody money.' Her hand flew to her mouth. She shouldn't have raised her voice or said *bloody*. They were both mistakes.

He was looking at her sternly, and she noticed the waiter staring at her open-mouthed, then the manager was speaking to someone on his phone, thumbing through his paperwork.

Turning round, she looked across the café towards the four people who were sitting at the table where, not thirty minutes ago, she'd sat with Zara. It seemed that apart from them the café had been abandoned.

'Can you lend me some money so I can pay my bill? Please? I'll give you the name of the hotel where I'm staying,' she called to the woman who spoke English. She delved into her bag, but of course her wallet had gone and inside the wallet was the Green Spa Hotel's phone number and address. 'It's the Green Spa Hotel. Room 11. I'll pay you back, honestly. I'll pay you double. I've been robbed. Now I haven't got a penny.'

But they were getting up from their chairs. 'You best talk to management, *fräulein*. I'm sure they'll help you sort it all out,' the volunteer interpreter muttered uncomfortably, sidling past her with her three friends to the counter, paying their own bill and leaving Jo alone to battle it out.

Screeches of laughter came up from the beach below and she saw a gaggle of women tossing a yellow and blue ball between them. She quickly made a decision. They couldn't keep her here. She was a guest in their country and had done nothing wrong.

'Look, I've told you where I'm staying. I've explained the situation. I am now going back to my hotel. I will pay you later in the week when I get some money sent over.'

She turned towards the long beach, to the hotel in the distance shimmering in the heat. Could she even find her way back to the Green Spa hotel? The journey here had taken nearly an hour. Maybe she would collapse from dehydration in the street. No identity. A wandering woman in a foreign country. She'd have to resort to begging, sleeping rough. She was panicking now. There'd been hundreds of lost Westerners in India. As a child, she'd seen them staring vacantly into space. Would she become like that? She stepped beyond the threshold of the café. A uniformed man on the beach was heading her way. As soon as he was standing in front of her, she recognised him as the man who'd told her off for using the hotel toilet.

'Miss Carr,' he said. 'You come back to our hotel.'

'How do you know my name?'

'I speak with Green Spa Hotel where you stay.'

With the hot sun blinding her, while sweat poured down her back, she tried to explain again.

'You come with me, ma'am. It is best.'

What choice did she have? She followed behind the uniformed man, trying to keep up with him, struggling across the lumpy sand while the sun worshippers followed her path disinterestedly with shaded eyes. With every step her leg ached more as she swallowed repeatedly, trying to muster up saliva to wet the inside of her mouth.

The hotel lobby gave out an aura of sheer extravagance. Beneath her sandals the marble floor shone under the chandeliers. The fountains spouted luxuriously. What would she give to dive into one? Three receptionists in orange saris and cream sashes stared at her as she left a trail of sand behind each step she took. The uniformed man was opening a door to a small side room.

'You wait in here.'

'This is ridiculous. How much was the bill?'

'Please, you sit and wait.' He closed the door behind him and left her there in that cramped space with only a desk and two chairs. It was painted beige and there were no windows, no air conditioning, no fan. Mildew crept down the walls and it reeked of sweaty men, tobacco smoke. But surely they hadn't locked the door? She turned the handle and opened it only to see a different man in uniform sitting in a chair cleaning his nails. He stood up. Was he going to force her back into the room?

'Wait,' he said.

'You can't imprison me here.'

'Wait.' He pointed into the room.

'For Chrissake, this is *absurd*!' She was shaking as he shepherded her back into the room and closed the door. She laid her head on the desk, closed her eyes, aware that she should stay alert, hold her ground. Images of imprisonment without trial – *torture* even – flitted across her mind and her heart began to race. But for an unpaid *café* bill: a few lousy rupees? She tried the door. This time it *was* locked. From outside the room came the sound of two men arguing. She couldn't understand a word and hammered on the door. What were they scheming? The door opened and she was alone in the room with the moustached man.

Keeping his eyes fixed on her, he moved in closer to her. 'On holiday alone, are you?'

'What is to you?'

'It is dangerous, pretty girl like you on her own. A lot of bad men in this country.'

Panic rose from her gullet. What did he intend to do to her? But she would not show her fear. Instead she began to get up from her chair. Quickly he rose and was soon round to her side of the table forcing her back down with his hand on her shoulder.

'Please, sit.'

'If you touch me again I'll scream.'

He was smirking as he placed a piece of paper on the desk in front of her and pointed to the bottom of the page with his forefinger. There were several lines of type. She didn't understand a word.

'You sign here, stupid girl,' he said and sat back in his chair, the whole time looking directly at her breasts.

She turned her body sideways, away from him. 'I don't know what it says.'

17

'You no pay. You sign,' he said. 'Your friend Raquel say she left you the money for bill, but you not pay.'

What was he talking about?

'Who is Raquel?'

'You sign here,' he said again.

'I need to know what I'm signing.' She *would* not allow him to bully her.

'That you pay bill before you leave our country. For now your hotel will pay and you pay them.'

'Christ, what a fuss over a handful of rupees,' she said under her breath and signed her name at the bottom of the page. Her prerogative now was to get out of here. 'I don't know anyone called Raquel and no one gave me any money to pay the bill. Just for the record. Can I go now?'

He indicated for her to leave then stayed close behind as she rushed past the fountains, past three cream leather sofas and several gilt tables with their onyx statues of naked women.

Out through the gate and onto the street.

2

Vehicles drove past Jo at speed as she stumbled along the stony road. The sun was blisteringly hot and her face flushed fiercely in the heat. Sleeping dogs sprawled across broken slabs, mixed odours of spices, fish, diesel oil filled the air. All she could think of was getting back to the Green Spa Hotel, the safety of her room.

She hurried between rumbling buses, fumes belching from rusted exhausts. Scooters drove round her, sounding their horn, so close they almost touched her, and sweat dripped from every pore. All the time Jo's eyes ached from looking for Zara, though she suspected she must be back at the hotel by now. Did she really think she'd get away with a theft like that? She walked as fast as she could. Hungry, thirsty, she followed the road, stopping and asking, desperately wanting all this to be a bad dream, searching each white face, just in case it was Zara.

She finally arrived at her hotel, and headed for the reception, aware of the pool man's eyes following her as she limped past. Making her way round the edge of the pool where four tanned bodies lay face down on sunbeds, she faltered under a palm tree for a moment of relief. High in the trees, birds chattered while the water gently rippled in the breeze.

In reception, she stood beneath the whirring fan, bedraggled and weary. She rang the bell, waited and stilled her breathing. A man, a slim Sri-Lankan with oiled hair stepped from the office behind. He smiled.

'Ah, good afternoon ma'am. We pay café bill for you. You no worry. We put it on your account. No need to return there.'

'Thanks,' she said, wondering if he knew the man at the other hotel, shuddering as she remembered him gloating at her breasts. 'But you know I was robbed by one of your guests, don't you? Did they tell you that?' She pushed her hair from her brow. 'Do you know where I can find Zara?' Her voice was harsher than she intended, she'd planned firm politeness. 'I must talk to her. Can you give me her room number?'

The receptionist moved his finger down the ledger on the desk. 'Zara? Sorry. Who is Zara?'

She leant over his giant ledger and said very slowly to be sure he'd understand. 'Zara. She's the woman who took my money and passport.' Pointing to the side of her nose, she said, 'She has a blue stud. And short blonde hair.'

Suddenly, he looked happy. 'Ah, *Raquel*? You mean Raquel?'

'She told me her name was Zara. From England. I met her at breakfast – Zara. Definitely Zara.' Yet hadn't the man in the cafe *also* told her someone called Raquel had given her money for the bill?

'Sorry, ma'am.' He touched the furrow between his eyebrows, put his head on one side. 'She return half an hour ago. Then she take her bags and check out. She not here.' He hesitated. 'Not Zara, madam – Raquel.'

'She's gone? Are you sure?' The room began to turn. Gripping the desk to steady herself, she leaned forward. 'Please check again.'

The man glanced at his large ledger. He didn't believe her. She could see it in his eyes, the careful withdrawal of expression, the direct quick gaze, then the look away. An explanation, she thought, then he'll understand. So she told him about the café on the beach, her visit to the café toilet, the realisation hitting her like a brick.

20

He cleared his throat, daintily raising a polite fist to his mouth. 'Have you checked your room? Perhaps you find the things you are missing there.'

She tried again, talking slowly, keeping herself calm. 'But *I* paid for the taxi. So I had my money when we arrived there.' She was thinking: the woman's probably long gone, sitting on a plane right now, drinking champagne, feeling satisfied: a job well done. How had she allowed this to happen? She began to panic again.

'I have to tell someone. You know, someone official. The police. The Consul. Stealing a passport is serious. Can you help me with that?'

He stared down at the huge book lying open on the desk, as if seeking inspiration from the list of names. 'Best you check your room, madam.' He hesitated. 'Raquel. English. Like you?'

'Assuming your Raquel is Zara. Yes,' she confirmed shortly. She was about to say that all English aren't honest, that thieves exist there too. But she decided to say nothing, Careful to hide her anger she turned, preparing to leave the reception.

'Madam, one minute please.'

She swung back. 'Yes?'

He handed her an envelope. Her name was scrawled on the front.

'What's this? Who left it?' she said, ripping the envelope open. Fragments of paper fell from the packet, torn pieces of a photo of Mark.

Her Mark.

He'd given it to her in the airport. '*In case you forget what I look like,*' he'd joked as he'd slipped it into her wallet.

A cold shiver snaked up her spine.

'It was left on the counter, ma'am. I am not sure who it is from.'

Jo's hands were shaking as she salvaged all the pieces of the photo and replaced them in the envelope. The receptionist vanished into the office and she heard the murmur of voices. In a daze, she left. And, exactly as before, the pool attendant with the scarred arm was watching her every move while she stepped across the paving, made her way round the sun beds, back up the steps to her room on the first floor.

The room had been cleaned, her bed made with a folded white towel placed on the red cover. She sat on the bed and turned the envelope over and over: *Jo. Room 11*. The handwriting was large and childish and an aroma of powerful perfume drifted from the paper. She stared at the blue Biro ink, her stomach churning again. She looked around the room, feeling as if she were being watched and opened the door to check outside. There was no one there. She thought of Zara's smile, the ease with which she'd ordered three beers for herself knowing Jo would be called upon to pay. Did she plan to steal her identity? Was that behind the theft? But why would Zara rip up a photo of Mark? *You've got a husband and you leave him at home?*' She'd claimed to be a loner: was she so jealous of Jo's steady relationship that she'd felt compelled to destroy the photo? Was he safe? Urgently she dialled home listening to the British ringing tone, feeling comforted by the familiar sound. No reply. No answerphone on. Was this entire episode some kind of punishment for wishing to spend some time on her own while Mark overworked at the hospital and his father lay sick and helpless in his bungalow?

She emptied the contents of her suitcase onto the floor. Just in case. Definitely no passport or blue leather wallet. Nothing except a change of clothes. Why was the hotel being so unhelpful? It was as if Jo were the perpetrator and Zara the victim.

She found the number for her credit cards which she'd thankfully written at the back of her diary and cancelled them. Zara, it seemed, had not tried to use them. Five minutes to take a rest, sort her head out, then she'd phone the authorities here.

She put the fan on, lay down on the bed, switched her iPod to Billie Holiday and tried to escape the day. Gradually

22

her mind closed down as the music took over and she drifted into a restless, dreamless state. Until a sound from outside, a child yelping, jerked her back to the room. Another track started up and she lay on the bed staring up at the ceiling, the fan rotating round and round, the gecko still on the wall near the bathroom, the sun peeping through the blind, the wardrobe and chair where her jeans and angora sweater had been dumped while Billy Holiday sang the Blues. She wished she'd listened to Mark. Why hadn't she agreed to cancel this holiday?

She re-dialled home. But the phone rang and rang again. She remembered the day in September, the day she'd got the e-mail at work explaining about a cost cutting exercise, reduced budgets and that her job, her department was being amalgamated into another team. She'd wanted a shoulder to cry on but Mark hadn't been home on that occasion either. Her rage had reached boiling point. She'd sat in their burgundy living room, cup of coffee growing cold, waiting for him to return. She'd felt chilled to the bone that time, even though the heating was full on, creaking and burbling despite the sky yawning clear blue and the trees stunning in their golden hues. There'd been another emergency at the hospital. There always was.

She took a slug from the water bottle and walked to the reception. The same man was still behind the desk. He was doing nothing. Staring into space. A crowd of German tourists were gathered in a knot. The men slapped each other on the shoulders and the women were comparing tans.

'Ah, hello, ma'am. You find your passport?' the receptionist said.

'No. I need to tell the police.'

He flicked his eyes to the side. 'They are closed today, ma'am.'

'The police are *closed*?'

'Yes, madam. Holiday. Full moon.'

'The police don't work because it's a full *moon*?'

'It is Buddhist holiday.'

23

How could she forget? Full Moon parties were a childhood favourite. 'What about the consul. The British Consul?'

'You have telephone number?'

'I thought you might. Or maybe they don't work on a full moon either?' she said and wiped her forehead.

'You wait,' he said. 'Please sit.' And he vanished back into the office.

She wandered out to the pool and stared into the water, then up at the array of rooms, at the striped blue and white hotel towels hanging out to dry on balconies. It was too hot to stand in the glare of the sun so she dragged a sunbed into the shade of the palm tree, perched herself on the edge, watching the pool man hurry across towards her. She heard voices coming from a ground floor room. A couple stood in the doorway, cases at the ready. They waved to her. 'Have a good holiday,' the woman called out and the man nodded his head, waved, smiled.

'Shall I move you more into the shade, ma'am?' the pool man asked.

'It's fine. Don't worry. I'm waiting for the receptionist. And it's Jo. My name's Jo.'

'You are from?'

'England.'

'Ah, like your friend, Raquel?'

'She was no friend. She stole my passport and money,' she said. 'It was her idea to show me this great beach. Better than this one, she said and I believed her. I was tricked.'

Hand stroking his chin, he studied her for a moment but made no comment. Maybe he was embarrassed by her anger, perhaps his English wasn't good enough to understand. Not his fault a guest of the hotel was also a thief.

'This beach very good, ma'am,' he suddenly said.

'Did you know her?'

'Who, ma'am?'

Was he being deliberately obtuse?

'*Raquel*. Did you get to know her? And call me Jo. Please.'

'She was here for two weeks. Swimming every day.'

Why had she called herself Zara? 'I'm going back to reception,' she said watching as the man looked at her, his head nodding and shaking.

'I am sorry, ma'am,' he said.

'*Jo*.'

'I am sad that she was bad to you, Jo.'

She paused, taking in his smooth skin and wide eyes, the long nose. 'Not your fault, but thanks.'

He brightened. 'Maybe you would like to visit Buddhist temple at 5 o'clock. Special festival. Full Moon. I take other guests. I drive mini-bus.'

'I must sort out my passport.'

'Maybe tomorrow is a better day for you? Festival is two days.'

'A visit to the temple might be a good idea. I'll see.' She headed back to reception from where a phone was ringing and ringing and she hurried, hoping it was Mark. She had to speak to him.

In the reception two children were bouncing on the sofa. They spoke to her in German, but she was in no mood to let on that she understood the gist of what they were saying. She guessed the boy was about eight and the girl was younger.

'Sorry. Don't speak German,' she said.

'We're springs,' the girl said. In excellent English.

'Great,' she muttered, defeated. 'That's great.'

'Can you be a spring?' her brother said.

'Not at the moment. Not feeling springy. Sorry.'

She stood there in the reception, waiting for the man to finish his conversation on the phone. There was a musty smell in there like the room she'd been put in earlier. She felt sick. The receptionist was talking in the local language, shouting down the phone while he patted down his oily hair. The two children were up close to her now, chatting to each other in

25

their mother-tongue, panting with delight, foreheads shiny in the heat. Each grabbed one of her hands. She wondered where their parents were.

'You sit there.' They were pulling her now. 'You sit there, so we can be springs round you.'

Allowing herself to be led across the terracotta tiles to the sofa, she took a backward look at the receptionist who was still on the phone. Briefly, he looked up, put his hand up, palm facing her and finished the phone call.

'Madam,' he called. 'I have the phone number of the British Consul.'

'Why've you got a funny leg?' the boy asked.

'That's my secret.'

'That's a *stupid* secret.' He started to bounce on the sofa again, spinning round when he landed so she had little choice but to sit between them, waiting until they had finished their game. Besides she was too tired to protest.

It took a long time to get through to the Consul. The line was busy. Maybe they'd taken the phone off the hook, tired of British tourists getting into trouble. Or, perhaps they had decided to honour the Buddhist holiday and close for Full Moon too. Meanwhile the two children were taking it in turns to try and yank Jo back to the sofa. Pretending to be cockerels now. One day, she always said, she would have children but she'd kept putting it off, was worried about the kind of mother she'd be, wary of making the same mistakes as her own mother. Like mother, like daughter: ending up on her own.

And these two weren't doing much to change her view.

The children had launched on a screaming competition, seeing who could reach the highest pitch. The receptionist ignored them, carried on filling in his ledger. A droplet of sweat from Jo's chin dripped onto his page whereupon one Biro word fuzzed into a spidery wet blob. She stepped back apologetically, but the man merely glanced up, smiled wryly and carried on. It was noisy and stuffy in there with the children yelling and her standing there, leaning against the reception, just out of range of the desk fan's flow, with her leg hurting and her eyes wanting to drop closed. Outside, the sun was beginning to set, her first day wasted.

No – her first day an unmitigated *disaster*. And it hadn't ended yet.

3

She got through to the Consul's ringing tone and waited. The receptionist looked busy, turning the pages of his giant ledger. His hair glistened with newly applied oil.

'Can you tell me Raquel's second name?'

He smiled at her, put his hands on the ledger, palms down. 'We are very sorry for you. It is difficult for us all to believe – a terrible thing.' With his forefinger he ran down the list of names in his ledger.

'Here it is, ma'am. Miss Raquel from the UK.' He put the tips of his fingers together making a steeple as he continued to look down the columns of the register.

'So there's no family name? She just called herself Miss Raquel?'

He snapped the ledger shut. 'Excuse me.' He disappeared into the office and she heard him talk to a woman in Singhalese.

No one had answered the phone. The receptionist returned.

'Sorry, madam. It is against hotel policy to reveal information about a guest who has checked out.' He put his fist to his mouth. 'I am very sorry I am not permitted to give personal information about Miss Raquel.' He lifted the flap on the reception, walked to meet another hotel guest who'd just arrived back.

'Welcome, madam. Was your shopping trip successful?'

'Hang on,' Jo said. 'I haven't finished. What am I supposed to tell the police if you're not *permitted* to give me Ms Raquel's surname?'

'One minute, madam.'

The other guest was holding up several plastic carrier bags and Jo watched her take out little parcels, begin to unwrap one while the receptionist looked on delighted, clapping his hands while the children tugged on her skirt. There was a man's voice at the other end of the phone. The consul had answered at last. Jo turned away from the scene. Missing out the visit to the toilet, she told him her story, decided not to mention that she'd voluntarily left her bag in the care of a woman she'd only just met. Not necessary that he knew all the details. Does the consul lend money, she asked. She had none, she explained. Not even a credit card; they'd been in her wallet too.

'You have to go to the police first,' the voice on the line said. 'They will record the crime and give you a form. Do you have a pen and I'll give you the details?'

'Apparently the police are closed today. And I don't know her second name. The hotel say they won't – can't –give me it.'

There was a brief silence and Jo sensed him take a sip of something. 'Do you have travel insurance?' He sounded tired of dealing with inadequate tourists. She imagined him leaning back in his chair, holding a cup of coffee aloft.

'I didn't get round to it.' It was too complicated to explain.

'We advise tourists to take out travel insurance.'

The girl was having a tantrum, screaming that her mother had bought the wrong thing ...what was that on the terrace? She glimpsed a glittering peacock, a slip of a multi-coloured sarong in the distance and dropped the phone, left it dangling from its cord, hanging there with the man repeating hello. As the voice vanished, the phone banged against the desk. For the briefest of seconds she looked towards the yelling child, turned back to the pool, but the woman in the multi-coloured sarong had disappeared. Was it a hallucination brought on by the heat? But then she was there again showing clearly through the glass door. She was at the far end of the pool, the colours of her sarong showing bright amongst the palms. The reception area was cluttered, and there were obstacles between the desk and the door – a chair and a plant. The receptionist, the mother, and two children were staring open mouthed, and dimly she registered the girl telling her mother that Jo had a secret. Reaching the door she grabbed the handle in the plate glass and pulled. From there she searched the pool area, up through the palms, higher still, the balconies set in a semi-circle round the swimming pool. The woman had gone again. It was so hot out there, the heat bouncing off her head. Behind her she heard the door open and the children were running towards her.

The girl grabbed her hand. 'We're going to the beach.'

'Excuse us, children can be such nuisances,' the mother said to Jo. Her hair was sun-bleached and fell in wispy curls to her shoulders.

The mother took hold of the girl's other hand, moved away down the side of the pool. The water shimmered in the sunlight. A palm creaked, fronds moving, settling. Jo walked round with eyes narrowed against the glare, searching for Zara. But there was no one there, no one except three sun bathers lying on their backs in black bikinis, eyes vacant behind silvered shades, and the man with the scar on his arm standing behind a pile of towels in a thatched shelter.

'I thought I saw Zara – *Raquel*!' she called out. 'Did you see her?' She walked towards him. 'Did you *see* her?'

'But Raquel checked out, ma'am.'

She closed her eyes and took deep breaths. After the accident she'd had panic attacks. It was a natural reaction to falling out of a window, a therapist assured her.

There'd been a couple of therapy sessions where she'd tried to work through her fear and it was a while since she'd had a full-blown attack. The few she'd had didn't appear to be linked to falling from a window – they arrived from nowhere and always took her by surprise. The window 'thing' apparently transferred, so the therapist had said. As she scanned the balconies, trying to see beyond each open door, she felt her heart working overtime, her pulse racing and a cold sweat drenching her body. 'Breathe – breathe.' She couldn't do it. 'Breathe', she told herself. Dizziness swept through her and she felt as if she was going to pass out.

'You not look well. You sit.' The pool man hurriedly brought a chair.

She flopped down and inhaled deeply again, focusing on her breathing like she'd been taught. Nearby, in a tree, birds chattered. She looked up and saw a flash of blue and red fly from the tree.

'Thank you for getting this.' She tapped the side of the chair

'I will get you water. Please sit and wait, ma'am.' He brushed down her chair using a towel while holding the scarred arm behind his back.

'I was in the middle of a phone call –'

But he was gone. And she was glad to rest her leg, hoped the panic attack wouldn't return. Sometimes she used to have three in close succession. She closed her eyes again. Someone was in the pool and she listened to the splashes as the swimmer's arms hit the surface. A vagrant breeze stirred a palm tree, making the fronds squeak like a rusty sign in the wind. It was cooler there under the thatched roof.

She wanted to go back in time and change it all.

There were footsteps approaching. The man with the scar handed her a glass of water, the ice clinked on the side as she lifted it to her lips. She drank fast, feeling the pain of the ice cold against her parched mouth. It was a glorious sensation and she felt better immediately.

'Thank you, but I must phone home,' she said. She handed him the glass and realised that he was observing her closely.

Then he turned away and slowly began to fold towels.

Back in her room she looked round and saw it was as she'd left it. But there was something different, a sensation she was aware of.

'Who's there?'

Silence.

Then she saw the door to her tiny balcony was ajar. But she'd closed it before, hadn't she? Stepping out onto the concrete floor, she looked out at the sea in the distance, at the path below from whence laughter came and at the beach in the middle distance where sunbathers lounged. She walked back across the room. With trembling fingers she opened the apartment door fully.

There was nothing except for the sound of chatter from the poolside.

'Has anyone been in my room?' she asked the receptionist when he picked up the phone.

'Cleaners, madam –'

'Since then?'

'Do you have problem?'

She paused. 'No. Doesn't matter.'

She got through to Mark on the second ring. At first she was angry. Standing on the red mat by the bed, she yelled down the phone at him.

'I've been *trying* to get hold of you. Where have you *been*? I thought something had happened –'

'Hang on. Why are you shouting at me? I phoned you earlier. Didn't you get the message?'

She took a breath and sat on the edge of the bed. 'I didn't get a message,' she said and switched the phone to the other hand. 'My passport, cards and cash have all been stolen, Mark.'

She told him everything. Except about being locked in a tiny room with that disgusting man. That could wait. He listened without interrupting.

'So, I haven't got any money. Can you send me some to the Western Union bank next to the hotel?' It struck her then that they wouldn't hand it over without sight of her passport. But that was for later: her next idyllic holiday hurdle.

'You've lost *everything*?'

'Stolen. Not lost.' She glanced back at the balcony door. 'I wish I'd never come here.'

She heard him sigh. Was he pointedly underlining how he'd tried to dissuade her from doing just that?

'Did you tell the police?'

'Have done,' she said. It wasn't such a huge lie. She stared at the phone on the cheap Melamine bedside table, at the peeling label stuck on with Cellotape, the list of numbers: Laundry, Reception, Restaurant.

'I met her at breakfast, you know, this Zara woman, the one who robbed me. And I thought she was OK. She was really friendly. I bet she thought I'd be easy prey: you know, because I can't run? She's gone now, checked out.'

She hesitated then, thinking back to the glittery peacock on the far side of the swimming pool. 'But it's horrible, Mark because she left an envelope with reception. She'd torn up your picture. Why the hell would she do that?'

The line went silent for a moment. Until, 'Really? Are you sure?'

'Of *course* I'm bloody sure! I'll keep it and show you if you like.' She paused and took a deep breath.

'Apparently her real name is Raquel. She's got this blue nose stud. It has to be the same person. *And* they say they're not allowed to give me her second name. Something to do with hotel policy.'

'That's helpful of them.' She heard him tapping on the phone. He always did that. *Tap, tap.* As if perpetually playing his drums, while in the background there was the chatter of conversation from the radio. If she told him about the open balcony he'd say she must have left it open or it was the wind. But she clearly remembered closing it and there was not an inch of movement in the air.

'Mark? You still there?'

'Of course I'm here.' His voice trailed.

'To be honest, I feel like jumping on the next plane back. But I can't even do that, can I? Not without a passport.'

'Once you've got yourself some kind of travel document, you won't want to. Try and forget the entire event. The consul will supply that, won't they? Then enjoy the rest of your holiday. I'll get some money to you right now. I'll transfer it to the bank. You're only there for a fortnight.'

'Oh...I really miss you –'

'Me, you too.'

'How are you?'

'Busy. Going to visit Dad a lot.'

'Is he worse?'

'Yeah, he's quite bad.'

'Sorry. Give him my love .'

'Got to go now,' he said abruptly. 'Already late for work.'

Then he was gone, the connection broken, and she wondered about his father. Mark liked looking after people. It gave him a sense of purpose. Now he was thousands of miles away, working overtime as well as caring for his sick father.

In the bathroom she splashed her face with cold water. There was a trail of ants gathering around a blob of toothpaste. For a second or two she watched them and thought about the ripped photo of Mark. Why would someone do that? The bathroom was white with a drifting aroma of mould. A mirror, which took up the entire wall above the washbasin, was lit by a fluorescent tube and distorted the reflection of her face.

The toothpaste was black, now. Submerged by ants.

Getting through to the consul for a second time was easy but she curtailed the conversation as abruptly as she could, then lay on her bed. Soon she was asleep. In her dream she was in a room with bars on the single window from which she could see circling vultures. There was someone else there, but she couldn't see who. Only their shadow across the concrete floor was visible and there was a powerful smell of musky perfume.

Someone was shouting at her but she couldn't understand what they were saying.

A cold wind blew from the window and she woke. The air conditioning was on full blast. She turned it off. It was dark outside and the only sound was waves beating on the shore.

Lying awake listening to the ebb and flow, watching the dawn sneak through the window, the image from her dream returned: the vultures so close she could see into their soulless, glittering eyes.

At breakfast she selected a table in the corner away from the other guests. She had no wish to befriend someone else. It was best to spend the holiday in her own company. Hadn't that been the plan? But then the restaurant filled up and a couple sat at her table. Both of their plates were laden high with English breakfasts. She groaned inwardly.

'Good holiday?' the woman asked.

On second thoughts, they looked OK. 'Yeah, great so far. I only arrived yesterday,' Jo said. There was no way she wanted to go over the nightmare scenario of the day before with two strangers.

'So did you miss the temple?' the woman asked.

'Course she did,' the man said. 'She only got here yesterday.' He cut up some scrambled egg on toast.

'But you could go today. It's really worth it. Isn't it a two day holiday, John?'

He nodded and busied himself with his food.

'There's so much to see. There's this huge golden Buddha and lots of little shrines,' the woman said. 'We leave tomorrow. Sadly. Got to pack today. Top up our sun tan round the pool. Nice chap, Senaka. He'll probably be the driver.'

'Thanks. I might well go, then.' Jo said finishing her breakfast. 'Good trip back to sunny England.'

The couple nodded and grinned as she pushed back her chair. She'd book a massage for the following day. If she had one now, she'd miss the trip to the temple.

The man with the scar was fishing out leaves from the pool when she emerged from the restaurant. He smiled and his face lit up.

'You come to temple today?' he asked. 'Special festival Last day.'

'OK. Why not? What's your name?'

'My name is Senaka, ma'am.'

'I just met a couple who you took to the temple yesterday. You were recommended.' She smiled. 'Please call me Jo, remember?'

After she'd got her bag, she waited while someone else came to watch over the pool then followed him out with four other guests were rushing towards them, thinking they were late. The guests were two couples who said they were on holiday together. 'We always get away in January, now the kids have left home,' one of the women said. 'Last year we went on Safari in Kenya. This is our last day.' She introduced each of them by name: George and Sally, Irene and Tom.

'I'm Jo. Short for Jolene,' she said and smiled at them all. 'I arrived yesterday.'

'On your own, then?' Irene asked.

Jo nodded, wishing that Mark were here.

'You should get Senaka to take you out and about. He's very good. Knows a lot about local culture,' Sally said.

'Lovely man,' Irene added.

They went out through the large iron gates out of the hotel grounds and passed the line of empty auto rickshaws. The drivers were sleeping while they waited for work. The road was narrow and rutted. The minibus in which she'd arrived was parked to one side and she slid into the crimson passenger seat next to Senaka, the single traveller's prerogative, while the others climbed into the back. They were all carefree, happy, the way a holiday is supposed to make you feel and their mood was starting to rub off on Jo.

Senaka seemed at ease in his role as driver, checking the mirror, turning the sound system on to play some tinny pop tune. She wondered if he'd taken Zara - *Raquel* - out like

36

this. Perhaps Raquel had sat where she did now, scheming, watching travellers, seeing who might qualify to be her next target?

Jo watched him steer with one hand, the other resting loosely on the gear stick. He drove fast, making a left turn at the end of the road, away from the beach where Raquel had taken her. They drove across a bridge with fast flowing water beneath them and she stared down into the brown silt, at the houses crammed together on either side, the little shrines on the edge of the road lit with candles. Women in white saris and scarves thrown round their heads held the hands of barefoot children running beside them to keep up. Mark would have liked this. He'd have preferred mixing with the locals over lounging around in the sun. She thought back to their conversation while he'd tapped on the phone. He tapped everywhere. 'Just keeping rhythm,' he'd say. Sometimes he tapped out a tune on her shoulder as she lay in his arms after they'd made love, asking her to guess the tune. And he'd said nothing about trying to persuade her not to go.

Senaka turned to look at her, then behind at the four other passengers. 'Everything OK?'

'Brilliant,' Sally and Irene chorused.

'Fine, thanks,' Jo said. 'A little tired, maybe.'

'Oh, cripes, I've forgotten my water,' Sally said.

'You can have some of mine,' said Irene.

'You've only got a bit.' She tapped Senaka on the shoulder. 'Can you stop a minute? We need to buy some water.'

Senaka pulled up. 'Wait,' Senaka said. 'I go and buy. You wait here.' He took some money from Sally.

'You're the boss,' came George's voice from behind Jo.

The two women giggled.

Jo wished she could loosen up. She looked through her window. Around the bus people tramped past and in the near distance she could hear chanting and the deep sound of gongs. She opened the sliding door, thinking she'd take a look around. The sun dazzled her. She saw the pavement was broken and a gap revealed an open sewer. She closed the door and looked along the road, blinking, holding her hand up to shade her eyes from the sun.

'Oh my *God*,' she whispered, hardly able to believe what she saw.

The woman was standing on the opposite side of the road, visible through a sudden gap in the crowd. Motionless. Staring. This time it had to be her. The same black dress she'd changed into on the beach the day before: hatless now, but the same pink flip flops Jo had heard slapping round the pool as Raquel had led her out of their hotel to an allegedly amazing beach, far from where they were both staying. She clambered to the door, pulled it open, jumped across the broken paving slabs and ran round the front of the minibus. With two water bottles in each hand Senaka was hurrying towards her, striding purposefully across the shattered sidewalk, but this time she wouldn't be diverted. Pushing her way through the chanting women, the sick-looking dogs and scrawny goats, she reached the other side of the road.

Suddenly Senaka was tapping her on the shoulder. 'Ma'am. What happened?'

'I *saw* her. She was just there.'

'It is best you come back to the bus. We will soon be at the temple.'

Pushing her way through the crowd, ignoring Senaka's cry of, 'You wait, Miss Jo,' she started searching, looking into a shop where brightly coloured kites and beach balls hung, glancing down narrow side streets where garbage lay strewn and a woman in a purple sari put out a shrivelled, supplicating hand. She smelt unwashed bodies. In the distance the gongs sounded again, louder than before. Which way had she gone? Then Senaka was beside her, his anxious face peering at her.

'Why do I keep seeing her if she's checked out?'

'Another girl. Not Raquel. You not worry.'

It was no use, Raquel could be anywhere by now and Senaka was gesturing for her to get back into the minibus, touching her elbow, urging her to hurry. She climbed back in as he started the engine. Deep breaths. Slow. She arched her back, rotating her neck, trying to release all the tension.

'Hey. You OK?' Sally said.

'Yeah, I'm fine. No actually I'm not. I had all my stuff stolen yesterday and I thought I saw her, the woman; the thief.'

'We go to temple,' Senaka said.

'God, how awful for you,' Sally said. The other three echoed their concern and Jo turned round to thank them.

... until, as her head moved to look at them all properly, about to explain what happened, she saw, jammed in the corner of the seat directly behind one of the women, a pink, wide brimmed sun hat.

4

'I see her everywhere. And now her hat.'

'Why you worry about a hat. Enough in the world to worry about. You see another girl. Not Raquel.' He was changing gear with the hand of his scarred arm. Pain flickered across his face and he drove fast, overtaking three vehicles at a time, his hand on the horn.

She didn't press it further. Was he perhaps right about the woman she'd just seen? He parked and the five of them followed him along the street to where the temple rose high into the sky. They all started the climb. Jo felt sweat soaking her T-shirt. Had this really been a good idea? It wasn't as if she'd never seen a temple before. The air was thick with smoke from incense and the chanting became louder as they drew nearer to the summit. Beside her, easy in his flip-flops, Senaka strolled up the steep incline, face upturned to observe the Buddha towering high above while George, Sally, Irene and Tom steamed on ahead.

She watched him when she should have been taking in her surroundings, the peanut sellers, the coconuts laid out bristling and hairy, ribbon sellers, flower stalls, holy men. She should have been listening in awe to the chanting of the monks, to the great gong calling the followers to prayer, but she was trying to work him out. He seemed so defensive about Zara. Almost as if she were a friend.

Senaka had stopped at a flower stall. 'This is for you,' he said. He gave her a blue lotus flower and she thought back to when she'd arrived. The receptionist had given her a blue lotus flower then – a welcome gift. Now it had wilted and died. 'You can offer it to Buddha,' he added.

'You can't buy me this. What about the other guests?'

'They have already.' He smiled at her. 'You have bad time yesterday.' He was standing at the bottom of a great stone stairway which led up to the towering Buddha. People were removing their sandals and climbing the steps in bare feet. He kicked out of his flip-flops.

She looked at the pile of shoes: more flip-flops; sandals; a pair of trainers with orange laces, and a pair of yellow, totally impractical high heels. She paused, couldn't face attempting the steps up ahead without footwear. She was still jetlagged, disoriented and it was only her second day.

'I'm not sure I can do this right now.'

'No need to remove shoes here. Not if you don't want to.' He pointed up the steps. 'Difficult. You take them off at the temple – yes? It is beautiful. You will see.'

Mark would have shed his sandals, made it up the steps in his large white feet with their soft soles. For the sake of 'going native' he'd have hidden the discomfort of climbing a rocky staircase with naked feet and disregarded his view of anything linked to religion. She could almost hear his voice at her shoulder: *'It's the architecture I like. All those carvings and golden statues. Aren't they amazing? And the atmosphere...not pious like the British churches.'*

If only he were here.

They started to climb.

'Thank you for waiting for me,' she said. Up and up while the giant Buddha looked serenely on and the harsh sun bore down. An ache was expanding down her leg. She looked above her at the tree and temple at the top of the steps.

Senaka was slowing down for her, his hand ever ready to support her.

'We think you are mistaken,' he suddenly said.

'Mistaken?'

'There are many poor people here, ma'am. They are not good people.'

41

'I *know* it was her. Why don't you believe me?'

Gongs played again and again and the chanting was getting louder and the smell of incense was becoming more powerful. She felt her heart beating rapidly and panic set in. The cicadas were buzzing and the odour of hot bodies and peanut breath was everywhere.

'Ma'am? – Jo?'

'I don't feel well.'

'We return soon,' he said. 'It is better. We go back to hotel if you are tired.' He was looking at her, worry lines creasing his brow.

The flower was still in her hand, crushed as she held it tight. 'Yes. I can't do this.' She was breathing fast now and her brain felt like it was spinning, frying in the heat. From the corner of her eye she saw the shadow of a bird flitting across her view while the chanting was getting even louder, deafening. 'Sorry. I should never have come here. I have too much to sort out.' A headache was blooming over her left eye.

By now they has reached a tree where mothers and their children sat in the shade. 'I'll wait here,' she said. 'I can't climb any further. I'm sorry.'

'No problem. It is not large temple. We all return soon.'

She waited for half an hour in the shade of tree. Children practised their English on her then mothers gathered them up and they began the descent.

She thought of Zara, remembering the ease with which she had trusted her. She hoped something equally bad would happen to her. She wanted her tormentor to suffer the same injustice as she'd doled out to her. She pictured the one she still thought of as Zara: the dyed blonde hair, black eye-makeup she'd been in such a hurry to repaint after her swim, the awful pink hat, that blue nose stud she was constantly fiddling with. All that rubbish about it being her that would buy the drinks. How could she have been taken in by a woman like that? Now she despised herself for her gullibility.

Then she saw the five of them coming back down the steps, Senaka in the lead.

'We've been worried about you,' said Sally. 'Are you not feeling well? It took me ages to get used to this heat. And I still feel like I've got stuck in a tumble dryer.'

'I could have hung round here for longer,' Jo said. 'You didn't need to come down right now.'

'Too crowded up there for me,' George said. 'We've had enough now. Time for a siesta.' He grinned sympathetically at Jo.

They all made their way back past the believers holding their offerings, their dainty feet barely touching the steps as they climbed.

They reached the minibus and she stood at the passenger side, waiting while the other four, joking and chiding climbed into the back. There was another traffic jam. Car horns blared. Senaka was resting his scarred arm on his lap, while the other one lay on the wheel, a finger tapping the plastic like Mark would have done. The air was sullied, no breeze from the open window. She put the lotus flower on the dashboard.

'Didn't quite work out as I planned,' she said.

'No problem. It is best you rest today.'

'I thought I'd be OK.' The traffic had started to move again. Her face was turned to the open window. She felt the breeze against her cheeks, erasing traces of tears remaining.

'Can I help you, ma'am? Is there anything I can do?'

'No. I'll be fine. But thank you, Senaka.'

'You must go now and rest,' he said when they reached the hotel and the other four guests had bid their farewells.

'You take care of yourself.'

'Don't be getting sun stroke.'

'Enjoy your holiday.'

'Thanks and safe journey back,' said Jo.

'You keep this.' Senaka handed her the flower and walked off round the back of the hotel, while the man with the oiled hair watched her every move from the reception doorway.

Her room was a mess. She'd forgotten how untidy she'd left it. Without air conditioning, with the windows shut, it was stifling and smelt even mustier. She drank hard and fast from the water bottle in her minibar while squinting round the room. Her case was on the floor, lid hanging open, its edge lowered onto a woven red mat. On her knees she began to search for the packet of Paracetamol as a headache grew. She started off methodically but was soon surrounded by clothes, more books, pens, creams, lotions and tampons scattered across the floor, rolling under the bed and wardrobe. She searched in each of the pockets. She hadn't realised this case borrowed from Mark contained so many. Inside one she even found a map of Prague. She opened it out, stretched out the creases, recalling the holiday that spring, not long after she had met Mark. Four days exploring the cobbled streets, reading about the revolution and afterwards lying in a four poster bed with down feather pillows and duvet. He wouldn't have stayed at home then, he wouldn't have let her to go without him 'Flu epidemic or not, he'd have found a way.

Someone was playing football on the beach. There was the rhythmic *biff-biff* of the ball. A child was crying. She stayed put on the blood red mat and watched another or maybe the same column of ants forming a dead straight line as they travelled up the opposite wall. Her possessions were lying in heaps around her and the case was empty. No bloody painkillers. She remembered then that they'd all been in her bag. Nose-stud had even taken them, too. She was sweating hard now, the humidity had increased but she didn't want to move. She was aware of the room darkening, of a cloud moving across the blue. The lights flickered.

From somewhere in the distance there was a deep long peal of thunder. Jo stretched out, feeling the concrete hard beneath the carpet. Her head was spinning. She needed sleep. She listened to the flash-rainstorm beating against the

44

corrugated iron roof, turned her head towards the window and saw only a gun-metal sky. She knew she should collect the stray tampons and get herself together. But it would take more effort to lift herself up onto the bed than to remain where she was. It was raining even harder now. She stayed on the floor, eyes closed, concentrating on the sound of the downpour, trying to empty her mind; to do otherwise would make the headache worse. A streak of lightning cut across the room. She sat up, listened to the rain bouncing off the roof. It made such a din. Suddenly the room was dark. It seemed the power had gone.

The phone rang and she scrambled to her feet with difficulty amid the chaos of her belongings.

'Hello?' she said.

There was no reply.

'Hello, hello, *hello* –'

She felt her heart banging against her ribs.

'*Hello.*'

Still there was no reply. She heard the intake of breath followed by air being expelled. The line clicked dead.

She dialled reception, peering at the extension numbers on the telephone: hoping the power outage hadn't affected the internal telecom system, 'Who was that? Who was that who called me just now?'

'Sorry ma'am?'

Her brain felt as if it was exploding. Teeth gritted, she repeated herself.

'We don't keep a record of incoming calls, ma'am. Sorry.'

'No, no. Of course you don't.' She replaced the receiver, sat on the edge of the bed, shivering. Had she imagined the breathing? Was it the state of her nerves, her imagination working overtime? She stared at the phone. There was no mistake. She shot up and ran to the door, shot down the steps. Senaka was under the thatched shelter, staring unconcernedly out at the deluge. Water poured through the coconut matting, cascading to hit the terrace where large

45

puddles formed. The sound of rain blocked out all else. A figure still swam in the pool – a man in blue trunks.

'You get wet, ma'am,' Senaka called out.

She was panting and her clothes were drenched. Her skin was wet and still her head pounded. She got to the shelter where Senaka had resumed sorting towels in the half light, chucking some into a basket, folding others, putting them on the table. His eyes were flicking towards the swimmer then back to her.

'What happened?'

'I – I don't know. There was a phone call.'

He stopped folding, stared at her. 'Is there a problem? Is everything OK, ma'am?'

'There was someone there. I know it. I heard her breathing.'

He pointed outside, beyond the shelter to where the rain was coming down in sheets and lighting slipped across the sky. 'Maybe because there is power cut –'

'I know it was Zara. *Raquel. I know* it was.'

He began to frown.

'You still think I am mistaken?'

'Sorry, Ma'am. How is it possible? Raquel no longer stay at this hotel now –'

'But she's still in the country. I know what I've seen. Why is she doing this?'

The swimmer climbed out of the pool and padded towards the shelter. Senaka handed him a towel. The man glanced towards Jo, nodded a greeting, then made his way towards a ground floor room. The rain was beginning to stop.

'I am not sure, ma'am.' Senaka pointed to the sky. 'Always there is sun after cloud. Your bad luck turn to good soon.' He turned towards her. 'Your husband send you money?'

'Husband?'

'He stay in England?'

'I didn't tell you that. Did I?' Now she couldn't remember. Not for sure. Whether she'd told him about Mark, or not?

Senaka was looking at her, rubbing the side of his nose. She stared at the swimming pool, at the ripples, the way each one caught the sunlight. Senaka picked up a broom leaning against the wall and began to sweep the leaves. The concrete had already dried now, the puddles shrunk. Frowning, she watched Senaka until he'd pushed his broom to the far poolside where he continued to sweep briskly, his body turned away from hers.

5

Days merged into one. Lying on the hotel beach wishing the holiday over, how could she possibly relax? Then one morning she was sitting in the back seat of the minibus again veering through stinking traffic. One of the waiters sat in the passenger seat at the front; he was visiting his family in Colombo on his day off. Jo's eyes began to close. She'd barely slept since the day of the theft although it was nearly a week now. Last night was another where she had lain in the cell-white room in the vast double bed while the rain poured endlessly, creating an unexpected chill. She'd needed a blanket to stop the fit of shivering that had racked her body in the small hours of each morning. The holiday was turning into a continuous nightmare. Now, on her way to the Consul with Senaka beside her, she felt strangely comforted by his presence, even though he still didn't believe that Raquel – their precious guest, was a thief.

The traffic was stop, go, stop but Senaka was calm as ever, unruffled by the chaos. A kind man. A man who believed where there was evil, goodness lurked close behind. Her face burned as she recalled the ease with which Senaka had paid the police with money borrowed from the hotel, telling her not to worry that it was no problem; that she'd be able to reimburse them when her money came through. At least they'd agreed to verify who she was at the bank.

Then at least, this morning, some money from Mark had arrived. More than enough to see her through.

Senaka was always there listening to her concerns about fraud now Raquel had her passport, his head on one side, telling her not to worry, that things would work out. He'd driven Jo to the police station two days before, without question, as if this was a task he undertook every day. As she contemplated the sunny day now, she remembered the grey bleak looking building and how inside, every chair in the waiting room was taken, all space on the floor occupied by family groups. The women distributed food to their children. The men stood around observing, saying little. Jo took her ticket and took her place at the back of the room, as far as possible from the curious stares. The walls were sepia, she recalled, the chairs with their peeling covers were dun brown and the air was stale, smelling of the many bodies that had passed through that day. Senaka had chatted to a man with a long moustache and cropped hair, occasionally stopping while they both gaped at her, making her feel even more paranoid. The wait was two hours, but Senaka didn't comment, he maintained the same beatific expression he had now as he drove along a packed highway. They'd been called in to a small room with mud brown walls, and an enlarged photograph of the president in military regalia set high on one wall. Four policemen with guns in their holsters watched her enter the room. In Singhalese, Senaka had spoken with accompanying hand movements. And now, she evoked how they'd gathered at a polished desk and opened drawer after drawer. Of course, there was a charge for the form which they eventually found. There was a charge for the photocopy and another fee for their time.

The minibus jolted to a stop and a man crossed the road in front, shaking his fist at them. In front of her the two men chatted. Then Senaka was weaving in and out of scooters, auto rickshaws and other pedestrians trying to cross the road. She leant forward to watch him, rubbing the wheel as if it needed a polish as he waited for the bus in front to move. When she got the money that morning, she'd wanted to take a bus to the capital to sort out the passport. She had relished the opportunity of being financially independent at last. But no. The hotel, then Senaka had insisted. While you were a guest in our country you were victim of a crime, Senaka said. We take you to Colombo. It was as if he'd taken her under his wing, the abandoned tourist who'd hit on some bad luck. He still would *not* admit Zara to be the thief, nor that Jo had seen the woman round the pool or in the street on that long hot day when they went to the temple. The police thought she'd got it wrong too: 'Bad people in this country. They steal money. Not work. Lazy,' they'd said. 'You must be more careful.'

'But it was an English person who took it,' she'd insisted.

Senaka had spoken at length in Singhalese then and they'd all ignored her when she asked for a translation.

But at least she had the form.

Outside the minibus was the sprawl of urbanised landscapes and she surveyed all the shops and factories, apartment blocks, squat houses and the occasional Western-style hotel. The towns merged, seemingly unnamed, unplanned. And while she looked out of the open window, the past few days of solid rain and grey skies just a memory, she allowed the hot wind to bat her face and tangle her hair. The sky was clear again, rain clouds dispersed.

They were entering the city metropolis, the haphazard shops and factories giving way to grand buildings from the Colonial period, massive redbrick Victorian mansions, delicate pillared Regency-style hotels. The auto rickshaws were fewer and there were no scooters. A large private car with tinted windows passed them close by and she wondered what criminal sat inside: the incident with the man in the beach hotel had coloured her opinion of this country and its men who wore uniforms.

She gazed out of the window at the city dwellers, at a man in a grey suit and black patent leather shoes.

A mobile phone was glued to his ear and he appeared to be yelling. Capitalism held its grip here too. Another car with tinted windows blocked her view. It passed and she watched a woman tottering on white high heels. They turned into another quarter where the inhabitants were poorer, the road rutted. A woman in a scarlet sari observed them while they waited in a traffic jam. Her face was lined, haggard. She stood outside a shop selling sacks of rice. The shop keeper was scanning the streets for customers. A group of men wearing sarongs and shirts stood nearby gathered on the sidewalk and she watched them as they drove past thinking that at least she had a home, that at least she wouldn't starve. The traffic jam loosened. He pulled over and the waiter jumped out. 'Goodbye ma'am,' he called out before he disappeared into the crowd.

'I hope you don't mind doing this. I hope the hotel doesn't mind you neglecting your duties looking after the pool.'

'No problem, Jo.'

At least he'd finally stopped, most of the time, calling her ma'am.

'No need worry,' he added.

She envied his serenity, his calm attitude, the belief that everything would work out, that there was no need to panic. It could have been worse, he'd said. She'd known he was referring to the tsunami but this simply made her guilt increase. It didn't take much to make her feel like this, although guilt didn't stop her trying to find out Zara's second name. Neither did it stop her feeling so helpless.

He drove down a dual carriageway bordered on each side by tumble-down houses, with sheets of plastic slung over the roofs. The odd chicken scraped at a grass patch along the side of the road. There was a powerful smell of rotting garbage, open drains and fish.

They drove away from the shanty town. Soon they were travelling in a wealthy district where modern glass-fronted blocks reflected the sky. He spent time looking for a parking space while she clasped the form from the police, folding, unfolding it, checking the indecipherable writing, hoping she wouldn't have to wait too long.

'You been here before?' she asked, for something to say, anything that would stop the sinking feeling in her stomach, the dread her mother liked to call her sixth sense.

'I took a guest here once before.'

'Glad it's not just me.'

He slotted the minibus into a space, got out, came round to her side. 'It's not far.'

She slithered from the minibus, looked up at the sky, showing yellow through her new sunglasses, bought on tic from the hotel. The hotel tab was larger than she'd reckoned it would be when she paid it all this morning. She felt like her ex-clients with their multiple debts, the list of excuses. But this was not her fault – if she'd cancelled the holiday – but this was no good. She needed to concentrate on the task in hand.

'It is there.' Senaka was pointing to a modern building behind a wall. 'Come on. You go inside. I wait over there by the fish pond.'

'Fish pond?'

But he'd walked ahead of her. She followed him along the gravel path. There were lush lawns on either side. Sprinklers tinkled as they watered. The high wall concealed the street outside and the shanty town beyond. The many windowed building, and the neat, raked path should have made her feel more secure with their remnants of Europe, but they had the opposite effect; she viewed them as another bureaucratic hurdle that she'd have to overcome and felt insignificant in the shadow of this monstrous building.

He was sitting on the low wall of a fishpond where giant carp swam.

'Are you sure this is right?'

'Yes. You go through there.' He pointed to a glass door. 'I wait over there.' Over there was a large tree, where others stood or squatted in the shade.

Once she stepped through the door, a blast of icy air cooled the sweat on her face. The floor was marble and vast windows looked out onto immaculate lawns. It was like another country, a touch of modernity, no expense spared. She followed the sign, took the lift, a conveyance that rose silently to the second floor. When the lift shuddered to a stop and the doors opened, she saw why it was so quiet down in the lobby. This was where the queues were, the disarray. She took a numbered ticket and walked to the back of the room away from the window and sat in a blue bucket chair in the draft of an air-conditioned breeze for a very long time. Silently, crossing one leg over the other, sitting sideways or legs straight together, she fumed and thought about Zara with her ready smile. How long had she planned the theft? Was it the minute she saw her, the first morning at breakfast?

It took her two hours to be seen by a woman whose smile was familiar to Jo: the smile of a woman tired of smiling at strangers.

'So you need a replacement passport?' the woman said.

'Yup.'

'And you've got a form from the police?'

'Yup.' She knew she was being rude and tried to counter it with the narrative of the stolen passport, money, credit cards and the hotel's downright refusal to give her the woman's family name. She slid the form across the counter.

The woman took it. A silver bracelet glinted. She was wearing a loose white designer blouse. An ethnic gemstone hung from a silver chain round her extraordinarily white neck. Her hair was styled perfectly; the woman was worry-free in her secure job with all the frills. And Jo knew she was thinking she was a fool.

A flash of madness suddenly took hold of Jo. She really wanted to rile this woman. 'So supposing I had no money. You know it having been stolen. Would you lend money until I get back to the UK?' Her voice was crisp, sharp, smartly concealing her fury at the woman for being in such a position of power.

'Sorry. We don't have that facility. Not here –'

Jo didn't let her finish. 'Nothing? But I might starve.'

The woman touched the collar of her newly pressed blouse, while her other hand fiddled with the mouse. 'An emergency passport. I'll print off the application form. You said supposing you had no money. Yes? So I am assuming this isn't the case.'

'But I might not and I pay taxes at home to support this – to pay your salary, to –' her voice was getting louder. 'You have a duty –' She had an urge to really rile this woman.

'No. *You* have a duty to take care of *yourself* if you choose to travel.' Her voice was controlled.

'You wouldn't care if I starve? You don't care if I have to beg in a foreign country.' While the words flowed, she knew she'd already gone too far. Why was she doing this?

'Please don't raise your voice. Take a seat and complete this application form for an emergency passport. You can apply for emergency repatriation here.' She handed Jo a leaflet. 'If you have no funds I suggest you go there. It is round the corner from here.' She got up, walked away to the office interior where a water fountain gurgled and a man stood watching, the bulge of a revolver visible under his jacket.

Jo sat, shivering, but completed the form rapidly, while goose bumps appeared on her arm and she sneezed in the cooled air. She waited again, freezing in her T-shirt, hugging her knees to keep warm and ignore the curious stares of locals who were also waiting. Other Brits looked away. The hand on the wall clock opposite turned another hour.

She would have dealt with a person like herself, immediately. Got her out of the office. Avoid more confrontation. She shuddered, horrified at her behaviour, looked down at the floor, up at the ceiling. Anywhere to avoid the sneaked glances and the sidelong looks and thought back to the times when she'd felt threatened in her old job, had dealt with a client badly, weary of trying to sort out other people's problems. With a daily case load of sixty, the clients' faces merged, their problems becoming their identity, the individual personalities not recorded in files.

At last she was called. She was stiff from sitting, from the effort of keeping warm. Her leg hurt and she tried to conceal her limp, didn't wish to give the onlookers another reason to stare. Subdued, she handed the man her form, marked time by staring at his bald patch as he fiddled around on the computer while she dreamed of home.

'One emergency passport,' he said without looking up. 'Is that all?'

She nodded, took it, muttered her thanks and left. It had all taken such a long time, she wondered whether Senaka would still be there. But he looked unruffled, was chatting to the waiter, who had returned, while they stood in the shade of a tree. There was a pinkish glow on the horizon. Soon the sun would set.

'Sorry it took so long.'

'No problem.'

'I got it. My emergency passport.'

'I am happy for you,' he said. 'We return now.'

'They told me I can request immediate repatriation there. If I want it.' She showed him the leaflet.

'We go there now?'

'No. No need.'

'We go back to hotel then.'

The return journey took longer, the rush hour was in full flow and not long after they drove away darkness fell and headlights from oncoming buses and lorries cut into her vision. For a while she watched Senaka drive expertly through the appalling traffic, seeing how the light reflected on his cheekbones and brow. She dozed, jerking awake suddenly when the vehicle bumped across potholes or swerved, knocking her sideways, towards the window. It began to rain again. Hot and sticky, the splatters bounced off the windscreen, made the headlights coming towards them appear

55

blurry, they seemed dangerously near. By now, she was wide awake, gripping the seat, watching the road ahead of her, until finally they swung left into a lane and the minibus stopped to let the waiter out. He banged on the vehicle as it drove away. She knew that soon she'd be back at the hotel.

'I think you will have missed the evening meal, 'Senaka said as they were driving into the grounds.

'Doesn't matter.'

He parked and she reached for her bag, checking that the emergency passport was still there, just in case. The rain was steady now, relentless, set in.

'I have a little food at home,' he said.

The engine was still running.

If she stayed here, she'd be alone in her room, listening to the rain hitting the corrugated iron roof, on her own and hungry; she hadn't eaten since breakfast apart from the snack of chick peas she'd had earlier on that day.

'If it's not too much trouble, you've done so much for me already, but if I've missed the evening meal –' She slid out of the van, covering her head with her hands, and looked beyond to where the restaurant was. Only the bar remained lit. Meal times were strict at the hotel; dishes packed away at the given hour while cleaners upturned chairs onto tables and began to sweep the floor.

'You like rice and curry?'

'Where do you live?' The rain was soaking her.

'The next village. It will be my pleasure.'

She thought how Mark would approve if he were here with her, eating with the locals, seeing how they lived. But on her own? 'You are very kind,' she said but she didn't clamber back into the van and still the engine was running as she tried to form the words in her head, not wishing to appear rude, after all he had done. But hadn't she allowed herself to be duped by Zara? Did she appear that vulnerable, just because she had a limp? All the same, her skin beneath her clothes was damp and she felt foolish standing out there in the torrent. But what if sex was a motive? 'So do you live alone?'

'I live with my cousin. She is cleaner at hotel. Our house is very small. We are poor. But you are welcome to share some rice and curry that my other cousin makes. It is very good.'

The hotel grounds were plunged into darkness. Another power cut. She was very hungry.

'Thank you. You are very kind.' She clambered back into the passenger seat, sat clutching her bag, feeling comforted by the outline of the emergency passport which she felt beneath her palm.

'You would do the same in your country?'

'Of course.' Would she?

They bumped back down the road, turned left and left again. The road was worse here, a track for animals and pedestrians, not cars. As they swayed, they were thrown towards each other, back and forth while the rain dashed on the windscreen. There were no lights from the houses in the village.

He pulled up, got out, ran round to her side, an umbrella had appeared from nowhere clasped in his hand. Lights from windows flickered on, then off, then on.

The room which the front door opened into was small, dimly lit and crammed with two large chocolate coloured sofas, a dining table shoved against the far wall, a fridge which hummed in the corner, a tiny Buddha shrine with pictures of deities. Had Zara been here too? She stared at one of the sofas and shuddered at the thought.

'You sit,' he said, raising his voice above the deafening sound of rain thudding on the roof. 'It is ready. I'll get it from the kitchen. 'My other cousin, she lives in this village. She does all our cooking. She looks after the house while we work.' He spoke quickly, nervously. 'I am sorry. It is very small. Please sit. I not long.'

For a minute, she did so, but was tired of being seated. To stand, walk around, stretch. That's what she wanted. And she was curious about the shrine. Walking across the room, she approached the fridge and peered up above it, to the shelf where the miniature carved Buddha sat, hands resting on the lap, eyes closed and at the two postcards of deities propped up against an incense holder. Prayer beads lay in a circle on the top of the fridge. The sound of rain and the peal of thunder in the distance muffled Senaka's footsteps coming into the room.

'I light candle,' he said. 'You tired. You sit.'

Overhead, thunder crashed. A flame sprang up from the candle, then within seconds, diminished. The lights were blinking in the storm. Dark furniture filled up every space.

It was the sequins she saw first. She stepped nearer and recognised the peacock, the swirled pattern on the cloth. A musky aroma snaked upwards. 'You've got Raquel's sarong in your house – is she here? Is Raquel in your house?' she repeated urgently.

He had his back to her, didn't seem to have heard her despite her raised voice.

'Please. Be calm.' He lit another candle, bowed his head to the shrine and she watched his shadowy form, feeling the colour drain from her face.

'Do you like fish curry?' he was saying. 'It is very good.' The candle was spluttering. From his pocket he took out a third candle which he also lit.

She felt her heart pound. She was dizzy. Her body was swamped in a cold sweat. She took a breath. Counted. Breathed. She did this several times. Shadows from the candle danced across the wall.

His back was still turned to her but she noticed a movement of his head as he turned it slightly. 'Guests sometimes come here. I invite.'

And she thought to herself, why not? It was none of her business if Raquel had been here. Nothing to do with her.

'So was she here?'

'Yes, ma'am. She came here for a meal. Like you.'

'You never said.'

'It is not important.'

'It is to me.'

He rubbed his scar. Up and down his hand moved as if he were caressing a memory. 'She is nice girl.'

'Nice?'

'It is very difficult here, in this country. We are very poor. We have nothing. I lost everything, my house, my brother. He was paying for me to study. The tsunami took everything. It is hard.'

'I'm sorry. I really am. And Raquel? What's this got to do with her?' She was shaking, perplexed, terrified at the realisation that Senaka knew more than he'd said about Raquel.

'Raquel.' He looked at her. 'She –'

'Is she here now?'

'No, ma'am. Raquel not here.' He picked up the prayer beads from the fridge and ran them through his fingers, switching his gaze rapidly to the ceiling, the floor, each corner of the room, back to the table where the sarong lay neatly folded. Of course, she'd stayed here. She understood that now. Felt foolish for not seeing it before.

'Why are you defending her? She took everything from me. I keep telling you she did. How can you defend a woman like that?' Dizzy with anger, she walked over to the table and picked up the sarong. A waft of heady perfume drifted from the fabric. She stared across the room at Senaka. What did it matter to her if they'd fucked? Why was it important? The rain was batting against the windows. The air was heavy with the storm. She looked around at the room, imagined Raquel sitting on the chocolate sofa looking benign, innocent, the gorgeous English woman wearing an exotic sarong with a blue gem in her nose. Did she leave the wrap here deliberately? A token of her presence? The scent was strong enough to remind him of her for a long time. Or had Senaka, besotted, asked her for a memento?

'Ma'am –'

'For Christ's sake my name is Jo –'

'She is nice girl. I don't think it was her. Maybe you are mistaken.'

59

'So why did you take me to the Consul today? Why are you pretending to help me?'

'You are a guest at the hotel. My cousin –'

'I think I'd better go.'

'But dinner?'

'Doesn't matter.' She wanted out of here, back to the hotel where she'd call Mark and be soothed by the sound of his voice, try to get something to eat at the hotel. Surely all the staff hadn't gone to bed? She swirled round in the dimly lit room searching for the exit until she glimpsed the front door on the other side of the room. Grabbing her bag, slinging it across her shoulder, she limped diagonally across the tiled floor, aware of Senaka following her, beseeching her to stay. The storm was overhead, rain coming down in torrents. She felt his hand on her shoulder, and shrugged it off.

'Please. You stay for dinner,' he said. 'I invite.'

'I'm going back. I should never have come here.' She would battle the elements alone. The wind slammed against the door and she pushed against the force of the gale, struggled out. Water soaked her skin. Lighting lit up the way ahead and she saw how the puddles had deepened. The hotel was close enough. Stepping down his path, making her way into the road, she heard Senaka call again. She carried on walking.

'Jo. Ma'am. Please you wait. I drive you. It is dangerous. We are far from the hotel.'

She heard the van door close, saw the beam of light. She ran into the jungle, hid behind a thick tree trunk. The engine revved. The minibus crawled past her while she waited in the rain.

6

She stumbled over tree roots trying to find the road back to the hotel. It couldn't be far. Stories of getting lost in jungles and never being found again swam round her head. Rain poured down on her like a wall of water and the dark shapes of tree trunks rose at every step. What was she doing here? What had happened to the easy package holiday she'd planned? She stopped and searched through the darkness beyond, watching out for Senaka's vehicle. She wished she'd stayed. What did it matter to her that Zara had been there? It made no difference to his hospitality. She thought of turning back, wasn't sure which direction to take. No moon. Nothing. Everywhere black, the only sound steady rain and her heart thudding against her ribs. Water trickled down her cheeks, sneaked into her eyes. She scoured the forest searching for a way through. At every step her feet sank into mud. Thunder raged and forks of lightening glimmered in the trees ahead. Was that a figure silhouetted by a sudden flare? For a brief moment she saw Zara, wet hair showing the shape of her skull, pink dress sticking to her form. Then she was gone.

Stepping forward, Jo zoned in on the jungle ahead. Nothing. Not a soul. Trembling all over. Breath catching in her throat. There was another blast of thunder, a lightning flash. She threaded her way through tangled undergrowth. She floundered, called out. No one there. Her teeth were chattering; she was shivering. Must keep calm, stay cool. The rain increased. The forest was thickening, closing in on her. She began to panic even more. Then she was on the road.

Breathing hard, she looked to her right. Specks of light set far back glimmered and she stopped to get her bearings. The way ahead was barely visible in a haze, a sliver of moon slowly appearing.

She wanted to be home, with Mark's body near to her. Not here, in the pulsing rain. But if she'd flown home now, she'd be giving up. Zara would have won. The moonshine vanished. The night was black again. A shot of pain ran through her leg as her foot hit something hard. She stopped and looked around at the murky scene. Nearby a chewing goat was tethered to a tree. Her breath was coming hard and fast. She quickened her pace. Was Senaka searching for her, frightened for his job, a tourist in his care wandering in a storm? But she'd been duped, hadn't seen through Zara's pretence that she was a thoughtful woman, that Jo's limp was nothing to her. She hid her true scheming self so well. She *could* go back, dry out, share a meal with him.   Lost everything, he'd said. Wasn't that worse than Zara snatching her money and passport? But how would she explain her change of mind? And what if Zara was there? What if she was pursuing her, aided by Senaka? She scanned the area around her, peering, seeking. Nothing. Not a sign of life.

A boom of thunder pitched across the sky. Her sandal slipped off and she hunted in the ground feeling for it with her fingertips while rain seeped down her back. She found her sandal deep in mud, muck and scree, limped, one foot naked, until she slipped the other sandal off, dangled the pair from her hand, sharp stones beneath her bare feet. How did she get to this? Exhausted – dizzy – water reaching her mid-calf – she thought of floods sweeping her away.

One step in front of the other, she counted each in time to her breath. Wanted to sink to her knees. Stop. Just stop. Let events take their course. No. Must get back. Best to keep going. Strands of hair whipped across her face, blown by the gale. Couldn't get any wetter. Couldn't get any worse. And through the din of rain and crash of thunder, she heard the sound of an engine stalling, starting up again.

A vehicle appeared through the mist, the image blurred by the downpour, its headlamps glinting through rain. It bumped across potholes and she saw how deep the water was, and how it swayed, how near it got to tipping over. Closer now, the headlamps blinded her. She waited. Her heart thumped. Panicking again. The vehicle moved suddenly, careering towards her. Senaka? The van slowed and she saw it was different, a red stripe painted on the side. It drew up alongside her.

'You want a lift?' The man wore a Bob Marley hat. His elbow jutted out from the open window.

'Thanks, but I'm fine,' she said and began to walk away.

Behind her, the vehicle started up again, then pulled up a way in front of her.

'Where you stay, ma'am?' he called back at her.

'Look. I'm fine,' she said, speeding up.

'Where you from?'

She paused and with the ball of her palm wiped her face of rain, so her vision was clearer.

'I no harm you, ma'am. Where you from?'

'England,' she called out through the tempest. Thunder rolled. A little distance away now, echoing round the hills.

'Another English girl stay up there. You know her? Raquel?'

'No.' Her throat tightened.

'I take you back. Long way.'

'I prefer to walk,' she said, strolling past him, trying to move nonchalantly so he wouldn't see her fear.

'You sure? Why you want to walk to hotel?'

'Please. I'm OK.'

He drove off down the road and the tail lights grew smaller until they too had gone and she was alone again. So *he* knew Zara too.

There was no one around when she reached the hotel. It looked nothing like the pictures on the website where the sun shone constantly and everything was like a dream come true – the perfect holiday. The lights to the bar were off and the pool unlit. Her room was cold, the air conditioning full on. No power cut anymore. Her body ached. She'd take a shower, crawl into bed, sleep.

The room had been cleaned and tidied since she'd left it in chaos that morning. That felt like an age away. Had it only been that morning? How was it possible? Her teeth began their chattering as hunger pains shot through her stomach. She peeled off her clothes, stuffed them into a bag, dumped it in the corner of the room, stood beneath the shower, soaping herself, tipping her head to the warm flow. Some of the cuts on her feet were superficial, one was deep and she imagined telling the story to Mark. They'd be in a pub sitting at the open fire where freshly-hewn logs would spatter and give off that earthy smell and Mark would be nodding, smiling, dropping kisses on her cheek. The hot water turned cold and she was back in the bathroom with the flickering strip-light. She stepped out. Dried herself. Padded into the bedroom again, rang Mark. No answer.

She looked out to sea. The tide was coming in. A couple were walking below her balcony, giggling at a shared joke. Switching her gaze back to the sea, she saw how the moonlight caught the edge of the surf and, for a moment taken by the scene, she tried to convince herself that she was safe here, back in the hotel. Turning back, towards the room, she closed the door, dialled reception. No answer. The restaurant. Same. Would she be able to sleep with this hunger? Should have gone back to Senaka's. Her mind was switching back and forth, the pink hat in his mini-bus, the sarong in his house. But she'd soon be home. All this behind her; a classic nightmare holiday. Outside her room the ocean smacked against the shore and in the distance the bass drum of disco music pounded. She dialled home again.

'I got the money this morning' she said once he'd picked up the phone. 'Thanks.'

'That's good. It's manic here. At work and I have to stay overnight with my father quite a bit.'

64

'She keeps phoning me. The woman Zara or Raquel whoever she bloody is – she keeps phoning me. I know it's her and the hotel say they can't do anything about it –'

'What does she say?'

'Nothing. Just breathes. It freaks me out. There've been three calls now. I got my passport and I could have got repatriated through the Consul but I didn't because then the whole damn holiday would be wasted.'

'Three times you say? How do you know it's her?'

'I know. That's all. I know. It's her – I can't explain.'

'You should tell the hotel.'

'I did. I just told you.' She stared up at the ceiling at a damp patch in the corner. From one of the other rooms, she heard a toilet flush. Mark still hadn't replied. Her stomach turned over. She felt sick. 'Mark?'

'Sorry. Just thinking – maybe you should get that repatriation package. Cut your losses.'

'Then she'd have won?'

'Who? The woman who stole your things? That's daft, Jo. You know it is. She was a chancer, a bloody thief. It's not a competition –'

'I'm not doing that.'

The balcony door banged shut in the wind.

'Forget about this woman. Enjoy what's left of the holiday. 'Got to go now. Late for work,' he said.

'But Mark. Hang on. Listen.'

'Really.' He said impatiently. 'I was on my way out. Take advantage of the sunshine. It's vile here. Speak soon.'

'Night then. Take care', she said. The phone was dead. He'd already gone. She was going to tell him about getting lost in the jungle, how frightened she was. But it could wait till she got back. She lay back on her bed, drew the sheet up and listened to the waves hitting the shore. She stared at the ceiling where a spider was inching its way towards the doors leading to the balcony. Why was Raquel harassing her? Wasn't taking her money and passport enough? Why the phone calls? Why did she keep appearing? Or was it all in

65

Jo's imagination? Was she losing her grip? Too much time alone?

From the damp patch on the ceiling water dripped. The drip steadily increased. She fetched a bucket from the bathroom and stood it under the leak, got back into bed and drifted to sleep leaving all the lights on.

7

A pale apricot sky woke Jo at dawn. The orange glow made last night's storm seem like a bad dream. She soft-shoed it to the balcony, ignoring the sting from the wounds in her foot and picked up her sandals, peered out at the calm sea. On the horizon there was a ribbon of grey cloud and from a disco across the way, still came the boom of a bass. Her sandals were damp, heavy with mud, evidence that the events of the day before were *no* dream. She showered and dressed, unlocked the door, focused on a palm tree stretching high - still, like a photograph. In the warm sunshine, with birds singing overhead, the air heating up to a sweltering day, the fear from last night seemed absurd. How had she got into such a state?

There was Senaka, as she knew he'd be, with his net catching debris from the swimming pool. For a brief moment, as if halted by her presence, he regarded her, then resumed his work. None of the other guests were around; empty like that, the hotel felt hostile as if the abandonment was somehow related to her. She stood on the edge of the pool watching the lone worker drag his net across the cool blue water.

She edged nearer. He stopped fishing, switched his gaze towards her. 'Good morning, ma'am.'

'Hiya,' she said, trying to sound indifferent.

He stretched out to harpoon a drifting leaf. 'You return OK?'

'Bit wet,' she said.

'But you OK.'

She sighed. A door banged open to one of the rooms on the ground floor and a man with a barrel chest and white towel wrapped round his middle observed the scene. So she wasn't alone here.

'It was a bad storm, wasn't it?'

'Yes, ma'am.' He picked up the handle to his net, shuffled along the edge of the water. 'A tree came down in the village. Lightning.'

Another leaf floated by. Reaching across, he caught it in his net. He dipped the net in the pool and they both watched the ripples travel across the water. 'The dining room is open,' he said.

'Right. Yes. See you.'

He snatched a look at her foot 'You should rest today.'

'I will. Thanks. See you later.' She walked away from him, towards the restaurant.

'Ma'am.' Behind her – she hadn't heard his footsteps.

'What?' Suddenly frightened, she flicked round.

'You need medicine for that cut.'

Was that all? She was *so* jumpy. 'I'm fine. Thanks,' she said.

'We have first aid kit. Risk of infection.'

Of course she knew he was right. Living with a nurse had its advantages. If Mark had come he would've packed that little green case from the back of the bathroom cupboard with liniment, anti-septic cream, anti-histamine and anti-diarrhoea pills. But in her bid to pack light, she'd left it behind. She looked at her foot. The worst cut looked inflamed, probably infected, with an angry red swelling.

'I'll get breakfast first,' she said, not wanting to converse any more with him.

She'd got used to eating alone. Today there was no one to observe. It was too early for normal holiday-makers, taking advantage of the opportunity to sleep-in. There was only one waiter. She ate a full breakfast as he looked on indifferently watching the pool that glistened in the morning sun, moving across the dining room slowly, picking his way between the chairs and tables, filling her cup of coffee, returning to his place by the door. She ate fast, wanting to see if the computer was working yet. All she could think of now was getting home.

She had a massage and felt the pain in her hip easing. The masseur stuck a plaster on the wound on her foot and she went back out into reception where the man with oiled hair was behind the desk, peering at his ledger. Standing a little way back from him, she saw him run his finger down the list of names. He glanced up at her, nodded and answered the phone. She didn't trust him but despised herself for not liking him. Wasn't he simply doing his job, probably an underpaid one at that? All the same there was something about him. He had eyes that shifted round, avoiding her gaze, always something better to do than listen to her. Then there was his refusal to give her Raquel's surname. Was Raquel special for him too? Was that why he'd defended her? She moved a little nearer, caught coffee on his breath. The two children she'd seen before ran up to her, each grabbing a hand; the boy tugged harder and they tried to pull Jo away. She felt like she was re-living a scene over again. 'Hang on,' she said to them. 'Hang on a mo.' The man was still on the phone. The children jabbered to each other in German, pulling at her hands. 'Please. Wait a minute,' she pleaded. 'Come on,' they said giggling. 'He's busy. He's ignoring you. Come *on.*'

'Wait. Please.'

They released her hands, ran off. 'I know your secret,' the boy shouted. And for a second or two she forgot what he was talking about. Then she remembered. It was the day she'd seen Raquel, when the children had been trying to get her to play with them, when everyone insisted Raquel had checked out and she appeared at the end of the pool. She swung her head round, though she knew who was watching her. Senaka met her gaze full on, before he moved out of view.

The man was still on the phone, his voice getting louder as he gesticulated with his hands, glancing at her, pushing his hair back off his face with his fingers. Taking the opportunity, she fixed her eyes on the ledger in front of him, tried to scan the names. He finished the call. Stepping back, away from the desk, she asked if the computer was fixed yet – since she'd arrived, the solitary computer for guests' use hadn't worked.

'It fixed. I give you key.'

She took it, walked slowly, conscious of the swelling wound, past the pool where a man now swam, his great thick bronzed arms beating the water. No sign of Senaka – past the line of cheaper rooms without balconies or sea views, until she reached a door and opened it with the key.

It was a tiny room, more like a box, a space without windows. Cell-like, as her room was, the walls white and bare. She left the door open for air, heard footsteps running down the corridor, the excited voices of the two children. She logged-on, found her e-mails. Sweat seeped from every pore. No fresh air to soothe and cool. With the back of her hand, she rubbed her brow, then, using both hands, lifted her hair from her neck. There were one hundred and ninety three e-mails. Two from Lisa and one from another friend, Amy. She flagged them to answer soon and scanned down looking for one from Mark, halted, her cursor hovering at a reply to a job she'd applied for before she came away. How many jobs had she tried for since she knew she was going to lose hers? An interview was set for three days before she arrived back home from her holiday. It was typical, or was it Karma? Sweat trickled down her face and she thought back to the first time she heard her mother talking about Karma all those years back. There'd been a woman in Marrakesh sitting on the street crying because she'd found out her grandmother had died and Jo had never forgotten the way her golden hair was long enough to touch the pavement. Jo's mother told her the woman had abandoned her baby to her grandmother in England while she travelled round Asia. 'That's Karma,' her mother had said.

There was one from her mother: *I hope this holiday was what you were looking for. We must get together as soon as you get home.* They would no doubt rendezvous in *The Enclave*, where they usually met, with its collection of unemployed philosophers, aspiring poets and the odd foreign language student. She sighed and scrolled to the invitation to the interview, clicked on the print button.

'Found you.' The girl grabbed the chair, swung her round, turning her like a merry-go-round.

'Not now,' she said. 'Just a minute.'

'She is important lady. Let her alone.' The boy tugged at his sister's arm. 'I want to go swimming. This is a horrible room.'

They began to jostle each other, reverting to German and sped away.

It was so hot in there without windows. She turned back to the screen. She would write to the charity, ask them to interview her when she returned. A blank monitor faced her. Fiddling with the keys, turning it off and on, she shouted at it, still the screen stayed blank. Karma, she thought. Her mother was right.

'The computer's broken again,' she told the receptionist when she was in front of his desk again.

He smiled wryly. 'Sorry madam. We will get it fixed as soon as possible. Sorry for any inconvenience. This is for you.' He handed her the printed e-mail from the charity which had offered her the interview.

'Great. Thanks,' she said, with a grin. Maybe he wasn't that bad.

The two children were messing around in the pool splashing each other with water, shrieking, while Senaka looked on. He waved to her, beckoning.

No harm, she thought. She walked over towards the coconut shelter where he was standing, while the sun beat down on her; she squinted in the bright light.

He was holding a tube and roll of bandage in his hand, waving them. 'For your cuts,' he said as she approached. 'To stop infection.'

'Thanks.' She smiled at him. 'This plaster's not really big enough.'

'You want help?'

'No. Thanks. I can manage.' She removed the plaster then took the tube from him, still smiling, shading her eyes from the turmeric shaft of sunlight that penetrated through the coconut roof.

'She say she know you.'

'Sorry?' she said. 'Who?'

'Raquel. She say she know you in England.'

The tube of ointment was in her hand, the top off ready to smooth onto the cut. She unwound the bandage. Overhead, a flock of birds soared, the children yelled at each other, the sun rose higher, sweat poured down her face. She squeezed some ointment onto the tip of her finger, heard a woman's voice calling, the girl in the pool responding. The air felt heavy, claustrophobic, another storm brewing.

'How does she know me? When did she say that? You said nothing earlier.' A blob of ointment, melted, liquid, was spreading across her finger. 'That can't be true. I'd remember.'

He was folding towels. Brown and white striped. 'She said you not remember her. So I think –' He stopped folding, looked over her shoulder at the pool. 'I think then it is not important.'

'It's very important. It's very *very* important. She stole everything from me and you think it's irrelevant. She said we might have met in another life. That's what she said, you know. She said that at breakfast on my first day.

Said she believed in the spirit world, was interested in all that. Huh! Christ, I wish I'd never met her. Don't care where.'

'She not bad, ma'am. I think you friends.'

Her finger continued applying the cream, overdoing the rubbing, making the wound sore. Another beam of sunlight broke through the matting roof, catching the corner of her eye. 'What?' she said. Though she'd heard him, hadn't missed a word. 'What are you saying? Tell me exactly what she said. *How* does she know me?'

A woman's scream, a shrill line of sound cut all other sound out, slicing the atmosphere like a razor. Senaka was holding a towel up ready to fold into four, in preparation to stack with the others. The towel was dropped and a corner brushed her shoulder, his arms held high for a fraction of a second as if he was about to prostrate himself right there in the canopy while the coconut matting creaked overhead. She saw the white scar on his arm flash as he dropped the towel, smelt his sweat as he pushed past the chair where she sat, the tube of ointment in one hand, the cream oozing out from the top. Her finger, her foot, covered in the stuff, the melted ointment forming a rivulet down her arm. She saw him sprint towards the pool. He moved like an athlete, the sound coming from his mouth a cry of war, of disbelief and anger. He jumped into the water. The mother was already on her heels at the edge of the iridescent blue swimming pool, slipping into the water, yelling so loud, shouting her daughter's name out and all the guests, all the hotel staff, were out of their rooms, rushing over from their breakfast, abandoning the buffet bar, leaving the food to go cold. Water splashed on their clothes, sloshed on the sunbeds and the bronzed man who'd been swimming up and down counting the lengths, doing his routine, was yanking the boy out from where the child been standing in the shallow end, transfixed, horrified at what had meant to have been a game.

Carried by Senaka, the girl emerged. She dripped water, her small body folded, head lolling over his shoulder as if there was no life in her. He laid her down on the concrete, the hard ground that surrounded the pool. 'Go back', he told everyone. 'Back, back. She need air. He was on his knees, leaning across, his mouth over the girl's, the mother was kneeling too, hands to cheeks, wailing. There was no other sound. Nothing. Breaths held, willing her to survive, they waited and Senaka breathed into the girl's lungs while the girl lay still, still as stone. Someone was praying. A man's voice carried on the wind. The girl coughed, vomited water. Senaka placed her on her side, the bronzed man put a folded towel under her head, the receptionist put a blanket over her. Collectively, the onlookers sighed with relief, returned to their breakfasts, continued dressing or showering for the new day.

Senaka was allowing the mother to murmur into her child's ear, to smooth her hair from her face, enfold her in her arms and kiss her. Jo observed him standing, unwinding like a spring, while her hand dropped from her mouth to twist the top onto the ointment. Then she saw his sleek form move fast towards the brother who was crying like a baby, sobbing, wiping snot and pool water from his face. Senaka gripped the boy's shoulders, shaking them hard. 'Water is dangerous', he yelled at the brother. 'Your sister nearly drowned.' Back and forth he jiggled the boy's body as if he wanted to make his bones rattle. 'Stop,' a man's voice called. 'He's only a child.' The boy gabbled in German, tore himself away, ran off whining, frightened of his own strength, and Senaka followed the receptionist, the man who'd given Jo the lotus flower, back into the hotel reception.

Jo wandered over to the woman still cradling her daughter in her arms, asked if there was anything she could do.

'They're taking her to the hospital,' the mother said wiping tears from her cheeks.

The girl put her arm out and gripped Jo's hand.

'What a terrible thing to have happened,' Jo said, thinking how trite this sounded, but she couldn't collect the right words in her head.

The woman didn't reply but looked over Jo's head to where Senaka was returning, keys jangling in his hands.

'OK. Ready?' he said to the mother and daughter, turned towards where Jo stood holding the girl's hand. 'Hang on,' Jo said. 'I'll come with you.' Despite what had happened, she was thinking she must find out what he'd been talking about. How was it possible Raquel knew her? Already he was heading off, away from the pool, towards the front of the hotel. She made a quick decision. The girl would be fine. And Jo had every right to know what Senaka was talking about. But how could she be thinking such a thing, *now*? As she grilled under the morning sun, she watched the three of them walking off, the girl's hair, wet, shiny like a seal's coat, the mother with arms round her shoulders. Was it possible she'd mis-understood him? Passing the pool-side, she looked down at the spilt water, remnants of the disaster. The path where the girl had lain was already dry, the incident erased, as if it belonged to another time.

'Hey,' she called out. 'I'm coming with you.'
The girl stopped walking and said something to her mother. They all waited for Jo to catch up.

8

The receptionist with the oiled hair now watched over the pool. Sometimes a waiter joined him. They stood at each end even when there was only one swimmer, sometimes when there were none. The days were hot, with pale clouds on the horizon. Not changing form. They remained nebulous wisps in the distance.

Every day Jo bandaged her foot again and wondered why it remained stubbornly inflamed. Should she get more medical attention? Almost as much as she feared sickness, Jo feared hospitals with their long dark corridors, their smells of cleaning agent, boiled onion. Strange that she'd hooked up with a nurse, her mother always said. But what did she know about relationships?

Jo only stayed long enough in the hospital to get her foot bathed, more ointment applied and a fresh bandage. She'd questioned Senaka further but he didn't have any more information about this alleged friendship with Raquel. She was disappointed as she'd been expecting an explanation from him that would make more sense.

The mother and her two children had left the day after the pool incident, caught an early flight home to the safety of their Western lives. No chance to say goodbye to the family. They'd been whisked away to the airport by another driver in the small hours. Senaka seemed to have vanished entirely off the scene.

Tomorrow she would leave: she didn't like to constantly ask when he might return. Didn't want to arouse suspicion and make her stay even more fraught than it was already. They told her Senaka was away on business. Business? She asked once, the question out before she could stop herself. The look the man with the oiled hair gave her said it was nothing to do with her. And of course he was right. It looked like she would never find out more about Raquel.

Now, after a few days, she began to doubt her ability to recall the exact conversation on the day Senaka saved the girl from drowning. That incident stayed with her. Not the moment when the girl coughed and spluttered to life, but watching Senaka leap into the swimming pool. She disliked herself for remembering this so clearly rather than the moment when everyone knew the girl hadn't drowned. She despised herself for being irritated because the moment when Senaka was going to tell her about Zara was snatched away. But it was the possibility that she'd never see him again, she'd never know more about the woman that bothered her. And she knew he knew more than he let on. It was in the hospital that she realised this and it niggled at her and kept her awake. Added to this was the pounding pain in her foot last night which had reminded her of how she'd felt with that first operation after her fall from the window.

Tomorrow she'd be home.

She decided to spend a last day on the beach and after a final massage in the Spa, donned shorts and T-shirt with her blue bikini beneath. She walked down the path towards the beach. Soaked with sweat, her new sun hat shading her face, she located a plastic lounger and dragged it out of the shade of a palm tree. She removed her shorts and T-shirt, lay flat, knees bent, the leg with the bandaged foot crossed over the other, face turned to the sun. She closed her eyes, felt the sun roast her pale flesh and made an attempt to drain her mind, concentrate on the sounds around her, the birds, the ebb and flow of the tide, an occasional murmur from nearby – but failed. Ten minutes was all she could take of this. Mark was right. A holiday spent on the beach equals boredom and skin cancer.

She slipped past the professional sunbathers with their lustrous tanned limbs. Her feet sank into the sand as she walked in a straight line, following the trail left by birds' footprints down towards the sea. It was a beautiful day, her last day on holiday.

A woman was coming towards her carrying a bag from which sarongs, scarves and skirts drooped, the ends trailing in the sand. Jo stopped, glad of the opportunity to buy more presents. Hand shading her eyes, she waited for the woman to arrive.

'How are you today, Jo?' the woman said when at last she stood in front of her, the sarongs, scarves and dresses flapping in the breeze.

'You know my name?'

'I give you good price.'

'How do you know my name?' Was she infamous here – the tourist who was robbed by a co-patriot?

'This one suit you very well. Look, blue to match your eyes.'

Behind her sunglasses, in the fierce light, Jo blinked. Amber, Mark had called them when they first met. *You've got amber eyes. Like the jewel.* This woman had deep brown eyes, almost black, the etchings of a lost beauty, a youth vanished too quickly. This woman, who knew Jo's identity, was delving into a sack, pulling out sarongs, one by one, holding each one up so Jo saw the colours and designs.

'But how do you know my name?'

'You friend with Miss Raquel. She gone now. Please you buy sarong. Not many tourist. No business. I have family - six children. Very good quality. You buy.'

'She wasn't a friend.' Why did *everyone* think they were buddies?

'She English. Like you. She say me.'

'Yes. But all English aren't friends –' she stopped. No point. Instead she fingered the sarongs. The woman had stopped pulling her wares from the sack and was now peering at Jo, observing the tremble in her hands.

Panicking again. Never mind it was the final day. The woman zoned in on the bandage on her foot and Jo curled her toes.

'I'll buy a couple. No. I'll buy four.' A silver shimmering sarong for her mother, one each for Amy and Lisa, green and blue, and a turquoise one for herself.

'You are good person. Thank you.'

The woman busied herself, folding the four chosen sarongs, slipping them into a creased plastic bag, piling the other sarongs back into the sack and walked back up the beach to the shade of a tree. Jo turned away, took a peek inside the plastic bag. *Friend*. As if... she couldn't rid herself of the spectre of Zara.

A breeze ruffled her hair as she approached the rolling surf and stood there on the edge of the sea, looking out. She tried to imagine a huge wall of water coming towards her. With her bad leg, she couldn't possibly have survived. She thought back to the shaky mobile phone recordings of the tsunami she'd seen on TV all those years back and shivered.

The sea was mirror calm. Children swam in the shallows and she saw the flash of scales glitter in the sun as fish rose to the surface before dipping down under the water. She sighed, thought what a mess she'd made of the last two weeks, tried to push Zara from her thoughts. What did it matter now?

Always before, she'd turned left along this beach where the gradient was less steep. Today, her last day, she decided to explore the area to the right where there were fewer people and the sand rose up from the sea in dune-like hillocks. The wind was against her and she was aware of the strength of the sun piercing her eyes. Feeling free, away from the crowds, she walked along the edge of the sea, dodging the water, jumping back as the tide flowed in. She gave up on keeping her bandaged foot dry. Tomorrow she'd be home. Totally alone, her mind drifted, emptied; she was aware only of the water, the gulls above, a container ship on the horizon, the sun on her face.

There was no one else around. The sand was less dense and her feet sank deep making it incredibly difficult to negotiate her way along the beach. She was nearing the remains of a blackened building set back from the sand dunes. As she got closer she saw green tendrils of weed growing up and around it. The sun burned her as she studied the edifice. She looked along the beach, saw a figure on the shore line. The tide was coming in fast, a wave riding up the shore, drenching her foot. The bandage was waterlogged, full of sand. She should turn around, return to her room, bathe the wound, avoid complications. But this, after all, was her last day. And the walk was good. Alone on the beach, she was happy in her isolation. She crouched, unwound the bandage from her foot, rolled it into a ball, stuffed it into the bag of sarongs.

The figure was still standing at the shoreline with water up to his knees, profile shadowed by the sun. She walked on, the wind tousling her hair, saw that the solitary person was looking out to sea. There was something odd, unnatural, in the stance. What was he doing standing there so still? There was no fishing rod, no line being cast out to sea. It took her a long time to reach the form, standing there immobile, watching the tide come in. She was uneasy about the man's intention. Who was he? She walked closer.

It only took an instant to recognise the face.

'Senaka,' she called. 'Senaka, what are you doing?' Her hat blew off her head and landed a few feet away onto the water, floating on the crest of a wave.

He continued staring at the waves. The water now reached his thighs.

'What's going on?' While spots of rain fell on her hair, she waited.

No reply. She looked to her left, saw the building, its blackened form rising from the dunes, to the right where the sky was turning pewter grey. Not a soul. Birds soared, rising on the wind. To the left again she saw dark specks, people, in the far distance, in the water and on the sand. Had she really walked so far? There was Senaka in front of her, unaware of her presence. The ocean swirled around her legs. She was scared.

She cupped her hands to her mouth and yelled across to him. 'Senaka. You can't just stand there. You'll drown.'

Nothing.

She waded deeper, reached out her hand. Not close enough. She stepped nearer, the tide surged.

She screamed his name. He turned. A fraction. But still he turned.

'What the hell are you doing?' She grabbed his shoulder. 'I'm not a strong swimmer and if we both stand here, we'll drown.'

Beneath her hand, his muscles relaxed. 'You think I want to drown, ma'am?'

The wind tore at her hair. Overhead a gull screeched.

'Get out of the bloody water. You're terrifying me. The tide's coming in. Will you get out?'

'I like to be in the sea when the wind is strong. When the waves are high.'

'It's dangerous here with the tide coming in. Why –?'

'You should go back, ma'am.'

Then she saw it coming, rolling along the surface of the sea, gathering pace. Water swirled around her and she tasted salt on her lips. The wave was gathering momentum, increasing in size. Above her sea birds were circling, crying out. Senaka was facing away from her watching the wave swell. She knew it would be large, that she should step back, knew she would, but for that moment was transfixed, unable to move away. The ocean rose. The horizon vanished into the sea and Senaka turned and looked at her, the expression on his face blank, the courtesy of the hotel worker gone. Contempt was in his eyes. He didn't care whether she lived or died, whether or not she went down with him. Water was surging around them, pushing them closer and she felt his hand on her shoulder, heavy as if he was forcing her under, as if he wanted to take her with him. His grip was tight, his eyes uncommunicative as he looked into hers, as if he weren't conscious. She tried to turn away from him, fight her way out of the ocean, terrified, while water churned around them white and frothing. The swell reached her chest and she thought 'this is it'. The weight of water was dragging her torso down and his hands were firm on her shoulders, pushing. Was this why she had been drawn to the holiday, to this place, to this part of the beach, to meet her end in the water with a hotel worker? Fate. Her mother's words. Aware of the birds above and the roar of the ocean, she was struggling, twisting and turning, fighting for her life. A larger wave was now a few seconds away, rising high from the ocean, a wall of water, full of sand and debris. Grit sprayed onto her face. 'Ahh,' she screamed yet still somehow managed to tear herself away from his grip. Then it seemed as if his hands beneath her lifting her high. Her breath caught in her lungs. She was coughing out water, tasting salt. Couldn't breathe. He had hold of her: one hand on the small of her back, the other beneath her neck. Breath hot on her face. He carried her through the water, pounded up the sand and she felt rain on her face, saw the dark clouds above, the sun hidden, vanished from view. Her heart was crashing against her ribs. What did he intend? 'Let me go,' she shouted, knowing it was useless screaming. He was holding her tight carrying her up through the ridges of sand though she struggled, tried to break free, used the heel of her feet to beat his thighs. Running towards the flotsam on the edge of the beach, he muttered something barely audible, his breathing heavy, then without warning, he dropped her. She ran off in the direction of the hotel. Her foot was on fire. Rain splattered her face and wind tore at her hair. She sprinted across the sand. The old blackened building wasn't far. An extra spurt, then she'd be there. She forced her legs to work harder, ignore the pain searing through her limbs. Run, she screamed to herself. *Run.*

Collapsing onto a tangle of a yellow flowering bloom, she sank to her hands and knees, crawled up the sand dune. She reached a wall of the building, the concrete streaked with decay. Seaweed, bird guano, the stink was overpowering. She retched, saw the ground rising a short gradient to the left of the building, far enough away from the smell, far enough from Senaka. If she reached the spot she'd have a wide view of the sea below. She groped her way towards the building, one hand forward, one knee to follow. Breath laboured, hurting lungs. She reached the hillock and sat, hands clasped under thighs. She breathed slowly, looked out. Where was Senaka? Had she managed to lose him? Why had he wanted to drown her? Or was she wrong about that too? But hadn't his hands been on her shoulders pushing her under? Her body was soaked in seawater, salt tasted in her mouth, on lips, on strands of hair whipping across her face. On the horizon, the clouds were dissipating, shreds of blue showing through. In the distance huge rollers gathered speed. She searched the sand at the edge of the sea. Somewhere beneath the water lay the bag and the four sarongs. A shard of plastic fluttered up ahead, before flopping to the beach as if exhausted. Up there on the dune, she felt the warmth of the sun on her face and breathed deeply, easier. As well as yellow there were some pink flowers amongst the weeds, the same hue as Zara's hat, and her mind flitted to its discovery lying all pert and innocent in the back of Senaka's mini-bus. Why did he want to harm her? The rain had stopped. Salt dried on her face. Behind her she heard the fall of footsteps and quickly swung round, ready to take off.

'Why you run like that?' Senaka called out.

'What?' Jo stood, prepared herself to get away.

'Wait. Wait. Why you run away from me?'

She couldn't put her weight on one leg, couldn't get up. The best she could do was go on all fours. Why was this happening *now*?

'I help you,' he said.

'Don't touch me.' Small stones pinched her knees, the palm of her hands. She gathered pace, dragged her foot behind her, then forced herself upright, began to limp, sweating, gasping.

'You are injured. I can help you back. The hotel isn't far.'

'No. I'm OK.' She sank to the sand, forced herself up again.

'Ma'am. I do not think you are fine.'

She felt him draw nearer.

Spots danced before her eyes. His voice wavered like a heat haze. She heard it become fainter. Get a grip, she told herself.

'I carry you back. You are sick.' He was standing over her.

'You just tried to drown me.'

'Ma'am?'

'You tried to push me under.'

'I do not understand.'

'You tried to push me under. Back there,' she said.

He sat beside her. 'Drown? Why you think I do that?'

Had she made a mistake in thinking that? Was it possible? Was this yet another misunderstanding? She shuffled a little way from him. Sat holding her foot, felt the heat of the sun dry out her hair. She licked her lips and swallowed. Had he been trying to push her under? Now she didn't know, wasn't sure.

'I hold you. The undercurrent is strong. I hold on to you. Not drown ma'am. No. Why I try to drown you? I save the little girl. Why I drown you?'

She turned to look at him. Crystals of salt glistened on his skin, the scar on his forearm red. Remembered him leaning over the girl's body blowing air into her lungs.

'Don't know,' she said, as she stared at a beetle staggering over mounds of sand. 'You weren't trying to drown me then?'

'No, ma'am.'

'Why were you there? In the sea with the tide coming in? It was really dangerous.'

The sky was clear now, a keen blue, the rain clouds gone. Up on the beach, near the hotel, two people emerged from the shelter of the bar. Beside her, Senaka was smoothing a pebble with his fingers. So she was wrong. Wasn't she? But of one thing she was certain, her foot was inflamed, the wound infected even more than before. Her thirst was incredible, impossible and her head swam. Just in case, she dragged herself further away from Senaka.

'They never found my family,' he said, breaking the silence.

'What?'

'My two sisters, my daughter, my mother. They don't find their bodies after the tsunami. They are still in the sea. I talk to them. Sometimes I hear their voices in the wind. It makes it better.'

'Christ, Senaka. Your family? I didn't know.'

'I tried to save my daughter.' His arm was stretched out and with his finger he tapped the scar. 'The wave threw me against a tree. It trapped me so I couldn't catch her.'

Deep from within her lungs, she blew out air.

'I lived in city. I am studying. On day of the tsunami I am visiting.'

She looked at the sea. She looked at him as he turned the pebble over. 'It must have been awful.'

'You cannot imagine. But it is long time ago. I look after my son. He is all I have now. I pay for him to have extra lessons. Everything is expensive. We have to borrow money.'

Was he going to ask her for some cash? As she thought this, she hated herself for contemplating this when she had so much more than him.

'You are a clever woman, ma'am.'

'Jo.' She sighed, began to rake her fingers through the salt in her hair. 'I'm not clever.'

I am a good Buddhist.'

'And?'

He was drawing shapes in the sand; large circles cut through with lines and his mouth opened as if he intended to say something. Then he closed it and carried on drawing pictures in the sand. Jo changed position so she was cross legged. The sea water on her body was drying out, making her skin feel taut.

'I know her from before. Why she steal from you? She said you are old friends.'

'Old friends? How? From where? And how do you know her? I don't understand. '

'She say you are friends. I didn't ask how.' In his palm, he turned the pebble over. Looked down at the sea, at the thin line of sand which lay between the water and the dune where they sat. 'She stay here before.' He chucked the pebble across the sand. 'You go to hospital again,' he said. 'The wound is still infected. It is dangerous. We go now.'

Jo hadn't noticed the sky changing colour, hadn't seen the lead cloud coming across the sea. It began to rain again. She remembered the phone call in the storm, the other two that she'd padded across her room to take, only to hear someone breathing down the phone. Nothing made any sense but it all seemed so irrelevant now. Compared to losing an entire family in the sea, everything was irrelevant. Senaka was staring at her, watching her every move. So difficult to read him. He'd got up, was coming across the sand towards her. Jo felt herself go dizzy, black dots jigged in front of her. She blinked a couple of times as the rainwater wet the salt from her hair.

9

Everything packed ready. At last the day had arrived. A ray of sunlight from the open balcony door fell across the bed and she took a quick look at the sea in the distance, calm and turquoise now. Should she leave the envelope with Mark's torn photo behind, forget it ever happened, forget about her holiday? Opening the drawer where she'd put it, she snatched the envelope and stuffed it into the back pocket of her jeans. She'd show Mark, though exactly why, she didn't really know.

There was a knock on the door.

She hesitated, listening, then opened it. Senaka. 'I thought you weren't working today,' she said.

The look on his face revealed nothing of their encounter on the beach. 'Good morning, ma'am,' he said and she thought how easily he'd reverted to ma'am.

'They told me on reception that it'd be someone else taking me –' She faltered, aware that she sounded rude.

Senaka looked at her bag and into the room behind her. 'Someone else? You have problem that I drive you to airport?'

'No. It's fine.' She thought of the other man who drove the bus with a red stripe painted along its side. Yesterday, she and Senaka had said goodbye as she stood clasping her newly acquired medicine, a stronger antibiotic. He had rushed off, embarrassed that he'd told her so much.

She took a quick look round the room, at her white cell with the blood red mat, now empty of her belongings.

'Your foot better now?'

'Will be. Thanks for taking me back to the hospital.'

'No problem, ma'am. This is my job. To look after guests.'

The emotion of yesterday had gone. She struggled with the image of him standing in water up to his chest…it was as if it hadn't occurred. Here he stood now all neatly dressed, freshly ironed polo shirt and jeans – she'd intruded on the system he'd built for himself, his way of handling the grief. He picked up the handle to her case.

'I can take that.'

'My job, ma'am.' He walked away, her case rolling behind him.

She caught up with him. Hadn't realised till then how painful it was to walk.

'Have to take my sandal off.' Swollen, red, inside the bandage her foot throbbed.

'Medicine will work soon, ma'am.'

'Seeing as you're taking me to the airport. Seeing as this is my last day. Can you call me Jo? I really don't like ma'am?'

He nodded, slid the minibus door open and put her case on the seat. 'Do you need help?'

'Aren't there any other guests getting this flight?'

'No, ma'am. Not this one. Only Germans in hotel now. Is it a problem?'

'No, no. Of course not.' She smiled at him. I'd rather sit in the front. If that's OK.'

He nodded again and opened her door, then walked round to the driver's side. He started the engine. 'OK. I call you Jo. Not ma'am. You call Miss Raquel, Zara.' He sneaked a look at her before swinging the minibus round, out of the hotel grounds.

'You said you knew her from before. So she's been here more than once?'

'We have many guests who return.'

She wriggled in her seat, and for a moment wished the other driver was taking her. She'd looked forward to a silent uncomplicated drive to the airport. Then the image of Senaka standing in the waves appeared in her mind. Tired of talking about Raquel, she said: 'You speak English well.'

'I was studying Engineering. Before the tsunami. I also study English. I talk to the guests,' he replied.

'But they're mostly German.' She thought how since the trip to the temple she'd not come across any other English tourists.

'Not always.'

'No.' Zara's name hung in the air, unsaid. So much she wanted to know. But she'd leave it, would never find out. By tomorrow the two week holiday would fade into the past. Soon, she'd forget. She thought about texting Mark, decided she'd leave it until she was safely ensconced in the airport lounge. It was hot again today, the sun's rays powerful. She was beginning to sweat through the air conditioning, the cold draught that dried the perspiration on her skin. The traffic was heavy, trucks, more taxis, auto-rickshaws, big dusty buses – the bullies of the road.

'You have good holiday?'

She opened her window, smelt gasoline and cow dung. From somewhere nearby there was a waft of raw meat. 'Yes. It was OK.' She snatched a look at the sky, screwed her eyes up in the bright sunlight. 'The massages were very good. The best I've ever had.'

'You come back?'

'Maybe.'

In silence they drove through the higgledy-piggledy town where broken shutters hid the rooms over shops, where dogs and cows wandered aimlessly along the street and men in sarongs hung around shops, watching the traffic, the animals, the day go by. Women carrying plastic shopping baskets struggled with the weight. The road was suddenly full of goats. A goat herder was urging them on. Senaka stopped the minibus and they waited in silence until the goats had been cajoled away from the traffic.

'Your husband meet you at the airport?'

'Yes,' she said, not wishing to explain. 'You know Raquel or Zara, whatever her name is, tore a picture up that I had in my wallet. She put it in an envelope and left it at reception for me. It was of Mark, the man I live with.'

'That is strange.'

'Why would someone do that? I mean it's as though she hated him.' Could she know Mark? Was she an ex-girlfriend or something? She'd been so occupied with cursing herself for allowing Zara to dupe her, this idea had never occurred to her before. Or was Zara simply furious with envy of her steady relationship – her pleasure in the single life, a front?

'But you have other photos of your husband?'

'Yes, but –'

'Good. I am happy for you.' He paused. 'I have no photos of my family. The sea took everything.'

She looked at his arm resting on the gear stick. What would it be like being pinned to a tree while the sea swallowed your family, your belongings, so you had nothing, no reminders of them? How would she have coped? Soon, she'd be seeing Mark. She didn't need a photo. 'It must be so hard for you,' she said. 'I'm sorry to go on like that.'

'You home soon,' he said.

'Yes.'

She could see him thinking, working out what to say, opening his mouth, closing hesitating. 'Raquel said she see you in England.'

'What?'

'I tell you before. She said she know you – the hotel – we thought you friends. We see you go to beach together.'

A creeping paralysis had taken hold of her voice. Zara in England. *No.* 'When? How will she see me in England?' Her voice was small, remote. She heard it more like a whisper. 'How does she know me?'

'She did not tell me.'

'Maybe you misheard her.' There could be no other explanation. Or else he'd not understood what she'd said. She stared out of the window at a dust covered bus passing. Her heart was beating fast. Not a panic attack. Not now. She opened the window and breathed deeply, closing her eyes, allowing the breeze to mess with her hair. She couldn't wait to get home. Mark was so sensible; he made her feel safe.

With the toe of her better foot she pushed one of her sandals round and round on the floor. She was remembering the day before, sitting with Senaka on the sand dune as if they were the only two people in the world. Had he entrusted only her with the details of how he dealt with his grief? Or maybe he'd told other guests too – she tried to imagine losing all your family and friends like that, in a few minutes, under a colossal wave. No more Mark, her mother gone, both her best friends Lisa and Amy drowned. Rob gone too...In her train of thought, she paused. There'd been a client once who'd lost his entire family in a gas explosion. She remembered she'd completed the housing application form for the man who was shaking so much he couldn't hold a pen to write. She recalled how efficiently she'd carried out the task, sitting at her desk afterwards, sipping café latte while she wrote a report. There'd been a joke going round the office. Laughing so much, she spilt latte all over the form. She'd felt so bad she'd taken the page home, washed off the coffee and ironed it flat. That, of course was before she was promoted to manager. Managers were paid enough to leave their emotions at home – unlike front-line staff.

Did Senaka tell Zara what he'd told her? Not the most sympathetic of women with her all-over tan, that stupid pink hat, ruining Jo's holiday. That picture wouldn't budge. Pretending to be good, the tourist who cared, how dare she?

'You liked her, didn't you?' Jo said. 'I mean everyone here seemed to know her and everyone thought we were friends. I find that very odd. But it doesn't matter now.' And she thought how easily she too had been taken in.

91

He suddenly turned right and parked outside a row of shops. She saw a muddy path which led to the open doorways. A woman carrying a baby appeared from inside the shop and looked on. She was wearing a long blue and black dress.

'We stop here. So you can buy sarongs.' He pointed to a shop. Torn pink plastic protected garments from the sun. Pink again.

'No. I don't need –'

'To replace sarongs you bought yesterday. The sea took them.'

'No. Look. I have to get to the airport.'

'Plenty of time.'

He was already coming round to her side of the mini-bus.

She wanted to stay resolute. But to do that might appear rude and she didn't want that, not while she had to spend the next couple of hours sitting next to him, not after she'd heard him tell her about the family he'd lost. Over her swollen foot, she slipped on her sandals, put the best foot on the ground followed by the bad foot. As well as the hip injury of old, her cut foot made her hobble.

'Christ,' she said

'Everything all right?'

'My foot seems to have swollen like a balloon.'

'Medicine work soon. No worry.'

'I hope you're right.'

A plastic chair was brought out from behind the counter. 'You sit, ma'am', they both said. There was no air in the shop. A broken fan stood on the counter. The woman, still holding her baby, opened the door to the glass counter, reached inside, pulled out one sarong after another, folding them out when Jo showed the slightest hint of interest. It was oven-hot in there, her face was like a furnace, hair damp. She longed for cold England at that moment. But there was no time for day-dreaming, she she had to choose quickly. Didn't she have a plane to catch?

'I'll have that one, that one and that one.' They weren't as nice as the ones on the beach, but she was past caring, just wanted to get going on the road. 'And that one.' She pointed to another one, a black glittery sarong that her mother would like.

'We have hats too. Plenty of hats.'

'No. I'm going home to England. It's freezing there. Don't need a sun hat.'

Hat upon hat was brought out from a display cabinet behind the counter. The woman brought out steps. 'No,' said Jo. 'Please, there is no need.' Still carrying the baby, the woman climbed the steps and brought more hats, tucked under the other arm. The baby began to whimper.

Jo touched a pink hat, like Zara's.

'You try it.'

'No. I was just looking at it.'

'You try. You try,' the woman said again.

Jo glanced at her watch. 'OK.' She put the hat on her head.

'Very beautiful, Ma'am. I give you good price.'

Jo sighed. 'No honestly. I never wear that colour.'

Senaka was talking to the woman as she folded each sarong, slid them into a plastic bag, idly chatting as if there was no plane to catch. Why did she agree to this? Why hadn't she stood her ground?

'What's she saying?'

'She say business is slow. It is difficult for her.'

Absentmindedly, Jo was fingering the pink hat. 'Sorry to hear that,' she said. 'But can we go now?'

'You take this? Half price?' The shop keeper said, pointing to the hat.

'Oh, OK.' She'd do anything to hurry up the process of getting back on the road. She paid and winced when she stood. 'Right. Let's go.'

She tried to put her weight on the better foot as she stepped back down the path. Four children approached her. 'Pens,' they said and stared at her feet. Their hands were outstretched, the whites of their eyes so pure. She delved into her bag, brought out a pen.

'Here,' she said. From the road, Senaka was watching her. She only had two pens and needed one. But thought how their need was greater. She placed some coins into each of the children's palms and gave her second pen to the tallest child, the thinnest one. 'Thank you, ma'am,' they said. They ran off laughing, their naked soles chafing the mud. Inside the minibus, she took her sandals off, waited for the air conditioning to cool her down. She thought how she could've given them more. Staring out of the window, clutching her newly acquired sarongs and hat on her knee, she turned to look out of the window at the street outside. 'You are good person,' Senaka said.

She didn't reply. 'Did Raquel say where she knew me from?' To save confusion she'd decided to call the woman Raquel.

'I didn't ask. Sorry ma – Jo.'

'You find it hard, don't you?' she said, smiling. 'I mean, calling me Jo?'

He glanced at her. Overtook a bus. And she watched the arm with the scar. The hand rested on the gear stick while the other one steered.

'It is no problem,' he said.

Late but not too late, they arrived at the airport. The sun was high. Clouds of exhaust infiltrated the smells of sweat from the travellers and duty free perfume from a shop set near the entrance.

He lifted the case from the back of the mini-bus, grabbed the handle, wheeled it towards her, reached down, took her bag, heavy with her book and emergency passport and the sarongs. Reluctantly, she wore the new pink hat. 'I'm fine now. I can take all this. Thank you for everything,' she said.

'I take it in for you.'

'No. Please. I'm fine,' she said. 'You've done enough. Honestly.'

He was in front of her. With his good arm he was trailing the case. The other arm hung at his side with the straps to her hand luggage clutched in a fist.

'Wait.'

Ahead of her he walked. Difficult to separate him from the other men wheeling their guests' cases. Why was he walking so fast?

'Hey,' she called out. 'Senaka. Wait.'

Her heart was somersaulting against her ribs, So many cases and trolleys to negotiate. So many bodies. She pushed through. 'Sorry,' she said again and again. 'So sorry.' And now her foot was agonising. Sandal cutting into the wound. The infection was spreading. She knew it. Had to get home. She felt panic tight in her chest. He wouldn't. Would he? She slipped out of her sandals, easier in bare feet. A man pushed into her, nearly sent her flying and she put a hand out to steady herself. The sandals were knocked from her hand. Barefoot, she struggled onwards.

'Senaka?'

People parted, allowing her through. He was there, standing by the automatic door, waiting, chatting to a man in uniform.

'I thought you'd gone.'

'Why you think that?'

The man in the uniform was looking at her. He rolled his eyes up and down her form, rested on her naked, swollen, red, dirty feet.

'No shoes,' the man said.

'Back there,' she said, embarrassment making her flush. 'I've injured my foot. I'm sorry I'm in such a state. I'm not usually like this.'

The two men spoke. With their palms open, they gesticulated, voices rising as they took in turns to gaze at her.

'No shoe. No travel,' the uniformed man said.

'Right.' She knew in countries where the economy was based on bribes, officials had a tendency to make up the rules on the spot and she took hold of her bag in one hand, case in the other. 'I'm going to retrieve my sandals.'

'I go. You wait here,' Senaka said.

'Please. Hurry.'

While the crowd jostled, pushed, knocked her foot; while she winced in pain, the man in uniform looked away. Tucked into his belt was a revolver. A hand rested on the butt. She noticed a small dark stain on his otherwise immaculate khaki coloured shirt. She was an hour late checking-in.

Through the crowd, Senaka appeared pushing a trolley. Her sandals were suspended from his finger and thumb.

'Thanks,' she said. She gave him a wad of notes. 'This is for you.'

'There is no need.'

'Please take it.'

'You are a kind lady. I come with you. To make sure everything OK.'

'Not necessary.' She grabbed the trolley and began to load it. 'You don't need to follow me, Senaka. You can go back now. Thank you for everything you've done for me...'

'Good luck,' he said. He smiled, turned round. Was gone.

She took her place at the end of the long queue. She sighed, puffing out air, could barely believe she'd made it. At last!

It was a small airport. Crockery clattered as it was washed somewhere in the back of a nearby café. Someone dropped a plate and she heard it crash on the floor. As she stood waiting to check-in she listened to the smashed crockery being swept off the floor. The queue moved along a fraction. The flight was supposed to leave in fifty minutes. There was a shop where carved elephants, tigers, replicas of Buddha, and peculiar looking beasts with three horns were displayed on a shelf. A rail of kaftans was set as near as feasibly possible to the end of the queue where Jo stood on her dirty swollen feet, waiting while she gripped her hand luggage into which she'd stuffed the pink hat, though now the zip wouldn't close. Five minutes passed. The queue was stuck. For more than ten minutes she stood waiting. She took a hand mirror out from her hand luggage and smoothed her hair, checked her eye make-up put on some lipstick. Still the queue remained static. She stared at the board with flickering flight numbers and sighed and swung her injured hip while holding onto the trolley. The massages in the hotel had definitely helped, even so she dreaded the long flight ahead...she yawned, feeling sleepy. thinking about the kip she yearned for, while overhead the strip lighting buzzed and blinked. Stretching her neck, she stood on tiptoe, tried to discover the cause of the delay. She took two steps out from the line. Just to find out, that's all she intended. A little curiosity – nothing more. Someone else was also stepping out of line to take a look. A woman wearing a pink sun hat. Jo stepped out a little further. Told herself it was impossible, that there were plenty of pink sun hats around, even she'd got one. She was a little jumpy. That's all. Then the woman turned round, was looking directly at Jo. No, thought Jo. No. No. *No*, she'd made a mistake. Jo left her case unattended as she walked down the length of the queue in the direction of the check-in whilst swinging the straps of her hand luggage on her arm. She was aware of some people staring at her; she reckoned they were asking themselves who this woman was with inflamed feet and a limp. She flicked a look at each face, noting only that they didn't belong to Zara. She must have been mistaken. For the pink hat she'd seen before had now vanished. But still she walked slowly, painfully, along the queue. She had to be sure. Perhaps the faulty strip lighting was playing tricks. Or could it be her imagination? She had reached a man standing behind a trolley laden with assorted sizes of boxes, tied with string. The boxes were piled so high they blocked the view of the person in front and his trolley was at an angle, sticking out in a disorderly manner. She skirted round it, forming a loop so she didn't miss sneaking a look at the person in front. Her breath was coming short and fast. She was then standing parallel to the woman who was standing in front of the man with the boxes. And there was the pink hat. The woman turned. Heavy make-up gave her a doll-like appearance. Raquel. No mistake. She stared at Jo. Blank. Did she plan to use Jo's passport?

'Right,' Jo said firmly. 'I'm going to get security. What you did to me. You're not getting away with it.' She looked back along the queue, to the place where she'd left her case. Everyone in the line was staring at her, their attention alerted by the possibility of an event breaking the boredom of checking in. There near the shop selling carved elephants and replicas of Buddha stood a man wearing a security uniform. She made her way towards him,

'Excuse me,' she said, trying to sound calm and speaking clearly. 'There is a woman in the queue who stole my passport and is maybe intending to use it now. That would be fraud, wouldn't it? She also stole some money and credit cards.' The man, who was short and stocky with an oiled moustache, clearly didn't understand her.

But by now another man in uniform with severe acne had joined them and she was asked to repeat what she'd just said. The two men talked to each other in Singhalese. They kept looking at her. Should she have reported it at all? Maybe she should have let it go. But the idea of Raquel getting away with it was intolerable.

'You show us.'

At last, justice would be done.

She led them to where Raquel stood smiling at the security men, her musky aroma infiltrating the air.

'Do you know this woman?' the spotty man asked her.

'Never seen her in my life before,' Raquel said, smiling sweetly. 'Is there a problem?'

'Your passport,' the man demanded.

Without so much as a glance at Jo, Raquel handed over her passport and the man thumbed through every page until he found the photo. He looked at the photo then back up at Raquel.

'Is this you?'

'Of course it's me,' Raquel said just as the shorter man took a call on his intercom. He spoke rapidly to the other man.

'You come with us, ma'am,' he said to Jo.

'Why?'

The man with the stain on his shirt joined them. They were all gazing at her.

'You come with us.' The man with the acne put his hand on her shoulder. She didn't like the stern looks on their faces. To make matters worse, the queue was moving, the check-in woman getting through the passengers at an alarming pace. 'Look. What is going on?'

Instead of replying they frogmarched her from the queue, past the shop and into a room next to the automatic doors, where before, she had walked through, happy to be at last going home. It was another small sweaty airless room. Was there a conspiracy? Had that bloody awful man at the beach hotel been in contact with these border police?

She sat where they pointed, on a small wooden chair in another beige room where the only furniture was a desk, a monitor, a mucky computer keyboard, two chairs. They asked for her passport.

'Here you are. It's an emergency passport. Mine, you see, was – look, that woman stole my passport *and* my money. Isn't it she the one you should be questioning?'

They weren't listening. The three men were talking to each other, passing round her document.

'My case is still out there.' She could barely breathe in this place. Already she was soaked with perspiration. 'Please. I cannot miss that flight.'

'Why you get *this* flight?' The man with acne frowned. As he gesticulated, as his body moved inside his shirt, so did the gun.

'It's the end of my holiday. I want to get home. Why else?'

Again they spoke to each other. One of them left the room. They still had her passport and the pink hat was bursting out from her hand luggage where the zip was unfastened. She extracted it and placed it on the desk. 'What's going on?' she said again.

'Ma'am. That is what we are trying to find out.'

The man returned with her case. 'Is this yours, ma'am?'

'Yes.' She went cold. Shivers were creeping down the back of her neck. She'd try again: 'Can I go now? Please?'

One of the other men was speaking now. 'Can you open your case?'

'Why? Yes. Of course.' Pictures of planted drugs flashed through her brain. Her hand was shaking so much she could barely unfasten the catch.

One by one, her pieces of clothing were lifted from the case: her knickers were shaken out, the pockets in her shorts turned inside out.

'Why are you doing this?'

Ignoring her, they carried on extracting her wash bag, the antibiotics she got yesterday from the hospital, a blister pack of painkillers which she'd finally located at the bottom of the pocket with the Prague map. 'They're ordinary painkillers,' she said. 'You can buy them anywhere.'

They said nothing, but continued removing her belongings from the case. She was trembling all over as she held a hand to her throat. Very soon, the case was empty. But no. There was more. What were they doing? She stared, feeling sick. A false bottom that she knew nothing of, that Mark hadn't told her about.

She gasped. 'I didn't know –'

It seemed they were peering at something inside this false bottom that was a surprise to her, this secret compartment where she was convinced someone had placed packets of heroin and cocaine. The room seemed to be closing in on her. An image of prison, death by shooting, the terrible beatings beforehand, fixed itself in her mind. But this was Mark's case. What was she thinking? She watched closely as the men pulled out sheets of tissue paper and shook each one. They laid them on the desk, one by one and smoothed them out with their fists. They looked at her and she couldn't read their faces.

The man with the waxed moustache began to replace her belongings into her case.

She breathed.

From the desk drawer the man extracted a form. 'You fill this in,' he said. 'Then you go.'

'I don't have a pen,' she said. 'I gave all my pens to some children.'

They searched her face and for a minute she wondered whether not having a pen was also a crime in this country. One of them left the room.

'Last call for Kandia Airlines flight 667 to Manchester.'

'That's my flight. Please. I have to go – please, can I fill this in on the plane? There isn't time now. I *mustn't* miss my flight.'

'Wait,' the man with the dirty shirt said, a nasty smirk spreading across his face. 'You have emergency passport. You must complete form. They should give you this when you collect your emergency passport.'

'But I've done nothing wrong. And the consul didn't give me any form.' Then she remembered how stroppy she'd been there. Had the consul omitted to give her the form to spite her? Or had she mislaid it, left it in the mini-bus, not realising its importance. 'If I miss my flight – Christ, what will I do?'

The door opened and a pen was thrust in her hand. 'You fill this in. Then go.'

'All of it? There are three pages. Why do I need to do this?'

Perspiration was dripping down the back of her neck. She flicked through the pages. How could she possibly do what they asked and not miss her flight? Rummaging through her bag, she plucked out a piece of paper with the full postal address of The Green Spa Hotel and began to write: passport number, home address, married or not, hotel where she'd

101

stayed, date of arrival, reason for travel, declared goods removed from the country. Stomach knotting, she turned the page over.

'Last call for Kandia Airlines flight 667 to Manchester.'

'That's my flight.' She saw the man with the stain on his shirt move to the door blocking any exit and felt her skin begin to crawl.

'Why are you doing this?' she asked uselessly. It took her another few minutes. But she answered all the questions on the three pages and thrust the sheets at the man.

'Thank you, ma'am,' he said, the unpleasant smile creasing his face again. Satisfied with what she'd put, he opened the door and beckoned for her to leave. No word of apology left his lips. Nothing. Not an utterance. With her case rolling behind her she sped to the check-in counter, now closed and knocked hard on the counter.

'Your flight has departed, ma'am,' the check-in clerk said, her eyes mournful. 'I am sorry.'

She felt weak, all her energy sapped. Raquel had got away with it again. 'Is there another one today?'

'No ma'am. Tomorrow morning. Three fifteen in the morning.'

Jo put her hand to her face. 'Are there any seats?'

'Yes, ma'am.'

After she'd booked a seat she looked around the airport. Would she really have to spend the next twelve hours here? But she would try and relax until she got home. No more nightmarish events. At least then she would be able to move on from this holiday and resume normality.

Part 2
Revelation

10

Air turbulence kept Jo awake through most of the flight. As the stewards passed down the plane, trolleys laden with food and duty free, she felt sure they were giving her odd looks. And she caught two of them observing her in disquieting way while they chatted. Was she on some kind of special alert? Did the authorities still believe she was carrying drugs? Was Raquel somehow in cahoots with the Sri Lankan authorities? In her exhaustion, her imagination ran riot. Perhaps she wouldn't be allowed off the plane without a police escort. Would she be locked in another tiny room and questioned again?

But no. At Manchester, she sailed through Customs. Not one security officer gave her a second look. It was good to be home.

Then Mark was hurrying towards her, nearly skidding across the floor of Arrivals. Smiling in that crooked way of his, he grabbed her hand and pulled her to him. 'At last,' he said. 'You made it. Lucky they had another flight so soon.' He was breathing hard as if he'd been running.

'I still had to wait seven hours in that bloody airport. God, it was awful. I'm never going on a package holiday again. I'm never going *anywhere* again.'

'Come here, my sweet.' They hugged and his body felt new, even though she knew him so well. She loved his spine, the gentle, almost feminine curve, and his strong legs. She reached up and kissed him. God. She'd missed him. 'It was a bloody awful holiday. They were bastards in the airport –'

'You look shattered?' With his finger, he traced the curve of her cheek. 'Still as lovely though. A tan suits you. Makes you glow.'

'You evil flatterer. ' She returned another kiss. 'I just want to get home.' She took a breath, was going to tell him in more detail about what had happened in the other airport, the man with the stain on his shirt that she now suspected was dried blood from beatings, her conspiracy theory, but changed her mind. It could wait for later. He pointed to her swollen foot. 'You didn't say it was that bad.' He seemed to have grown even taller, his lean face sexier-looking than ever. 'I'll take a look when we get back. But you must have got something out of the holiday. Surely? I bloody hope so –'

'I'll have to think about that.' Where could she start? The girl nearly drowning; seeing Senaka on the beach? Or should she begin by telling him about everyone knowing and liking Zara and the way she felt under suspicion? Being locked in a room *twice*? Too exhausted to go through all that again, she decided to save it all. 'But I *have* got an interview the week after next.'

'That's great. Who with?'

'A housing association. I'll tell you all about it later.'

Once inside his old blue Golf she dozed fitfully, surfacing from her uneasy sleep when they stopped or started at junctions and traffic lights. Momentarily, she woke to Mark's fingers tapping on the wheel in time to the low music in the car. Then she slept again. The rain was steady and the swish, swish of the windscreen wipers became, in her dreams, the sound of surf hitting pebbles and sweeping back up the beach. Zara was there too. A figure in the distance in a multi-coloured sarong. Through her dreams, her foot throbbed and became a red sun on the horizon.

Jo woke fully when the car swung into their road and stopped outside the house in Meresbridge, her home for the last two years. She looked up at the Lake District mountains shrouded in mist. Even without their full majesty as a backdrop, the street looked just as amazing with the rows of tall slate houses. Their house was larger than the others with a garage and an extension and a converted loft. Mark's wife – now dead – had had a reasonable income writing for women's magazines and the house was inherited from her grandfather. Not in a thousand years had Jo imagined she'd ever live in an upmarket street in Meresbridge. Dragged around all those exotic countries when she was little, she was the envy of her friends. Such a brilliant interesting childhood, they all said. Envious of her switched-on mother, they didn't understand the reality of being a child constantly on the move.

She watched him stride up the steps, two at a time, lifting her case as though it contained nothing but air. She followed him and brushed against an overgrown bush, drops of water scattering on her jacket. In a daze, she looked round the hall. He was stroking her hair, tipping her face up to his, kissing her hard. His mouth was full on hers and he supported her as she lifted her legs so they circled his waist. He carried her up to the first landing, bumping the landscape paintings on the way, took off her coat, put his lips on hers and she felt the excitement run through her body. Up the next flight. He pulled her T-shirt over her head. To the top floor and into their bedroom and she was unzipping her jeans, straining to ease the fabric apart. The envelope fell from her back pocket. Fragments of his photograph scattered over the wooden floor. For a second, he stopped unhooking his belt, glanced at the shreds, then his mouth was on hers again. They were embracing, licking, tasting each other, moving to the wall and his bare chest was pressing against her breasts. For a split second her mind was distracted as an image returned, the circling vultures from her dream, before they were on the bed together, naked. She felt his penis hard against her stomach before he was inside her, then as her passion completely consumed her, she thought of nothing else besides the sensation of him pushing deeper inside.

He rolled off her and she lay on her side, nestling into the crook of his arm.

He ran his fingers through her hair. 'The sun's made your hair golden. My golden Jo. I wish I'd been there with you.'

'Never mind. Back now,' she said sleepily. Across from his shoulder she could see the scraps of paper that had fallen from her jeans. She was so tired. She closed her eyes and heard voices come up from the pavement; not English. Suddenly she was back in that tiny room in the beach hotel with the two men shouting at each other while she tried to explain. A dog barked repeatedly. The yellow painted room came back into view.

He picked up a shred of the paper, examined it, and sat on the edge of the bed. 'Have to get you another photo.'

'Got the real thing. Don't need one.' She stretched her arm out and tugged his leg. 'Come back to bed.'

'Sorry. Got the bloody late shift.' He hurried into the bathroom and she heard the whoosh of the shower. For a while she lay there thinking how good it was to be home, making love with her man in their comfortable Queen-size bed.

It was a large room, dramatically changed from when Mark used to share it with his wife. Jo had insisted. Gone was the divan, replaced with an oak framed bed and a cotton filled mattress. She'd disposed of the ornate reproduction Georgian furniture. She had so disliked the gold trim. Mark had bought two matching chests of drawers in antique pine, a mirror which swayed in its frame and two wicker chairs to celebrate their relationship.

She decided to join Mark in the shower for some soapy sex. Opening the door to the en-suite bathroom, she saw Mark towelling himself.

'Sorry. Bit of a crisis at the hospital. I took the day off yesterday.'

She pulled him to her. 'They'll have to wait.'

'Stop tempting me. I really have to go.' He cradled her face in his hands. 'You know I cooked a special romantic dinner for you last night –'

110

'That was a nice thought. Can we have it tonight, then?'

'I'll cook another one tomorrow. A better one. You'll see.'

'Brill,' she said. Slipping on her robe, she went to the dormer window and looked across at the roof tops where smoke drifted from chimneys, then down at the street. A sheepdog was being led across by its owner and she watched its progress. A woman in a black coat was standing across the road. Yellow blonde hair cut short. Standing motionless. She looked up at Jo and held her gaze. The blood drained from Jo's face and she pressed herself to the window. Was that Raquel or Zara or whoever she was? She gripped the sill, watched the woman walk down the road while looking back towards her. But how could she see her there on the third floor? And how could it be her? The idea was pure madness.

Mark was rummaging in a drawer, pulling out underwear.

'You should cover that wound.' He put a roll of bandage and a tube of ointment on the bed.

Without focusing, she looked at the gauze, saw Mark hurriedly dressing. It couldn't be Zara. She had to get a grip.

'Making some tea,' she called to Mark as she stepped out of the room, passed the Windermere landscape, then the blue and white vase on the next landing, the familiarity of both so comforting.

'I'll make it. You stay in bed.'

But she was already in the hall, opening the front door, exploring the street with her eyes. Up and down. She stepped out. Nothing.

Could she have imagined what she thought she'd just seen? She went into their living room and sat on the blue sofa pushed against the window. Was she having some kind of hallucination, brought on by spending seven hours in an airport followed by twelve hours on an uncomfortable flight trying to sleep, trying to make sense of it all? Twisting round, she took in the road outside where her red Peugeot was

111

parked. Rain water rolled down the road filling gutters and forming rivulets on the tarmac. The slate of the houses opposite shone and dripped and the hedges glistened, the leaves showing bright against the grey surroundings. The dark clouds hung so low they looked like they might soon touch the ground and from nearby came the sound of a damp engine trying to start. A black cat dashed across the road and took refuge under a car parked opposite. She felt warm and safe in the constant rain and mist. It was exhaustion that had interpreted the woman she'd seen from the bedroom as Zara. The holiday was behind her. Nothing could harm her now. She closed her eyes and heard Mark coming down the stairs, the familiarity of his footsteps making her feel at ease. Was that a low roll of thunder moving across the far-off mountains? Nothing seemed to have changed in that respect.

The doorbell rang.

'I'll get it,' Mark said. It rang again.

She heard him open the door and strained to see but it was impossible from that angle. The door slammed shut. Mark's voice, angry, the words borne away in the wind and rain.

'Who was that?'

'Jehovah's Witnesses. Told them where to get off. They've gone now.' Kissing her, his mouth lingering on hers, running his fingers through her hair, he hugged her. 'I'm sorry, baby. I wish I didn't have to go.'

She remembered how his mother had been a Christadelphian. Ruined his childhood, he said once.

'So do I,' she said.

'And I've got to go to my dad's after my shift. I'm sorry.'

She untangled herself from the embrace. 'When will you be back?'

'I'll have to stay over with my father. A carer's got this flu bug. But you'll be fine, you'll sleep. You do understand, don't you?'

'I could meet you at your dad's.'

112

'Thanks but he gets very confused. Get some sleep, babe.' He was moving round the room, picking up newspapers, closing his laptop. 'I'll be back as soon as I can. Try and keep me away from you.' He laughed.

'But –' she began. He'd gone into the hall, into the kitchen already and was out of earshot. She turned her gaze to the road outside. A woman with a pink umbrella was standing in front of Mark's car. She thought of how Zara had stood waiting for her on the beach while the sea birds cackled overhead. How could it possibly be her? Moving closer to the window pane, she willed the woman to raise her umbrella but the face remained concealed. All she could see was the fingers clasped round the umbrella handle; clutching, tightening. Jo put her hand to her mouth. It couldn't be. *No*.

Mark was back. In one hand he carried letters and a roll of bandage, in the other, a cup of tea. 'You OK?'

'That woman out there with the pink umbrella. See.'

He followed her gaze. 'What about her?'

'I think it's *her*. I think it's Zara, the woman who robbed me.'

'What? Jo come on, how could it be? You're home now. In England. That's all history.'

'Looks like her.' She focused directly on the woman, hoping to stare her out, make her feel uncomfortable, so she'd get the message and go. 'I wish she'd fuck off.'

'Hey –'

'I'm completely freaked out. It's like something out of a horror film.' How could she be the same person? This was all going wrong. When she'd not been worrying about why the air stewards might be watching her, she'd passed the time daydreaming about seeing Mark again, how they'd fuck all night and sleep late the next day. She moved her foot so it was lying flat on the sofa. 'I was looking forward to spending a bit of time with you.' She knew she sounded sulky, but couldn't disguise her disappointment.

113

'I wish I could stay.' He walked to the window. He was standing close so she could smell the laundry soap on his polo-shirt. 'She's just an ordinary woman.'

'Why do you reckon Zara tore your photograph into shreds?'

'She must be deranged. You said yourself she seemed really pissed off that you'd left me behind. You said she was jealous you were in a relationship. She's gone. You're not going to see her again. Ever. You had some bad luck and I know it must have been bloody terrible, but she's not going to follow you home –'

'How do you know?' She felt like her mind was exploding and she jumped up, snatched her new pink hat from the table and stuffed it into the waste paper basket.

She sat at the table opposite Mark. 'Bloody hat. Bloody foot. Bloody holiday.'

'God, Jo.'

'*She* had a pink sun hat. And I kept on seeing a bloody pink hat everywhere; then I was cajoled into buying that one by this woman who said her business was doing badly. I didn't want it.' She paused for breath. 'I really think she must have followed me her. She would have arrived in the UK yesterday.' She moved closer to Mark. '*Please*, can't you stay?'

'No one's going to harm you. You're home now. Whoever she was is out of your life.'

'I don't mean anyone. I mean *her,* that Zara, *Raquel* woman.'

'Look. You're tired. You've had an awful experience. But that can't be the same woman, Jo. I mean, how could it be?' He was fiddling with the bowl of fruit, rearranging the apples and oranges. 'A lot of the staff are off sick, so I couldn't change my shift. I had yesterday off because – I'm really sorry.' He gathered some papers together, stood gazing at her. 'She looked quite ordinary to me, probably just looking at houses. There's a few on the market in this street. You'll feel better after a sleep.'

114

'Houses are selling then, are they? The market was dead before. We could put this on the market then, couldn't we? Raise some cash if we're short. You always said there were too many memories here.'

'We can talk about that another time. OK sweet? Right now I have to go.'

'Fair enough. Shame though. I mean shame you've got to go.'

Drawing her to him, he kissed her firmly on the lips then she heard the letter box rattle as he closed the door and she watched him speed down the steps, open the car door and drive off.

By now her tea was nearly cold but still it felt good slipping down her dry throat. She lay back on the sofa and closed her eyes for a few minutes before she remembered her post. A load of junk mail, a bank statement, a union circular and a letter inviting her for an interview to replace the one she missed. Fourteen days gave her plenty of time to prepare.

The only sound was the rain. Pitter-patter on the window. A slow drip from a gutter, a stream of water emptying into a drain outside. The grandfather clock, inherited by Mark's wife, ticked in the hall. She had died a year before they met. Ovarian cancer, the silent killer. He'd nursed her till the end. He told her the first time they'd shared a Chinese, on their first date. Dates were not something she was used to. Meet at a party, fall into bed, meet a few more times till the magic wore off had been her way. Apart from Rob, but he was different. She and Mark had talked all night and watched the dawn rise over the mountains. She fell in love. Moved in six weeks later. She had immediately packed away all the ornaments and rolled up the sheepskin rugs. The rose patterned Marlborough sofa was next to go, replaced by a long blue three-seater with huge animal print cushions, though the floral chair, opposite the TV, a wedding present for Mark and his wife had remained. The fireplace needed renovating, the green paint stripped. She had plans. Mark wasn't particularly interested in interior design. Her mother would have preferred Jo to hook up with a guitarist in a rock band, someone more interesting. But she'd never known the extent to which Jo was wrecking her life before she met Mark. *You're turning all bourgeois* she'd seen her mother thinking on her first visit to the town house with the trimmed hedges and shiny four wheel drives parked along the street. In an attempt to seek her mother's approval she'd told her about Mark playing the drums and how they'd met but didn't say he seemed to have lost interest in his drums and they'd been abandoned in the garage.

She turned over on the sofa and floated. The burgundy walls blurred as her mind closed down. Sleep took her over and she only came to when her hip began to ache. Pain shot down her leg. She lay flat again, adjusting her position so she would have a clear view of the street while the rain bucketed down. She closed her eyes and hoped Zara would never appear again. And she remembered Senaka's words: *Raquel say she see you in England.* But how could the woman with the pink umbrella be Zara? She stared at a print of a snowy mountain opposite, at the retro chair she'd bought on impulse before losing her job. The room was hot and stuffy.

The cold damp air streamed into the centrally heated room when she opened the window. A man strode past, parka hood up. He slowed down to look at Jo before hurrying on and a car sped by, water spraying from its tyres. Was that the same woman with a pink umbrella at the end of the road? The figure was coming back towards their house. The phone rang and she slowly made her way towards it. The ringing stopped. No message. Number withheld.

She looked out at the street, expecting Zara's face to be there. Rain, more rain, the sound of cars from the distant main road. The hand of the grandfather clock clicked as another minute passed. Hand trembling to such an extent she could barely sort through the drawer in the kitchen, she found a bread knife, returned to the window and watched through a crack in the curtains for the woman to appear outside the house again. She had another dream: She was back in the

116

airport, an interrogation light blinding her. The airport shrank to the size of a cell and she heard rats scuttling.

They were scampering up her legs, heading for her face. Zara was laughing: *You left your husband at home. You stupid fucking cow.*

Bathed in sweat, thinking she was still in the airport with the strip lighting flickering and fatigue popping her brain, she opened her eyes. At home. In Meresbridge. With Mark.

Slowly she came to, barely remembering climbing the stairs and getting into bed the night before.

She got up and went to the window. It was still dark. Her foot throbbed. It was a steady, set-in, sensation of pain. There was heaviness in the air. It would rain again soon. By the light from the lamp post she saw Mark's car drawing up outside. She watched him park, get out and lock the door. He rang the bell. Half asleep, she went downstairs and opened the door.

'Sorry. Left my keys at work. I saw the light on.'

'Bit late aren't you? It's four.'

'Sorry,' he said again. 'Shift from hell.'

She returned to bed, closed her eyes, drifting into an unsettled sleep, hearing the pull of the wave, the tide ebbing and flowing – Zara drinking her beer, scheming, planning. Why would she be here? Could Senaka have been mistaken? Or was it that she'd misheard him? Mark was in the bedroom undressing. 'You OK?' He drew the duvet back and slipped into bed beside her.

'Can't sleep. It's better now you're back.' She'd already decided not tell him about the knife. In daylight her fears of last night seemed absurd. The nightmare was fading fast. She drank the tea Mark had brought up. Hot and strong. 'How's your dad?'

'Same as ever.' He turned over.

Aware of him beside her sleeping, she stayed awake watching the shadows, remembering how Zara had chatted to her that first breakfast in the hotel, bringing her coffee, telling her how she could read palms, how they had met in a previous life, pulling Jo to her like they were old friends, laughing at Jo's stupid jokes – had she really followed her here? Why? In a restless dreamless state she slept then woke to see Mark getting out of bed, making for the bathroom.

'You awake then?'

'Sure am.'

She watched him shaving, could easily see his reflection in the mirror over the basin and she observed him plug his razor in, smooth his cheek. He moved closer to the mirror and glanced at her. She smiled, then looked up at the sky through the velux window. The rain clouds were clearing and a small patch of denim blue could just be seen in the corner of the frame. In the bathroom mirror, their eyes met. With a finger he wiped at something on the mirror, a blob, some toothpaste perhaps.

'How d'you fancy going away for a smoochy weekend?'

'Mmm. But can we afford it?'

'Be nice to get away. Paris or maybe Prague again?'

'Or somewhere in this country?'

'Sure thing. Whatever you want.' He gave her a big smile then switched the shower on and vanished from view. Jo watched the mirror steam up. No sound emerged. He usually sang under the streaming water. Maybe while she was away, he'd stopped. Perhaps the empty house had reminded him of how it was when his wife had died.

Above her, a weak sun shone through the window. She'd get up, go for a walk, she needed fresh air and exercise. Mark came back into the bedroom. He smelt of mint. Was fumbling through the chest of drawers, dressing at the same time: black trousers, bottle green polo shirt, pushing his fingers through his hair. He kissed her. Then he was speeding down the stairs, a hurricane on the loose.

Always in a hurry. Never enough time, he always said. Chasing my tail. He liked to say that: *Chasing my tail.*

She heard him in the kitchen, opening doors, banging them shut, and imagined him standing in the middle of the kitchen eating from a bowl of cereal. He never sat when the job in hand could be carried out just as well upright. In the living room, now doing the rounds, picking up this and that. 'Byeee.' The front door slammed.

She went across to the window watching him drive off. There was no sign of the pink umbrella. Well of course there wasn't. No need for an umbrella now.

The phone rang. She went to answer it, the phone stopped ringing. So she dialled number recall. Her mother. First she'd take a walk.

A bitter wind hit her straight on. She hunched her shoulders against the cold and pulled her hood up. Even when she stepped carefully, putting the weight on her uninjured foot, it was still painful to walk. With her face nuzzled into her collar, she battled against the gusts while her eyes watered and her lips turned numb. The street was long and curved gracefully with similar tall narrow slate houses branching off. At the end there was a playground and a small patch of grass, a couple of picnic tables.

There was a mother and toddler in the play area of the park, both bundled in scarves and hats. Jo watched from afar while the mother pushed the child on the swing. From that point at the edge of the green, Jo had a clear view of one side of their road.

She wondered which houses were on the market, which had sold. Maybe once she got a job, they could move. She walked back down the street. As she approached each house she searched the drive, the windows and hedges for estate agent boards. No *For Sale* signs. Lots of houses on the market, Mark had said. It didn't necessarily mean anything, him saying this, but then it obviously wasn't the case. And why shouldn't someone wander around in the rain with a pink umbrella? She walked back to the park and took a look at the houses there. Nothing for sale.

11

The sky was bloated with rain, the clouds uncomfortably low. Feeling claustrophobic, without the usual comfort she got from the solitude of being alone in her car, Jo drove nervously along the motorway, her injured foot still bothering her. Then rain started to descend in sheets, the tarmac glistened dangerously and the fields around her looked sodden, the colours muted, compared to the bright colours of Sri Lanka. She had wanted to cancel, meet up with her mother another day. There was so much to do at home. It was Mark who'd said she needed to get out. Although he didn't add 'and stop looking for Zara', she knew he meant that, thought she was becoming obsessive.

But *he* didn't have Senaka's prediction ringing in his ear.

The road ahead was hard to see through the thickening mist, and the repetitive swish of cars speeding drowned out the music. She turned it up to full volume, trying to keep herself alert. The mist cleared. She glimpsed sheep dotted on the fells in the distance. There were fields on the side of the road, puddles catching sunlight on the ploughed soil. The hues were muted, dull in this weather, so different from the bright colours in Sri Lanka. She thought of the jumbled streets, the open drains of the other city that lay thousands of miles away. Blinking rapidly, she forced her eyes to stay open. The beach where Zara had stolen her passport and money was there again; the sour-smelling room in the hotel, the man ogling her breasts. Was Zara watching the house now, waiting for her to return?

As she neared the city, she could see the snow line on the mountains through wedges of cloud; the sun came out, temporarily blinding her. Turning off the motorway, she followed her mother's directions and drove into the city centre, on and on until she turned into a narrow back street with peeling posters announcing long-gone gigs and faded anti-war slogans scrawled across a grey broken wall. The street was deserted and she could see the wall backed onto derelict houses. She checked the address, as she crawled down the road with barely enough room for one car. What had happened to The Enclave, her mother's usual stamping ground? She'd been looking forward to visiting the old hippie place again. She scanned the buildings searching for the place her mother had told her about and stopped at a green door with a large 46 painted across it in black. Was this the place? She shivered. The door looked familiar. Had she been here before? Jo searched around her, cut the engine and listened, but there was only the wind whipping along the narrow street.

There was no indication of what lay beyond the green door, no bell, nothing, and she rapped on the door. An icy sharp wind bit her face. A. A jolt ran through her. A sudden recollection. Then it was gone.

'Yes,' he barked.

'I'm meeting Janice Butler here,' she said.

'You are?'

'Her daughter, Jo.'

The door swung open and her eyes took a while to adjust to the interior. Loud music thumped. 'Aren't you expecting me, then?'

'Through there, darling,' the man said and indicated with a thumb. He returned to his chair at a table where *The Sun* lay open at page three. She bit her lip. This was not the place for an acid comment.

Dance music bounced off the walls. A few trance-like figures rocked to the rhythm and a bar lit up by purple and red

121

fluorescent lights glowed through the gloom. Her eyes gradually became accustomed to the dim light and she saw a cave-like room ahead of her and tables with little red shaded lamps set in their centres. A stage was to the left where two women dressed in sparkling leotards were dancing to the music. Why was it so familiar? And why the hell was her mother here?

'Darling. You got here.' Her mother had appeared and grabbed her arm. Gone was her mother's long hair that used to cascade down her back. The amber and turquoise beads removed too. Bangles made from Indian silver had been replaced by a flashy watch. And instead of the silk tunics and heavily fringed scarves, she wore a tight shiny number. Her hair was dyed black and cut short. She still looked amazing.

'Mum. What *is* this place?'

'Come and sit over here, darling. With me. Then I can hear all about your holiday.' She hooked Jo's arm and shepherded her across the room.

The room stank of booze and male sweat. It was difficult to stop herself staring at the twisting bodies on the stage. Had she really been here before? She darted a look round the room, felt her face flush. There was a memory here. A time when she was off her face, an insane night when she'd shed her clothes, danced on the stage, then recollection slipped from her grasp and she stared up at the stage. What was happening to her head? Was she going insane?

A few men sat around, faces tilted towards the tiny stage, observing the women. Apart from the four people bopping on the dance floor, there were few customers and their absence made the club seem even seedier.

'Bit of a dump. Why are we meeting here?' She followed her mother to a small table where a tiffany style lamp gave off a low glow.

'Don't be such a prude, darling.' She leant across the table and kissed Jo on the cheek. 'I do shifts here sometimes, you know, to help out on the bar and Baz asked me to fill in for one of the girls this afternoon. She'd gone off sick

122

suddenly so it was an emergency. We'll meet somewhere else next time… I so wanted to see you. It's *such* a long time and I have *so* much to tell you.' She took Jo's hand from where it lay on the table and clasped it. 'I noticed you're limping.'

'Those women. God, mum. And no, I don't go to places like this.' If she was lying, her mother would never know. She was the new Jo, the cleaned up Jo. She'd never look back again to the mad druggie days before she fell from the window – before she and Mark got together. But her mother? Here?

'They're only dancers, there's no funny business, you know.'

'I bet. You must think I was born yesterday.' Even though it was hot in there, she pulled her coat tighter round her 'I'm not a prude.'

'Sorry darling. Didn't mean it. Don't be cross.' She waved to someone at the bar. 'What you having?'

'Coffee, please, and I've limped for years. You know that –'

'You're limping differently, dear. I am your mother. I notice these things.'

'I hurt my foot on holiday.' The music stopped and she watched the two women slink from the stage, disappear behind the bar. She should have worn her biker's jacket. She knew they'd be meeting in a private club. Her mother had said so, but she'd imagined a basement with curtains drawn and cushions on the floor, tapestries draped on the walls, oriental carpets on bare floorboards. Somewhere to talk about the good days, get a little stoned in private, do deals. Her mother had a thing about living on the edge. Maybe she'd never been here before, it just reminded her of all the similar places she used to frequent. Her mother was staring at her while she rotated liquid in a long glass with a cocktail stirrer.

'So what's wrong with *The Enclave*?' She couldn't work out why she felt so irritable.

'I've moved on from there, darling. I had a bit of an altercation with Dick, you know, the owner.' She touched her hair. 'I do miss my curls.'

'Mum, that's awful. You've known him for years – why d'you get it cut, then?'

'Baz prefers my hair short.'

'You know, you shouldn't cut your hair to please a man.'

Her mother pouted and Jo felt rotten for getting at her mother's Achilles heel.

'Don't you like the new look, darling?' Her mother smiled a broad smile, all red lips.

'You look great, mum.' Then she remembered the present she'd bought her mother and handed her the blue sarong folded in tissue paper.

'It's beautiful, darling. How sweet of you. How was the holiday? Did the massages help you?'

'They were great. Yes.' Now she was here, she didn't want to share the awful events with her mother. It was always the same. The reality of her mother never quite met her expectations.

'Did you meet? Forgotten her name.' She rolled her eyes to the left and placed the cocktail stirrer to her lips. 'Now what was her name?'

'Who?'

'It'll come to me. Someone you knew at school apparently.'

'Who are you talking about? Did I meet who?' she urged.

'I'll remember in a minute. I'm so glad you had a nice time, darling.'

'Who do you *mean*?'

'Don't keep on. The name will pop into my head if I don't try… I couldn't believe my daughter was going on a package holiday…still, I knew this one'd be for you.'

'*This* one?'

'A place with a spa and all that sort of thing. Pampering. Everything laid on. What's got into you? Why are you so jumpy? I thought you'd gone to relax. I still don't see why you couldn't have just gone off on a plane with nothing planned, like we used to. We never went on packages or used guide books. Everyone has to have a guide book these days.' She turned to take another look round her.

Jo said, 'Maybe I've had enough of staying in flea pits, of sharing a toilet with a hundred back-packers. I've done all that. I wanted sea and sand.'

'Travelling enriches the mind.'

'Don't feel very enriched.' She thought of how she'd run from Senaka's house in the storm, how Zara's figure had appeared momentarily, a spectre lit up by lightning, the rain plastering her hair to her scalp, how she couldn't be seen in the next lightning flash. Till then she'd forgotten about this and the memory sent spirals of fear snaking down her spine. Had the woman really followed her to Meresbridge?

'Honestly, darling, you should take it more easy. You're so wound up.'

'I'm not.' She knew her jaw was clenching. Also knew her mother would've noticed. 'You told me you met someone. Am I going to meet him?'

'Baz's brother owns this club. He's a business man.' Pointedly, she looked at her watch. 'Baz'll be here soon. He's *very* generous. Bought me this. It's designer.' She picked up her glass and over the edge, locked onto Jo's eyes. 'And how's Mark?

'He's absolutely fine. Thank you.'

'Still playing the drums, is he?'

'Doesn't seem to these days.'

'That's a shame. That's how you met, isn't it?'

'I've got to find a job, you know.'

'You'll get one, darling. Are you looking for a similar one?'

'Yes. That's what I have experience in, Mum. So who's this Baz?'

'They should never have let you go. Gold dust, my little Jo,' she said. 'But the planets are on your side, my sweet.'

Jo reddened, licked the coffee from her lips. She said nothing, smiled across the table, bathing in this hint of motherly love. She wasn't sure what to make of this new look but her mother was always changing her image depending on which man was in her life. It *was* a while since they'd met. The last arrangement cancelled by Jo – too depressed at losing her job to face her mother – the one before that cancelled by her mother with no reason given. Before that her mother had been in hospital with a gall bladder problem. Surely that wasn't the last time they'd seen each other. Jo thought hard, her mind flicking back through the months. It must be seven, if not more.

How did that happen? She glanced up. The two women, now wearing petrol blue bikinis and matching feather boas, were stepping back onto the stage.

Her mother nudged Jo. 'There's Baz over there. He'll be coming over in a minute, darling. He's been dying to meet you.'

'Has he?' Jo turned her head in the direction where her mother was gazing.

'Don't stare, sweet.' She touched the mole under her eye.

Jo swung back to face her mother. 'He's different, isn't he?'

'Different?'

'Yeah. Different. Not your usual type.' The men her mother usually took up with were wheelers and dealers, dabbling in the barely legal end of antiques, and in dope, losers with a good yarn. Or men who'd travelled round India and South East Asia in the 1960s and acquired wealth through questionable means. Baz didn't resemble any of them.

'He's got money then?' Was that the attraction? Had her mother finally given in to material possessions? 'How did you meet him?'

126

'You remember Jackie? She introduced us. Baz is a good man. He takes care of me.'

'I'm sure he does.'

It seemed the sarcastic tone hadn't escaped her mother's ears. She twiddled her cocktail stirrer between finger and thumb and glared at Jo. 'Baz is a sweetie. Underneath all that leather is a real teddy bear.' She nodded across the room, gave a little wave. 'He's coming over now, sweetie. He often asks after you. "How's that daughter of yours," he says. He hasn't got kids.'

The man walked like a cowboy, swaggering towards them. He was tall and bulky, wearing a brown leather jacket over a white T-shirt. There was a gold ring in one ear and as he approached, Jo noticed a gold watch like her mother's. He stared at her, then looked at Jo's mother and back again at her. Where had they met before? He put his hand out.

'Happy to meet you. Jo, isn't it? You look so like your mum.'

She smiled, shook his hand, trying to remember, willing him to say nothing about any prior knowledge of each other. Or did he simply resemble someone she knew?

'I'll just say hello to you two lovelies. Then I'll be off.' As he spoke he put his hand to the back pocket of his jeans and took out a phone.

'Darling. You've only just arrived.'

'Business,' he said. 'Sorry, babe.'

'You be long?'

He was already punching out a number. 'Back in thirty minutes.' He whipped a look towards Jo. 'You still be here?'

'Probably not.' She took a breath. 'Things to do. Places, you know.'

And her mother switched to Jo, gave her a warning shot. But Baz was walking away, phone glued to his ear, so he wouldn't have heard Jo say anything even if she'd chosen to ask him what his business was – which she wouldn't. Especially as she knew they'd met before. Her mother was gazing after Baz, following his every move, waiting for him to turn at the doorway and reciprocate her wave.

'You don't like him, do you?'

'I only met him for five minutes.'

'You didn't really tell me how that man of yours is? Young Mark. I was quite surprised at him letting you go on holiday on your own.'

'It wasn't a matter of him letting me. We talked about it – because – because he had to work overtime at the hospital. There were other reasons, but honestly Mum, it was a joint decision.'

They talked about the disagreement her mother had had with Dick in The Enclave. Apparently he'd not liked a photograph of a sunset her mother had donated to the café. She told Jo she'd found the original dress worn by Celia Johnson in the 1945 film *Brief Encounter* in a market and sold it for a fat profit to an American collector.

'My little retro shop is doing quite well. I think I'm getting quite a name for myself,' she said.

'I must see it again,' said Jo, wishing she were doing as well.

Jo told her about the temple she'd visited and how Senaka had bought her a flower to present to Buddha. She said nothing about the theft. There didn't seem any point. They lapsed into silence while the music played on and the dancers appeared again in sparkling black leotards. An image of the airport crept into her mind, the acrid stifling room where she'd been interrogated, the night spent stretched out on plastic chairs, too frightened to attempt sleep. She shook her head trying to dispel the memories and read the time on her mother's shiny new watch. Despite an hour passing, Baz hadn't returned.

'Another drink, darling?' her mother asked for the second time.

'No thanks, mum. I really must go now. Got a lot to do.'

'What a shame. Aren't you going to wait?' She paused. 'He's a good man, you know. Baz. He's got a big heart.' She beckoned to the man behind the bar. 'Just walking my daughter to the door. Same again for me.'

Her mother linked arms with Jo as they weaved round the tables. They'd reached the doorman sitting behind a table. Arms crossed over his chest, head down, he appeared to be dozing, but looked up sharpish as the two of them approached.

'My daughter's going now.'

The man said nothing, but slid open a couple of bolts, unfastened a padlock and opened the door. The eye watering wind was still blowing down the alley. Jo pulled her coat to, watching an empty cigarette packet skittering along the gutter.

'Bye darling. Phone me.' She kissed Jo on the cheek.

'Brass monkeys,' she said and shivered. 'Parked far?'

Jo was fastening her coat. 'Just up there.' She gave her mother a hug, felt the wind slap a strand of hair against her face. She wanted to get away from that place.

'Raquel. That was her name,' her mother said, grabbing Jo's arm. 'Told you it'd come to me. That was the name. Thought you might have come across her on your travels. God it's cold.'

'Raquel, you said? Raquel?'

Her mother had her arms wrapped round herself. She put a finger to the side of her nose. 'She wore a nose stud. Bloody hell. It's freezing. I'm going back inside.'

'Wait. Please mum. How do you know her?'

'Darling, don't you remember? I'm sure that was her name. Maybe you didn't meet her though I thought you did. It doesn't matter if you didn't come across her. I was only asking out of curiosity. Look I really don't want to stand out here. I'll catch my death.' Already she'd stepped back across the club threshold. 'Phone me when you get back. OK, darling?'

Her mother's face was turning white from the cold, but Jo persisted. She *had* to know the truth.

'Please mum, this is important.'

'Are you going to stand in the doorway letting all the fucking cold air in or what?' The door man was glowering at Jo.

'Phone me, sweet.' Her mother blew a kiss. Then she was gone, door shut and bolted. She knocked on the door again and just as she thought no one was going to answer it, the doorman drew back the trap door and unbolted the door.

'I need to see my mother again.'

With his head he indicated for her to go back into the club. Her mother was talking animatedly to Baz. Jo moved quickly.

'Darling, you're back.'

'Hello again,' said Baz.

'Excuse me, mum. Can you tell me who Raquel is?'

'Raquel?' She tittered with exaggeration, obviously for Baz's sake. 'An old school friend. I told you.'

'But why would I meet her in Sri Lanka?'

'I'll be off, then, babes. It seems that you two lovelies haven't finished catching up –'

'Yes we have. Isn't that right, my sweet? Can I phone you later? Would that be OK?' Her eyes pleaded at Jo.

What could she do?

'It's important. As I say. I'll phone you later then.' She turned and left.

For a minute Jo stood outside the club. Why didn't she insist? But she knew why. Her mother was an expert at emotional blackmail and Jo was always a sucker for it. It was so quiet standing there all alone in a back street with the light dimming in the rain-filled sky. But what was her mother talking about? How was it that everyone knew Raquel? A school friend from which school? The name rang no bells.

She started off in the direction of her car. From somewhere nearby there was a bang; an exhaust backfiring? A firework? A gunshot? She turned the corner, ran into the main street to her car. Sitting at the wheel, she put her head in her hands. Her hands shook as she inserted the key into the ignition. But how could she drive in this state? Calm. Breathe. Slow. Breathe. She started the car and soon she was back on familiar roads with the motorway up ahead. She relaxed, checked in her mirror, saw a black car with a dent in the bonnet behind her. A green ball bobbed from its rear view mirror. She indicated right to move out of the slip road into the motorway. Thirty minutes at most, and she'd be home. She kept in the left hand lane, allowed traffic to overtake her, and remembered Raquel in that multi-coloured sarong, that bloody peacock glinting. How was it possible her mum knew this woman? Was there some connection with her and the club? What did someone she knew at school want with her? She crossed over to the middle lane, was driving at a steady pace. About to switch lanes, she checked her mirror. The black car was still behind. Dent in the bonnet.

She switched to the left lane. Black car there again, the lime green ball swinging from the rear view mirror. Back to the right lane. Was it following? Left lane. Car tailgating. She would try again. Right lane now. Her hands were so clammy. The wheel slithered through her fingers. In the mirror she could see the black car getting closer. Foot hard on the accelerator, couldn't go any faster, the engine juddering as she pushed. She swung onto the hard shoulder, brakes squealing, skidding to a stop. Horn screaming, the black car whizzed by; her car rocked with the rush of air. Rigid, a rock of tension, she felt the blood rush through her veins, a pulse vibrate in her temple. Had she been followed from the club? What did her mother know? She phoned her, left a message. Deep breaths. Steady. Slow. She checked round her and turned into the road. Their junction was next. The first of three markers zipped past her. Traffic lights ahead, lights changing to red the minute she approached. Ten minutes and she'd be home. She waited, looking out for the car, willing the green light to show. A queue of cars was backing up behind her. Was the black car one of them?

Amber. Why was it taking so long?

Green. She shot forward, looking in the mirror, her stomach tying in knots.

12

Panic was still threading through her gut, heart pounding. Was she going crazy, imagining everything? But she *had* been run off the road. She *had* been followed.

Mark handed her a glass of Sauvignon. His lovely lean face was puckered with concern.

She drank without tasting. 'God. I need another one.' She sat on the blue sofa by the window.

'So where did this car start following you?' He walked to the end of the room, picked up his phone and turned to face her. 'Did you get the number? We should get the police involved –'

'I couldn't write the number down. I was too busy trying to get away.'

He took her empty glass, stroked her hair. 'After everything else that's happened.'

'It's completely freaked me out. Why would anyone be following me? ' She bent to remove her boots, trying to shut out the thoughts racing round her head; she closed her eyes, sinking into the zebra print cushions. 'My mother asked me if I'd met Raquel on holiday. I'm going to phone her in a minute. Ask her what she meant – apparently she's someone I knew at school. Can't remember anyone called Raquel or Zara. Plus I went to three different schools.'

'You never told me that.'

'Yeah. My mother was always taking me out to go off travelling. That's why I never did well. Went to uni as a mature student – I told you. I'm sure I did. Not that it matters now.' She leaned back and closed her eyes. There was a slight disturbance of air as Mark left the living room. Footsteps resonating on the tiled floor, he went across the hall into the kitchen, leaving both doors ajar. She listened to him opening the fridge, pouring more wine into two glasses. Then there was no sound except the hum of the fridge, the tick of the grandfather clock.

'Hey. What're you doing? Crushing the grapes?' She got up and absentmindedly examined a framed black and white photograph: Meresbridge in 1918. Life was simple then, she thought.

'Be right with you.'

Mark returned to the living room, handed her a glass and went across to the window. 'I can't see a black car now.'

'Course you can't. It's gone. Why would it hang around here?'

'I thought I might see something.'

Allowing the alcohol to swill round her brain was good. She followed Mark's eyes to where he was looking, saw a flock of birds migrating across a bruise coloured sky.

'You OK?'

She nodded, drank her wine.

'I got something for you. It was supposed to be a surprise. Well, it still is,' he said.

'For me? I should have got *you* something – I did think about it – but then it was your money I'd be spending – but that gorgeous dinner you cooked the other night was enough for me.'

'Here it is.' He stooped and kissed her.

'You didn't have to do this. God it looks expensive.' It was a small parcel done up in blue shiny paper. Gold string and a silver bow.

'Can't I buy you a present? Isn't that permitted?'

'That's not what I meant. Of course. But I should have got *you* one.'

'No need. Not with the holiday you had.' The way he smiled made him look even more handsome, his face outlined

134

by the burgundy wall, a ceiling spot lamp shining on his head, halo-like.

She returned his smile and thought how lucky she was. 'Open it, then.'

The string untied easily enough. Next was the paper. Careful not to tear it, she removed the packaging. 'Perfume. Wow. This is a treat.' She sprayed some on her wrist. Orange Blossom, she read on the bottle and sniffed the spot on her wrist. 'Thank you. It's –' Her voice drifted.

The room spun. The smell was taking her to another place. She suddenly felt woozy as the scene returned to her. At a party where she'd decided to sit on the kitchen window sill to cool down. She recalled as if it were yesterday how the smell of orange blossom had filled her nostrils, how the warm night breeze had fanned her face, how she'd seen the city spread out in the distance: lines and lines of twinkling house lights climbing up the mountains far away until they vanished into a pinprick. Up there she'd felt free. The music coming from the party sent her mind soaring. Everything was perfect. She swung her legs and wiggled in time to the music. She'd made a half turn then looked back towards the kitchen where Rob was coming through the doorway. 'Hey, why don't you join me?' Beckoning to him, shuffling along to make room, she'd heard a meow, from a tabby kitten on the neighbour's ledge. She'd inched towards it, heard another frantic meow, seen how tiny it was, its tail upright, its saucer eyes and she'd watched its white paws pad stealthily towards her. Hand outstretched, she'd leaned towards it, felt herself slip, had heard her plastic wine glass bounce on the patio below.

'Jo..........'

She'd heard Rob call out just as she felt herself go. The wind soared past her. The smell of orange blossom flooded her brain. In silence she fell and felt her body land on concrete, felt the pain sear through her.

Then nothing....

'You all right, Jo?'

135

She gazed at Mark, remembering where she was. All that belonged to a different time, another era of her life, and she'd never seen the point in telling Mark all the details. He knew about her falling from a window and breaking her leg. She'd told him about the two operations which followed the first. No need for specifics. She'd never told him the precise details of the party; the drugs and alcohol that had swarmed in her brain and now she was still remembering the fall, the party that she and Rob had gone to, how she'd got so hot that sitting on a window ledge had seemed logical. Never mind that the flat was on the first floor.

'You're a million miles away,' he said, his eyes on her.

'Sorry. I was remembering that fall, you know, from the window.'

'Why d'you think of that now? It was a long time ago.' His brow furrowed with worry.

How could she tell him the perfume he'd bought her had reminded her? 'Maybe it was that bloody car bringing it all back, the panic. But thanks Mark. It's a really nice present.'

'You like it then.'

'Course I do. It's lovely.' She drew him to her and kissed him on the lips though she was still reeling from the memory. How could a scent have that effect?

Extracting her mobile from her bag, she called her mother.

'Who you phoning?'

'My mother. I want to find out how she knows – Mum, hi.'

'Hello darling. You got home safely, then. Lovely of you to call so soon. Sorry about before. Baz was explaining something important to me.'

From the table, Mark was watching, listening as he opened up his laptop.

'So you asked me whether I met Raquel on holiday. What d'you mean? And which school?'

'Darling. If you don't remember who she is, why does it matter?'

'Because it does. Do you know her second name? I might remember her then.'

She could hear her mother sighing and pictured her, finger to lips, eyes raised to the ceiling. Mark was staring at his laptop screen, hands on his hips, his chair at an angle to the table.

'Bannister. That was it. Raquel Bannister. I thought you'd seen her there. But come to think of it, the curtains were always closed around her bed in the ward, so maybe you didn't. I assumed she meant The City School.'

'What bed?' She turned away from the room and stared out at the street, watched a black car speed by. A four wheel drive – not the same as the one which had followed her.

'She was in the bed next to mine in hospital. You know, before I had that ghastly operation. Strange you not meeting though. She said she'd look out for you.' Jo heard voices in the background – men's. 'Glad you phoned though, darling. I was on the point of phoning you – funny isn't it? Telepathy. We always had that, didn't we, sweet? Didn't tell you, forgot, well, you know, we hadn't seen each other for such a long time.' She paused. 'Baz is talking about renting me a swish apartment near where he lives – that's what we were talking about when you came back. I'm sorry –'

'Doesn't matter, mum. Bannister? Is that what you said?'

'I think – to be honest darling, I'm not entirely sure. Did you hear what I just said?'

'I was only at City School for six months. It couldn't have been there. What did she want anyway?'

'Honestly, darling. What is the matter with you? Why aren't you more interested in what I'm doing? '

'I'm just trying to understand what went on with this woman.'

There was silence then and she heard Mark tapping the keys on his laptop.

'I wish you didn't get so cross with me. Baz is good for me. You know life gets very difficult as you get older. You'll see what I mean one day –'

'I'm not cross. And I'm really pleased Baz makes you happy. But is there anything else you remember about this Raquel?'

'There's nothing more to tell. But if I think of anything I'll let you know. I'm meeting Baz soon so I must get ready. We'll see each other soon, won't we, Jo, darling?'

The line went dead. She watched Mark's fingers. He was pointedly staring at the screen. Was he sulking? Hadn't she made a big enough fuss about the perfume?

'Raquel Bannister,' she said. 'That was her name.' Her head was hurting. Why did nothing make sense? 'Mum said she met her when she was in hospital. That must have been last April.

Without really seeing it, her eyes were on the sideboard where she'd replaced Mark's wife's gold and blue painted tea set with her own collection of studio pottery. 'Mum said this woman, Raquel Bannister –' she went across the room to her bag and scrabbled round for a pen, '– was in the bed next to her when they were doing all those investigations of her stomach.' Back across the room, her foot niggling, feeling inflamed again, she grabbed a chair, sat opposite Mark. 'So naturally, I'm concerned. I mean why would a woman who was in the next bed to my mother in hospital be in the very same hotel as me?' She reached across the table, picked up a newspaper, wrote RAQUEL BANNISTER on the top of the page, and underlined it. 'And I just wondered did you come across her yourself, you know, while mum was laid up.'

'How could I? You know which ward I work on. She must be someone nasty you knew at school. You said that already.'

She pulled out the chair next to her, rested her legs on it. 'Thought you were on the same ward as my mum for a while.' She put the pen to her lips. 'In the general ward,

138

wasn't it? That's where she was and you – I remember you were there when I visited mum –'

'My ward's very near that one. I popped in whenever I had a minute. Your mum was quite popular with the male doctors.' He reached across her to pick an apple out from the fruit bowl, with the other hand he picked up a magazine. He got up and moved to the chair overlooking the garden. 'Got to go and visit my father in half an hour. Carer's still sick.' He laid the magazine on his lap and examined the piece of fruit.

'Right,' she said. 'But you must have *seen* this Raquel woman too. Don't you remember her?'

'No. Don't think so.' He flicked over the front page of the magazine – Classic cars. He was mad about them, like his dad who owned a Morgan – always polishing and stroking it.

'You sure?' she said. 'It's important. As you know.'

'No sorry, the name means nothing.' He took a bite of the apple, munching slowly. His quarter profile was visible and she could see the muscles in his mouth masticating.

'But surely? '

'I meet hundreds of patients. How do you expect me to remember this particular woman and if she is the same person who took your stuff, who was someone you knew at school, it has to be a coincidence.' He returned the magazine to the table. 'Have you ever considered your mother could've made a mistake?'

'She's not stupid.'

'I'm not saying she is. Of course I'm not saying that. But she can't remember much about this woman can she, so maybe –'

'You think she's lying?'

'No. I didn't say that. But she might be embroidering the truth, you know.'

'No. I don't.' She went into the kitchen, opened a carton of vegetable soup, put it in the microwave. She filled a glass with water and drank. Easy for him to think everything was a coincidence. She poured herself a fresh glass of wine and heard Mark stomp out of the living room, go into the hall,

139

pause at the kitchen door. She didn't turn round. She was angry too. No need for him to get like that, throwing magazines onto the floor, stamping round the house. A little understanding wouldn't go amiss.

He was going upstairs, two at a time. His feet made the house shake as he ran up the steps. Raquel Bannister. She tried to recollect the bed next to her mother's and all the girls she knew at the schools she'd attended. But she'd never stayed in touch with any of them. But why should she have noticed anyone in the next bed? Her mother had worn a black lace nightie, a collectable, she'd said, a Marilyn Monroe styled 1950's original. She remembered *that*. And her mother reading all the nurses' palms, telling them what colour their auras were. Raquel in the bed next to hers? What was her mother talking about? How did she know about Raquel being on holiday? Fetching her phone, she Googled Raquel Bannister. Nothing. She tried Facebook. One in Toronto. Two in Ohio. Not *her*. She tried Zara Bannister. Nothing.

She heard Mark in the first floor bathroom. Putting some soup in the microwave, she suddenly felt uncomfortable sitting there in the huge Farmhouse kitchen with oak panelled doors and fake marble worktop. She wouldn't have selected this sort of kitchen. Now the house seemed alien. But Mark was as solid as they came. Wasn't he? Through the glass door of the microwave, she surveyed the rotating soup and remembered Senaka's insisting she knew Raquel before the holiday. None of it made any sense. It took her a while to locate the phone numbers of the schools she attended and they all said they would check the records and get back to her. But wouldn't she have recognised the name? She drank some water, and phoned Amy.

She would understand and know what Jo should do.

'Hi Jo, you're back then. Did you have an amazing time?'

'Not exactly, no. Can we meet up sometime?'

'That'd be great. I'm not working tomorrow. We'd planned to go to London, but John couldn't get time off. So I'm free. What happened?'

'Not on the phone.'

'Wow. Sounds serious.'

'It is. Kind of.'

'I could get to you.'

'Surely it's a bit far.'

'It'd be good to get out of the city.'

'What about Zino's?'

'Great. Say ten?'

Mark descended the stairs, slowly, carefully, she could tell. Then he appeared at the door, hair tousled and wet, running his fingers through his hair, shaking his head to dry out his locks. 'I hate it when we argue.' He pulled her to him and kissed her on the lips.

She sighed. 'Me too.'

'Got to sort out my dad's carers in a minute. I've got so much on my mind. I'm sorry I had a go at you. But sometimes I feel you forget what I'm up against, but I'll see what I can find out about this woman from work. That might put your mind at rest.'

'Would you? Thanks. That would be brilliant.'

He stood stooping slightly as if his height was wearing him down. Was his face thinner too? Could that happen in two weeks? Should she give him more emotional support? Was she expecting too much of him, now she had no job? He absentmindedly scratched his chin. 'Dad doesn't like the carers that are coming in at the moment. They're always different. He says he can't remember them, there are so many and they don't have time for him. Which they don't. It's hard for him.'

'I guess.' A rush of guilt made her face flush.

'Need to make a phone call, Jo. I can't be his carer and work double time too.'

In the kitchen, getting out a couple of soup bowls from the cupboard, she listened to him talking to someone about the

141

problems with his father's carers. She heard him explaining about his father's illness and his work, how he couldn't take time off. Was she being too mean to him? His wife would've helped out. She imagined emptying his father's bedpan, washing him, and knew she didn't have it in her.

At last he finished. 'They say they'll sort it. Staff shortages, as usual.'

'I should help really,' she said. 'I'd be useless though.'

'You hardly know him.'

'Neither do the carers.'

'It's because he's missing my mum, that's why no one's good enough.'

'Sometimes I wonder what your mum would have thought of my mum if they'd met. You've got that nice picture of her on the beach with your dad and you and your little sister wearing that sailor's hat. You know the one? 'I know your mum was a bit of a religious. But I bet she was really motherly.'

He was stroking her hair, the touch gentle, a caress. She moved away, confused about her emotions.

'I think my mum would have thought yours was very glamorous,' he said. 'My mum was a home bird. She lived for the family and the church. For my dad, for my sister and me. But I used to think she put the church before us.' He laughed. 'I remember she used to hate travelling, you know, she'd take a supply of tea and her favourite biscuits to France on our holidays. Said she didn't trust the food there, even though we camped and we never ate out. She said the shops all had a funny smell and that the French were heathens.'

'I bet she loved you to bits.'

'You saw so much when you were a kid. I mean you travelled so much –'

'Everyone says that. "You've had such an interesting life" they say. What they don't seem to realise is that trekking round Asia with your mum while she's on the hunt for another romantic encounter isn't that brilliant. And she's still at it. She still looks fabulous, even when she should look tarty, like today.'

'You remember that nightdress she wore in hospital. All that black lace and low neckline. Christ! The doctors didn't know where to look.'

'So you do remember?'

'Well, yes. Of course I do. Your mother was doing all that stuff with Tarot cards. She caused quite a stir.' He moved away from her towards the worktop and began to cut some bread. 'Look, I got a lawnmower. I found it in my dad's shed. Ours is broken and I thought I might as well take it now.'

'So, if you remember my mum in her black lacy nightdress, it follows that you must remember the woman in the next bed who happened to be Raquel, the very same

Raquel who stole my passport, my money, my credit cards. The woman who says she knows me from school. You said you didn't remember my mum, you told me you don't remember working on that ward.'

'I didn't say I don't remember her. Christ, Jo. What is the matter with you? I said I didn't remember the woman in the next bed, whoever she was.' He abandoned his bread cutting and left the kitchen. The wind shrieked like the devil as he opened the front door.

'Where you going?'

'To get the bloody lawnmower,' he yelled back at her.

She had a sudden urge to apologise. Waiting till he got back into the house just wouldn't do. There she was accusing him. Of what? Not remembering the woman who lay next to her mother all those months before? She stood in the doorway, hanging onto to her hair blowing across her face. She stepped out onto the path, down the steps, hugging her body as she went, feeling the cold slap her face. The lamplight across the road shed a pool of light onto the parked cars. Rain was belting down. Water-filled storm drains gushed down the road. Her boots stepped in puddles and dirty water splashed her jeans. He was on the phone, shouting, gesticulating.

She began to cross the road, was so near to calling out to Mark to tell him she would help him with his father. She was so close, the words were already formed in her mouth. Mark was really shouting. The wind was strong enough to blow away his words. He saw her and cut the phone call. She was soaked. Mark had hold of her.

'Jo? You're drenched.'

'Who were you talking to?'

'The hospital. Why are you spying on me?' He began to lug the lawn mower across the road. Two at a time, he mounted the steps. His hair was soaked, plastered to his skull. Rain was dripping down his face. She followed him in.

He pushed past her into the kitchen, half-dropping the lawnmower.

'I've never known you get so angry with your work before.'

'You don't believe me? Is that what you're saying?'

'No. Yes.' She put her hand to her forehead. 'Sorry, don't know what got into me.'

The landline was ringing. Silently she watched him pick the receiver up and sit at the table, head in hands. He was listening without speaking, his face turning whitish grey.

'That was the hospital. I knew he had another scan yesterday,' he said when the call was finished. 'They said they'd let me know as soon as – the cancer's spread to his lymph system. He hasn't got long.'

She walked towards him.

'And his mind – it's going, really going. He thinks Mum's still alive.'

She was there by him. She was holding him in her arms, smoothing his hair down, kissing each cheek. He held her so tight and she waited till he stopped, unwound herself from the embrace, looked into his eyes, saw the raw misery.

Was she becoming paranoid, suspicious of everyone in her life?

13

Amy was there already in Zino's, which was surprisingly packed for mid-week, mid-morning. She was easy to spot with her orange earrings, her mass of curls. So glad to see her, Jo rushed across the café to where her friend sat. In front of Amy was placed a glass of chocolate topped with ice cream. Her hand was clasped round it; as she brought the spoon to her lips Jo saw the opal ring she always wore. They kissed each other on the cheek.

'Nice perfume. Did you buy it duty-free? You look terrific. Must have been a good holiday.'

'Well actually, not that brilliant. The perfume was a present from Mark.' She sniffed her wrist. 'Nice isn't it? It's great to see you. You're looking good. I'll just get myself something.' Already she felt better for seeing her friend.

The walls had been painted since she was last here and were now peppermint, while the tables were black and the two men serving wore similarly co-ordinated jeans and T-shirts, giving the café-bar an edible look. An enticing smell of fresh coffee and pastries only made her wish for a time when her life wasn't so fraught. How would she explain to Amy about Zara? Would she too think her friend was half-crazy, imagining it all? She glanced back at her, the friend who'd always been there. She was engrossed in a paper. Jo felt a twinge of envy at the contented look on her face.

It took her a while to get to the front of the queue. Ample time to look round at the sea of faces and check. In the middle, sitting at a table on her own, a woman. Short blonde hair. Black jacket. But she had her back to Jo. How many women have that look? But still she watched her, even as she paid for her coffee, even as she threaded her way through chairs and tables and took her seat opposite Amy.

'You sounded frantic yesterday. What's wrong?'

'Nothing – well, yes.' She took a deep breath. 'Long story. First, how's life treating you?'

Amy hesitated, giving Jo a questioning look. 'I'm good. That hideous sickness has finished. And I have one of these whenever I can.' With her finger, she tapped the glass. 'Baby's unperturbed by the chocolate overload and I haven't put on more weight than I should, so here's to chocolate.'

'You look amazing. You've no idea how good it is to see you. How's the job?'

Amy shot Jo another puzzled look. 'Do you really want to know?'

'Yes. I do.'

'Well – It's brilliant. It really suits me. I love working at the university, even though the office manager's a bit of a headache.' She touched Jo's hand. 'So? What's happened?'

Jo took a sip of her coffee then brought out a packet from her bag. 'This first, Amy. I brought this back for you.' She put the wrapped sarong on the table and while Amy unwrapped the packet, Jo glanced round. The woman in the black jacket was getting up and Jo stared at her following her every move, ready to pounce, get her. She turned back to Amy. 'I got one for Lisa too. How is she?'

'It's gorgeous, Jo. Thanks. I didn't expect anything. It's really beautiful.' She fingered and patted it. 'Can't wait to wear it.' She leant across the table and kissed Jo on the cheek. 'Lisa's fine. Busy. She's off to Morocco next week. What's wrong, Jo?'

Heat spread into her face. 'I thought that was her.' She nodded towards the figure exiting the café.

'Who? What are you talking about?'

'God, it's been bloody awful.' Tears were welling; she blinked them away, saw concern spread across Amy's face. Adding sugar to her coffee she told Amy about the theft, the

146

ripped photo…here she hesitated, watching Amy's look of horror. She continued, telling her about Senaka, her mother, that she knew Raquel. That was enough for now. The relating exhausted her, as if she were re-living it all. 'I can't believe I allowed myself to be duped like that. Why didn't I question her when she said I must take my passport and money with me to the beach? She said I needed to carry ID round with me and I didn't think twice about it. *And* I believed her when she said some of the cleaners were suspected of pilfering from the rooms. Why wouldn't I? I thought she was looking after my welfare. Would you have done the same?'

'Jeez, Jo. I guess so. I haven't travelled half as much as you. She must be a good con merchant. Why didn't you email me? Out there on your own.'

'The bloody computer kept going down –'

'Not such a brilliant holiday then –'

'There's more.'

'Isn't Mark there for you? He's a caring kind of guy –' her phone rang. 'I'll just get this.' Listening to the easy conversation Amy was having with John made her gut ache. Why indeed wasn't Mark being more supportive? But hadn't he bought her the perfume? Maybe that was his way of being there for her while her world was turned on its head. Then there was his father… She jolted round, felt someone's eyes on her and she saw a woman's head turn away. A different woman. Or was she the same? Was she going crazy? Had they been her footsteps she'd heard behind her as she'd walked to Zino's? She stared at the back of the woman's head, at what she was drinking. Beer in a bottle, no glass. Blonde short hair. Black leather jacket. Pink umbrella rolled up and placed on the table. Was that her?

'Sorry about that,' Amy said. 'Jeez. You've gone really white. What a bloody nightmare.'

Jo swallowed. 'Apparently I know this woman. According to the guy at the hotel. And my mother too.' She told Amy what she'd learned from her mother about the encounter in hospital.

147

Once more, Jo swung round. The woman's face wasn't quite visible. Still she couldn't be sure.

'They said you know her? Your mum and this guy in the hotel?'

'That's right.' Her hand was shaking so badly, she didn't dare lift her cup. Instead, she picked up Amy's newspaper, smoothing out the front page, attempting to quieten her nerves. 'My mother was told by this Raquel woman that she knew me from school. Why is she stalking me? What the hell did I do? Most of the time I was miserable at school. Couldn't make any solid friendships. My mother was always taking me out to go travelling with her. Then I'd have to go to a different school when we came back to the UK.'

'You never told me about being miserable in school – I didn't have such a good time either.'

'Didn't you?' She smiled at Amy. 'I never go back to that time now. No point in dwelling on the past.' She paused. 'I think that's her behind me.'

'Where?'

'Short blonde hair. Pink umbrella on the table.' She put her hands to her face as Amy bobbed around trying to spot the woman.

'She's got a nose stud. Thin face. Is that her?'

Jo felt her face drain of colour, felt her stomach tighten, her pulse race.

'Why don't you ask her, then?'

'Don't know. Scared. It might not be her.'

'Shall I?'

'Don't.' Jo put her hand over Amy's. 'Please. I want to be sure.' And she told Amy about the incident in the airport. She finished her coffee, now cold.

'You want another?'

'That'd be great.' She watched as Amy slid out from her chair, then turned round so she could see the woman in the black leather jacket, she was swigging from the bottle and Jo remembered Zara on the beach, her sarong riding up her

148

thighs, falling open to show off her tan as she tipped her head back swallowing beer from the bottle, then ordering another. Someone dropped a plate. Jo was back in Zino's with raindrops smearing the window and a draught as someone opened the door. The room looked brighter, the chatter magnified like surf in a storm as adrenalin rushed through her. This might be her only chance. She waited for Amy to get back. Adrenalin was rushing round her body making her mouth dry. She was so sure. Did that mean that it was Raquel who was *really* following her? Amy returned.

'I need to know if it's her.'

'I'll come with you then – safety in numbers and all that.'

'You don't have to. I can handle this alone.'

'Come on.'

They walked across the café. Jo stood over the woman in the black leather jacket. Amy stood to the side. Raquel was texting.

'Raquel? Zara? Which one is it?'

The woman looked at Jo steadily, her gaze flickering coolly; she returned to her texting. 'Aren't you going to introduce us?'

'It *is* you.' Jo was surprised at how calm she sounded.

The woman picked up her beer. 'Did you want something?'

For a minute, Jo was stunned, her false tranquillity abandoning her in an instant. She hadn't expected an admission. But it was so obviously *her.* The woman was wearing a tight red low cut top and large hooped earrings. The blue stud glistened in her nose. Her mouth was painted scarlet like a gash on her face. Jo could barely believe who she was seeing right there in front of her. So many questions. Calm. Breathe. 'Why are you harassing me? Why are you following me?' Her voice was high pitched, going wobbly. The woman's eyes drilled into her. A coil of fear tightened round Jo's throat.

'I'd say it was the other way round, wouldn't you? Just quietly having a beer and this woman comes up to me and asks why I'm harassing her.' She was speaking in a low threatening voice, barely audible above the chatter of the clientele. Taking her umbrella from the table, she got up.

'Why don't you leave her alone?' Amy said.

'Excuse me,' Raquel said ignoring Amy, pushing past them both.

Rage soared through Jo's veins and her voice returned 'You followed me here. It was you who ran me off the road, wasn't it? It's you that's stalking me. What do you want?' She was shouting, fragments of the incident in the airport shattering in her brain.

Calmly putting black leather gloves on, flexing her fingers. Raquel was heading towards the exit and Jo was following her, aware that people had stopped talking, knowing that she was being stared at. Then they were both standing at the door and Jo was blocking the way out.

'Come back to the table.' Amy linked her arm.

'Excuse me,' the woman said again, coming close, bloodshot eyes meeting Jo's, and squeezed past her, treading on Jo's toe.

'Everything OK?' a man said to Raquel, giving Jo and Amy alternate filthy looks.

'Just trying to leave,' Raquel said smoothly.

Nothing else for it. Jo stood aside. Was she going to let her go? No. *No.* Out of the café, onto the street. Rain getting into her eyes, wind whipping her hair. She walked fast along the street, got to the corner, searched everywhere for the woman. Had she got away again? How did she vanish so fast? And what did the woman want?

Despite the cold, she was sweating, felt an unhealthy heat in her body. She turned back towards Zino's. Amy was approaching. No sign of Raquel.

'The bloody woman's gone.'

'Come back inside.'

'I can't. I made a fool of myself in there. Everyone was staring at me.'

'Ignore them. Come back. Your coffee will be getting cold.'

Head down, she followed Amy back to the table, aware of the hush as she sat down. She said nothing but sipped her coffee while Amy waited for her to calm herself. The chatter had resumed its low hum. The windows were steaming up as more customers arrived and she saw the queue was snaking round the café bar.

'You OK?'

'I knew I was being followed here. She loiters round the house too. And a black car ran me off the road yesterday.'

'Jeez. Have you told the police? Stalking's a criminal offence, if that's what she's doing.'

'What can I tell them? She hasn't harmed me...yet. And I didn't get the number plate. You know what they're like.'

Amy spooned ice cream into mouth, then tapped the air with the utensil. 'She looked weird. She must have emptied a bottle of perfume onto herself. And I reckon those boobs were falsies. Christ. Did you see the size of them? I thought *I'd* grown enormous!'

Despite everything, Jo laughed.

'You're not in touch with anyone you knew at school then?'

'Nope. Not a soul.'

Amy covered Jo's hand with hers. 'You need to take precautions then in case she intends to harm you. Surely Mark can help you with that?'

Jo was taking deep breaths, making fists, releasing them. 'Yeah, you're right.' Why hadn't she wanted to tell Mark about sleeping with a knife under a cushion the first day she'd got back? Was it just his enormous sense of logic that was getting in the way of her really confiding in him? 'It's such a relief to be able to talk about it,' she said. 'Mark's not that good at emotions.'

151

'Still –'

'He says he doesn't remember her when she was in the bed next to my mum's.'

'Well, why would he? He sees hundreds of patients-'

A waitress in a peppermint T-shirt with *Zinos* emblazoned across, began to clear their table. 'Mark's as solid as they come,' she added.

'His dad's really ill.'

'Oh yeah, I remember.' From her bag, she pulled out a packet of tissues and handed it to Jo. 'You sure you've never met her before?'

'Absolutely.'

'One of your ex-clients?'

'*And* someone who knew me at school?'

'Why not?'

'I'd remember if she was an ex-client.'

'But you saw so many. I used to work there, didn't I? You were all tearing your hair out with those enormous case loads. I mean I know I was only a temp, but I know it was constant. How could you possibly remember them all?'

Jo moved her chair to give the person behind her more room to move, suddenly realising how hot it was in there. Of course Amy was right. How could she remember all her ex-clients? She thought back to the time when Amy was perpetually searching for files. She'd been studying part time for a Masters in Economics and now she had a job where there'd been over four hundred applicants. But somehow she didn't think she'd forget a client like Raquel, something about her…an animal quality, a dangerous charisma. She wouldn't forget her.

'You could ask Rob.'

Jo looked up. 'Ask him what, precisely?'

'Jeez, don't be so – sorry – but you two. He still works in IT doesn't he? I mean he's still there?'

'Yes, but –'

'Ask him to look up the name. Then you'd know for sure.'

She sighed. 'Not sure that's a good idea.'

Amy moved her half-empty glass to one side and leaned a little closer to Jo so her almond shaped eyes were looking straight at Jo and despite Jo's efforts to wriggle from her gaze, she saw the look of concern, real friendship. 'Look, Jo. You have to find out who she is. At least you might have an understanding of what's going on in her head and more to the point, if there's anything fishy on her file, it would give you ammunition to go to the police.' She stopped and drew back. 'So call Rob. He'd do anything for you. You know that.'

'Do you think I should tell Mark first?' Though she knew the answer. And yet – she was so confused, didn't know what was best. But she loved Mark, shouldn't she tell him? Would that make him understand how bad it was?

'Up to you. Not as if you're thinking of shagging Rob, is it?'

Despite herself, Jo laughed. 'OK. I'll ask Rob. See what he can find – you do like Mark, don't you?' Not sure why she would ask such a question, she felt her face glow.

'He's a great guy and he'd do anything for you too. Two men who adore you. Lucky you!'

She laughed. 'Don't feel very adorable right now. I'll ring Rob. And I'll have to give telling Mark some thought. I hate to go behind his back.'

It was time to leave. On the street they kissed each other's cheeks again then Amy headed off to where her car was parked. For a while Jo stood in the cold, damp air filling her lungs. She looked in both directions before she set off for home and at every corner she stopped, held her breath and waited, watching out for the woman to appear.

14

The phone rang twice before Rob answered.

'Jo –? This is a surprise.'

She paused. 'You OK?'

'Yup. Fine. You?'

'Good. I just wondered, Rob – you can say no if you want.'

Was it really a good idea to phone him?

'Spit it out.'

'Can you do something for me?'

'I was in the middle of something.'

'Oh, sorry. What you up to?'

He sighed. 'I'll phone you back – two minutes.'

'No, I'll wait,' she said. 'If you've no objections.'

She switched the phone to loudspeaker, closed her eyes. How had she allowed Raquel to get away yesterday? Why hadn't she been more forceful? The woman must think her a wimp, bullying her like that. Would Rob refuse to help her? Tell her he didn't want any more to do with her, remind her how she'd finished with him, the row, her accusations? And how likely was it that Raquel was an ex-client? Wouldn't she remember her? She paced the room and scenes of times with Rob skittered across the surface of her mind; when she'd worked on the fourth floor and he in the basement, an IT man and a union rep; how after the fall from a window during that party one hot summer's night, frightened she'd never be free of pain again, she gave up drinking, stopped doing drugs, set her life on another path; how she'd met Mark, applied for promotion, joined middle management, sat at meetings with

154

senior management. While Rob, the union rep, sat at the other end of the large oval table. Jo stood and stretched, looked across the street at the other slate houses. Where was he? Stalling, she thought. Keeping her waiting deliberately.

Rob's voice interrupted her thoughts. 'Sorry 'bout that.'

'I need a favour.' She managed to keep her voice level.

'How's life with the doctor?'

She didn't correct him. No point. Instead, she told him about Raquel Bannister.

'You were on holiday without the doctor?'

'Yes,' she said and continued with the story.

'So not going too well with the doctor?'

'Please listen a moment. Please, Rob.'

She walked round the living room and sat back into the sofa. She told him what Amy had suggested.

'So. Let me get this straight,' he said. 'You want me to look up a client on the system?'

'And if she's there, can you track down her file? Your office is next to where they're stored. It wouldn't take you a minute.'

'Highly controversial. You know what they're like about confidentiality.'

'I know it's a lot to ask, but it's really important –' her voice trailed.

'Could get me the sack.'

She looked out of the window. 'It doesn't matter,' she told him. 'I'm sorry to have bothered you. I don't want to get you into trouble.'

There was silence from his end. He was waiting for further enticement, she knew. But she had nothing to offer him except her desperation. What would be her next move if he refused? Wait till the woman attacked her, then call the police?

'You could meet me first,' he finally said.

'Yes,' she said. She'd known he would suggest that. They'd been very close and she was quite good at pre-empting him. 'Where?'

He named a pub, one she'd never heard of.

Phone call over, Jo rang her mother, but didn't leave a message. She wandered through to the kitchen and filled the kettle. She put her hands to her cheeks and felt the fire in her face. Why could her life never be normal? Rain beat on the windows and she stared out at the gloomy day. In the distance, lighting flickered and the wind battled round the house. She pulled the curtain closed. *She say she see you in England,* Senaka's voice was there again, close by, in the room. She shuddered and remained in the kitchen away from the front of the house. She felt vulnerable there, as if she were being watched.

She filled a glass of water, put it to her lips, spun round as the doorbell went, dropped the glass on the floor. It smashed. She heard the light tinkle of glass sliding, settling onto the hard grey tiles. Water spread out across the floor.

She stared at the expanding water, the slivers of glass and went out into the hall. There was no one at the door. She ran down the steps searching the street, her heart thudding, nausea rising in her throat. Was that Raquel? What the hell did she want? 'Raquel? Are you there?'

Who had been ringing the bell? Stopping, standing still, she listened. In her ear, her pulse raced. There was no one there. Must have been kids messing about. She returned to her house, to the kitchen, to the broken glass. Swept the floor, picking up the larger pieces of glass, thinking about meeting Rob. Should she cancel, find another way? Go to the police? But say what? That she was scared?

The front door slammed. She swirled round.

'Hi. I'm home.'

'I'm in here,' she called.

Then Mark was in the doorway, drops of rain sliding off his all-weather coat. 'What happened?'

'Broken a glass. I was just about to clear it up –'

156

'You're shaking.'

'I'm on edge.'

'You've cut your finger. Let me take a look.'

He led her over to the sink.

'It'll stop bleeding in a minute.'

'Thank you doctor.' Her mind flitted to the conversation she'd had with Rob. 'I didn't hear you come back last night.'

'Didn't want to wake you.' He took his coat off, slung it on the kitchen chair.

'I met Amy yesterday.'

He was filling the kettle. 'Is she well? How's the baby?'

'She's absolutely fine. Wonderful in fact. That woman was there. No doubt about that. Definitely Raquel Bannister. Having a beer. It was horrible.'

He turned round, stared at her. 'You *saw* her? Are you sure? Why didn't you say before?'

'Telling you now. She was there, all right.' She remembered trying to find her, how she'd disappeared, as she always did. 'She was really quite threatening. I wasn't mistaken. I'd know that face anywhere.'

'What else did she say?'

'It was her manner – she obviously hates me.'

He gave her an odd look, came closer. 'Did she harm you, threaten you in any way? '

She shook her head. 'No. She made out *I* was following her. She made sure everyone in Zino's thought that too.'

'I should have been here when you got back –'

'So, no point in going to the police. Everyone in Zino's would say it was me. What does she want, Mark? Why is the woman I met on holiday – the bloody thief. Why is she here? How does she know me from school? What's that about?' Tears welled. She dashed them away with her hand.

'It'll be all right. She'll get tired of it. She can't keep it up.' He put his arm round her and pulled her to him.

157

The phone rang. She rose from her chair. In several strides Mark was across the living room picking up the phone, saying 'hello' and she thought it might be Rob. She imagined the conversation, Rob sounding so friendly, familiar, sussing Mark out. Should she tell Mark about her arrangement to meet Rob? He'd understand her need to find out if Raquel was an ex-client. But there seemed no point in causing him more worry. Didn't he have enough to deal with?

It was her mother. She listened to Mark's side of the conversation, while in her head she filled in her mother's words. He had a special tone for her mother, a doctor tone.

'Yes,' he was saying. 'I understand. I see.'

She beckoned and he passed the phone to her, sat at the table, then immediately got up and left the room.

'I lost my phone, darling. Sorry.' Her mother's voice was high pitched and breathy.

'How are you?'

'You should see Baz's house. You must come over. There's a swimming pool, you know.'

'You don't like chlorine.'

'There's a sauna too. Actually I'm sort of living with Baz. You must come over, sweet.'

'But you've still got your flat over the shop, though. I mean you've not actually moved out, have you?' She was remembering Baz, the brown leather jacket, grey ponytail. The way he'd looked at her, the awful familiarity, and she thought of the women dancing on the tiny stage, twisting the feather boas round their skinny bodies.

'He treats me like a queen.'

'What *does* he do?'

'Baz is a very clever man. He's a businessman. Really, Jo, sometimes I wonder which of us is the mother and which of us is the daughter.'

'That makes me feel great. Thanks, mum.'

Mark was putting his coat back on. She heard the back door bang shut, Mark whistling. How odd. He never did that.

158

'He's got a gym too. And a personal trainer. He's going to get one for me –' her mother continued.

'Mum. You know, I've been trying to phone you. I must have left half a dozen messages.'

'I've been so busy, darling. Sorry. And I only found my phone, yesterday and I meant to phone you then, but the shop's been frantic. Was it urgent?'

'Urgent? Christ, mum, I'm your daughter. Urgent? No wonder I'm so messed up.'

'Sorry, sweetness and light. Don't be angry.'

She looked outside to check for black cars and make sure Raquel wasn't waiting for her ready to pounce.

'It's just sometimes I feel that I am the least important person in your life.'

'Jo. Darling.'

She pressed her face to the cold window and remembered how left out she used to feel, how much like a spare part.

'So why were you phoning? I mean was there a special reason?'

'Yes. That Raquel Bannister woman's been following me.'

'Darling –'

'She was in Zino's when I met Amy yesterday. I don't know what she wants. Do you?' She couldn't think straight. It was as if her mind was unravelling. 'And how did she know where I was going on holiday? When she told you she'd look out for me. Can't you remember which school she knew me from?'

'You get so wound up, Jo. Why shouldn't she be in Zino's, though it is strange her going all the way out to Meresbridge. But you must remember her? She told me about this wonderful spa place and I knew you and Mark were arguing about where to go and what to see. You said you'd add it to your list –'

'It was *her*?'

159

'To tell you the truth I thought that's why you decided on it –'

'What?' She was remembering the list. All those months ago before she knew of Raquel's existence, before she'd had any inkling she was about to lose her job, in the days when she and her mother drank herbal tea in *The Enclave* café, when she and Mark had been natural together, as if they fitted each other perfectly. The list. She thought back. There'd been a big row about where to go on holiday. Their first holiday together – apart from a quick trip to France and a 'romantic getaway' to Prague – seemingly doomed. For weeks, the subject was vetoed. Couldn't decide. Couldn't compromise. It was Mark's idea. "We'll make a list. Your preferences and mine. Destinations. Form of travel. Reasons for and against. An evaluation at the end."

'I shouldn't think she'd be following you. You must have imagined it, darling.'

Only half listening, she dug at the recesses of her memory, wading through the other stuff: the redundancy, Senaka, the beach, Raquel in a multi-coloured sarong, her lost passport, the pink umbrella outside, Rob, the perfume – her mother in hospital in the black lacy nightdress, Jo sitting on the edge of the bed, being told off by a nurse, her mother going on and on about how travelling enriches the mind, how she couldn't understand a daughter of hers preferring a package holiday and that Mark was right – such a surprise – they should just get a flight and go. Like she and Jo used to.

'You told me it was a *good* friend that told you. I remember now. *She* wasn't a good friend. She was in the next bloody bed to you. Somebody who said they knew me at school. Why didn't you introduce us, mum?'

'I intended to, my sweet. But she never felt up to it. She was a very sick lady.'

'You know none of the schools I went to have any record of anyone by the name of Bannister. Why did you say a *good* friend told you?'

'Well, she was while I was in hospital. She could have married and changed her name. You know she told me both her parents had died in a plane crash. She said she had no one. I felt quite sorry for her. I thought she was nice.'

'Plane crash? Nice? Bloody hell, mum. How can you call her a friend? And she told me she wasn't the marrying kind.'

'I do wish you wouldn't get so angry with me, Jo. *I* haven't done anything wrong. Look, darling, I've got to go now. I've got a customer. Why don't you come to my shop? I've changed it round. It looks quite different.'

Jo didn't reply, was remembering her mother in hospital, drowsy after the operation. She was right. Raquel turning into a thief and a stalker wasn't her fault.

'Sorry for yelling at you. I'll come and see your shop soon.'

She walked towards the window, sat on the sofa, and put her head in her hands. She thought of her mother in the hospital bed painting her lips ruby red, pouting in a hand mirror. There had been curtains round the next bed; blue and green striped. Jo hadn't asked. Why should she? All the same, her mother filled her in, urging Jo further up the bed, so she could whisper and Jo had smelt the soap she'd bought her, jasmine. 'Bruises', her mother said. 'All over her. Broken ribs. Doesn't want anyone to see. Domestic violence.' Jo had had enough domestic violence cases at work; file upon file, paper case notes on her desk waiting for her to read, waiting for her to decide on their future while they lingered, rotting in a damp bedsit, sharing the toilet and bathroom with five other families, waited their turn to use the microwave in a mouldy, dank kitchen. But why should she have shown interest in the woman in the next bed to her mother? What was all this about? She took deep, long breaths, closing her eyes, visualising a beach, the sea rolling in, as the therapist had taught her. Distraction, she'd said. Breathe. On the edge of the visualisation, Raquel was walking along the shore, her multi-coloured sarong flapping in the breeze. Jo opened her eyes, feeling someone's gaze on her. There was no one in the room with her, no one outside. But still she felt as if she was being watched, her every movement scrutinized. Mark called to her.

'You finished on the phone? I reckon we should plant some daffodils. Come outside and take a look.'

Shrugging into her coat she went out into the garden. So bare, no flowers, the lawn overgrown and muddy. She shivered.

'What do you think?' He squatted, examining a large empty pot. 'Some could go in here. We could put them near the window so we can watch them grow. We should treat the lawn too.'

She was staring at him. 'My mother just told me that it was this Raquel who – '

'Jo –'

'Listen to me. It was she who told my mother about the hotel in Sri Lanka. She deliberately wanted to entice me there. Who the hell could she be? Do you think she told my mum she knew me at school to get in with her? '

'D'you want to know what I think? That you're getting really wound up –'

'And you're surprised?'

'Look. If she appears again, we'll go to the police. Together. Right? But I don't think you'll see her again.'

'Why do you say that?'

'Just a feeling.'

'You?' She laughed. 'You got a feeling!' By the lapels she pulled him to her. 'You'll be saying you've got telepathy next!'

'Oh ye of little faith. Shall we go to the garden centre?' Mark said.

'I'm not sure.'

'Come on. Think about something else.'

It seemed like the entire population of the Lake District was milling around the Garden Centre. She and Mark wandered round the aisles, ostensibly looking for winter flowers, seeds

162

that would bloom in the summer, bulbs which would reveal their colours in the spring. He walked ahead. She dawdled behind. The shop was over-heated and the lights too bright. She wasn't in the mood.

After they'd bought a few items they sat in the café. As she waited for Mark – he was queuing at the self-service counter – she remembered when she first saw their garden, how excited she was. Never before had she lived somewhere with one to nurture. It was in a state: covered in brambles. Apparently it was abandoned when his wife got sick, though he'd say no more than that, only describing how it used to look when Jo pressed him.

'We'll have it different. ' Mark had said. 'A complete change for our new life together.'

After they'd cleared the brambles, they'd come to this garden centre. Hand in hand they'd walked down the aisles.

'I've never been to a garden centre before,' she'd said.

'You've never lived, then.'

'I want lots of flowers.'

'We shall have lots of flowers then.'

They'd grabbed a trolley and loaded it with shrubs, trees and flowers and the following Sunday had planted, mulched and watered them in. She'd been like a child, full of glee. Then there'd been champagne and sex.

Now he returned to their table: two coffees, two slices of chocolate cake.

'Thought it might cheer you up.'

She pushed a lock of hair from her eyes, murmuring 'thanks', and sipped her coffee. 'So you really think I won't see Raquel again?'

Slurping coffee into the saucer, he put his cup down suddenly, pushed his chair from the table, deliberately looking way from her. She could see the impatience expanding, taking hold of his expression. Did he expect a few pretty flowers to make everything all right? What was the matter with him? Even if his father was terminally ill, why was he trying to diminish her obvious distress?

'Why don't you eat your cake?' he said. 'It's really delicious.'

She cut the cake into four. 'The thing is, Mark, I don't believe she'll go away just like that.' Picking up one the cake slices she regarded Mark. '*I* have a feeling. I'm sure I'll see her again.'

15

Half an hour early, Jo took her orange juice to a table in an alcove where there was only enough room for two. It was an old pub with exposed beams and framed political cartoons on the wall. Trendy looking university students were crammed together in groups. She would have liked the woman behind the bar to slip a little vodka into her orange juice, but she wanted to have a clear head and stirred her drink with the plastic stick, while inhaling the cigarette smoke which drifted across to her from an open window at the back. The music was the usual, in-house electronic type.

She took a gulp of cold orange juice and tossed it round her mouth as if she were testing the bouquet of an expensive and rare wine, remembering the time she and Mark had gone to France to revisit his childhood haunts. They'd taken a chateaux tour and played a stupid game: which one of them could retain the wine in their mouth the longest, which one gave in to swallowing first. Full of wine, they'd staggered back to their room in a hotel and collapsed, giggling, on a creaking bed. She fiddled with a broken nail. The holiday seemed so long ago, much longer than the couple of years it actually was.

Rob walked through the door. Cargo pants, denim jacket, trainers. Same as before. He waved. She waved back, smiled and as he made his way across the floor, she noticed a crease down his cargo pants. She never knew he possessed an iron, never mind an ironing board.

Leaning across the table he gave her a business-like peck on the cheek. 'Drink?'

'Got one, thanks.'

He walked off to the bar and she gazed after his figure, deciding she preferred his trousers creased.

'Didn't think you'd turn up,' he said, after he'd sat down and taken a long drink from his pint of Guinness. He waved to a man wearing a black sweatshirt.

'Well, here I am.' She gave him a smile. 'Did you find anything on Raquel Bannister?'

He was staring into his beer. 'So what's going on?'

'This woman, Raquel Bannister, is stalking me.' The words were out, no hesitation. Surprised, she felt heat rising to her face, anger at being put in this position. What the hell was she doing here?

He put his hand to the top of his scalp, that age old gesture. 'Bit heavy.'

'Could say that.'

'Why is she stalking you?'

'Wouldn't be here if I knew that, would I?'

From the inside pocket of his jacket, he took out a tobacco pouch and began to roll a cigarette. 'How long is it since we saw each other, Jo?'

'Eight, nine months. Why?'

'Well, you know. You phone me out of the blue and ask me to look up a name on the system, one of your old clients, you said, because she's *stalking* you. And that's all you say. How are you Rob? How's life treating you? No nothing like that. Bit much.'

She pushed her hair from her forehead, puffed out air. 'God. I'm so sorry. It's really getting to me. How are you? I meant to ask.' Feeling incredibly guilty, she touched the middle finger of the hand that clasped his pint. 'Sorry,' she said again. 'How's work?'

He offered her the tobacco pouch. She shook her head. He put the rolled cigarette in the top pocket of his jacket. The music had changed: hard rock.

'You don't mean it, though, do you? I mean really you're just saying that to shut me up.'

'I do. Really I do. I still care about you even if we've been out of touch – but being stalked isn't much fun. Have you ever been stalked?'

'Can't say I have. What does the doctor say about it?'

'Mark's a nurse.'

'So how's the nurse? Still playing the drums?' He looked away from her. He'd been envious of Mark's ability. She knew that, though Rob had never said.

'When he gets a gig, yeah.' She wasn't going to tell him that that part of Mark seemed to have disintegrated, that he didn't even practise anymore.

'And? What's his view, you know, on you being stalked?'

Nearby there were raised voices. Two men jostled each other. Another man came between them. No one else seemed to have noticed the commotion. There were four men in the knot of bodies, each of them with stomachs hanging over their belts, working jeans. They looked out of place amongst the other clientele and she wondered whether perhaps this pub had been their local before it was invaded by students. Was this Rob's preferred pub now? His old haunt had been a biker's watering hole, not far from where he lived. That was a long time ago. She gripped her glass. She was so tense. And what exactly was Mark's view on her being stalked? He didn't believe her, but she wouldn't tell Rob that.

'He thinks it'll all stop.' She drained the glass of orange juice. 'That she'll get tired of it. Something like that. Go to the police if it carries on. So you didn't tell me how work is.' She played with the plastic stirrer in her drink, rotating it round the glass. 'And how's the love life? Anyone special?'

'To the former enquiry I'd say same as ever. Apart from a major breakdown of the server which lasted four days and was a real pain in the nether regions, but I shan't bore you on that account. To the latter enquiry, the answer is zero.

167

How's yours? Love life, I mean. You're looking good. Positively glowing.'

She felt herself blush.

'I'm going outside for a fag. You going to join me?' he said.

It was cold and rainy, a misty rain. Other smokers huddled together, sucking on their fags, the tips glowing briefly on each inhalation. The four men who'd been arguing came out with them and moved a little way from the pub entrance. One of them poked the other in the chest, shouted something.

'You still haven't told me what you found out.'

His shoulders were up near his ears. He was shivering and she thought that he should wear a hat, having no hair, being so skinny. She always used to tell him this, she remembered.

'It's bloody freezing. Hang on. I'll just finish this. Can't think in this temperature.' He took a final pull on his ciggie, threw it to the pavement, squashed it with the heel of his trainer. 'Right. Let's go back inside.'

Of course, their table had been taken so they had to stand. Rob fetched their drinks and swallowed the remains of his Guinness. Her orange was long gone.

'This all right for you? I mean we can go somewhere else. If standing is, you know.'

'I'm fine.' Though she had to admit she was quite touched that he'd considered her injury. He'd been there when she'd fallen from the window. Not exactly there. Not precisely sitting on the window sill, but he'd been in the kitchen looking for a bottle which still contained some wine. It had been her and him at the party, plus some woman who worked in the *Apple* shop who fancied him. Plus a load of other people neither of them knew. And one of those hot sticky summers that only lasts a few days yet feels like it went on forever. They'd been drinking since they'd left work, so Rob told her. The party was heaving when they got there, apparently. She'd thought nothing of climbing onto the window ledge and strumming her legs on the wall in time to the music. And then there was the kitten. There'd been a moment that she still remembered, when the night began to sway, when the street lights blurred and became one, but the week prior to the fall was a blank.

'I'll get these,' she said and pushed her way through bodies, mingling, sweating, heaving, intoxicated. Thrusting a £10 note at the man behind the bar eventually got her served. She was desperate to get this drink, to find out what Rob had discovered, though part of her was scared, didn't want to know the truth, if the truth involved an increasing level of the nightmare that had begun three weeks ago. She bought vodka and orange for herself – she'd have one –no more. Rob took his pint from her. He'd been texting. He put his mobile away, took a gulp of Guinness.

'I had a look on the system for your stalker.'

She was pushed nearer to him by a woman trying to get to the bar. 'And?' She had to shout above the music. Her voice came out more like a squeak.

'She's there.'

'Christ. She *is* an ex-client.' After all this time, she could barely believe what she was hearing. The thoughts in her head multiplied like bacteria. Of course, she'd hoped desperately, almost convinced herself during the time it had taken to get the drinks, that this would be a wasted journey, that after she'd met Rob she could go home and bury herself in the life she shared with Mark, that the woman who called herself Zara was just a nasty piece of work.

'I've got to sit down.'

He took her drink and led her to the far side of the pub where there was a snooker table. They squashed on two chairs at the end, near the Gents. At the other side of the snooker table there was a group of drinkers and one of them had her back to her and Rob. Her pink sweater was fluffy, short, showed off a couple of inches of the woman's deeply tanned lower back. Her hair was short, dyed blonde. She was laughing, throwing back her head, putting her weight on her

169

left leg, standing all nonchalant, like she knew nothing. Jo craned her neck forward.

'You all right?'

She was thinking, I'm going to get her; I'm going to teach her a lesson. She was aiming a look at the woman, like she could shoot bullets from her eyes. The woman turned round, stared at Jo, swung back round to her friends.

'Jo?'

She gulped her drink back, feeling her brain filling with alcohol.

'You OK?'

'No. Actually I'm not.' She could feel her pulse racing, she took deep long slow breaths, spied Rob, over the top of his glass, observing the woman in the pink sweater, switching his look back to Jo.

'I see her everywhere.'

'Do you?'

'I am *not* going mad. You found her on the system, didn't you? I mean that's evidence that the woman exists. She was an ex-client, so she might well have it in for me. There've been cases of clients stalking social workers. God, I think one was killed. I know I wasn't a social worker but –'

He was looking at her closely.

'You think I'm imagining it all?'

'Did I say that?'

The woman who was crammed next to her, who'd been in deep conversation with someone else, turned, switched her eyes to Jo. Rob put his hand on Jo's knee. 'Fuck. You're really freaked out.'

She stared at his hand feeling the warmth through her jeans. All those memories – she pushed them away. 'What did you find out? '

He removed his hand, looked straight ahead. 'There was an asterisk by her name. Doesn't that mean AKA, also known as?'

'Christ.'

'Do you really not remember her?'

'Do you know how many cases I signed off in a week? I never met clients when I was the manager, did I? Have you got the file?'

He was watching the game of snooker. The woman whose turn it was leaning across the table, eyeing up the ball. She brought her cue back from her body and shot the ball across, hitting it neatly. It glanced off another ball. Rob turned back to Jo.

'No, I only looked her up.'

'You didn't think to look for the file?' She knew the room where the old files were stored. Some of them went back fifteen years, yellowing, the ink on the hand written case notes fading, smudged, the type written notes curled and thumbed at their edges. It was in the basement, next to the IT room where Rob worked. There'd always been talk of going through them, of destroying the records if they were more than seven years old, but no one ever had the stomach to do it, the occasional temp was brought in, but never lasted, such a tedious task. So the ancient files stayed put, holding on to details of every person who had entered the building.

'You would have recognised her before you were a manager –'

'If you're having a go at me, now is not the time –'

'I'm just saying,' he said. 'That's all. Just making conversation.'

'This isn't funny.'

'I'm not laughing, Jo. Maybe your bloke is right. If you're being stalked and threatened by an ex-client you should go straight to the police. Especially if she followed you thousands of miles away and nicked your stuff. '

'You don't believe me either, do you?'

'Yes. I believe you. Go to the police.'

'Oh, yeah. I'd look a right fool. Can you imagine? Anyway she's not threatened me. Not exactly.' She watched a pool player chalking his cue, blowing the dust off, leaning across the table, eyeing up his aim.

'Can you get me the file so I can have a good look?'

He put his hand in his inside pocket and pulled out his tobacco pouch, a nub of tobacco and a packet of papers. He rolled the cigarette very slowly, tamping down the tobacco with his thumb, licking the paper with precise practised movements. 'I could do.'

'But?'

There was a brief silence as the track came to an end and Jo heard the noise of the pub, all the chatter, the laughter. She smelt the warm odour of beer, heard the ease of chat, the camaraderie of the drinkers and felt envious of their happiness.

'You'd have to come to my place to read it. There's no way I'm bringing it to a pub.' His eyes locked hers and she saw the little flecks of gold in them. She knew what he was thinking, what was whirring round his head and she paused before she spoke, she stared into the bottom of her empty glass. Did she have a choice?

'Ok, then. I will. It's good of you to do all this. You're a true friend –'

'Don't push it, Jo.'

'I mean it.'

He sighed, drained his glass. 'I'll be off then.'

They weaved their way through the crowds, went out into the freezing night.

'I go this way.' Rob said.

'See you soon and thanks.'

Turning round, he nodded, then hurried off.

In the distance, a car alarm began to wail. She walked quickly towards her car, the alarm becoming louder the closer she got. Before she turned into the street where her car was parked, she knew. Raquel had followed her here. Had she been in the pub, eavesdropping on her and Rob's conversation? Was Rob in danger too? As she approached her car, panic filled her gut. The noise was coming from *her* car. There was shattered glass strewn across the pavement and road, a shrieking alarm. All the side windows were smashed. Broken glass covered the seats. She knew it was Raquel. For a second she stood staring at the damage not knowing what to do while the alarm screeched madly in her ear. Every sensible thought drained from her. How could she stop this noise? What should she do?

'This yours?' a man who'd been approaching her asked. He had a shaved head and wore a denim jacket. He was peering at her anxiously. 'Can I help? You OK?'

Reality seeped into her brain. She opened the car door, searched for a switch that would stop the noise, couldn't find it. The street was deserted; no other pedestrians. Traffic zoomed past. The sound was unbearable. She wanted to cry. 'Do you know how to switch it off?' She hated being the useless female, but what did it matter now?

'You do this,' he shouted above the screaming alarm while leaning into the car. The sound stopped. Apart from the rumble of passing cars, all was quiet. 'Bloody kids probably. You should tell the police, you know, get a number for the insurance.' He was looking at her questioningly.

She thanked the man. Reached for her phone, called Rob, told him what had happened, where she was. Wasn't he closer to hand than Mark? Didn't that give her good reason to phone him before Mark?

'Be there in two tics,' he said.

She phoned Mark, left a message, feeling thankful that his voicemail was switched on. What would she have done if he had said he would get there now? But why was she worrying about that while Raquel demonstrated her hatred by breaking up her car?

By the time Rob arrived she'd already called the police and the man wearing the denim jacket had gone.

'What did they say?' Rob asked.

'It was that bloody woman. I know it was. What's she trying to do?'

'Did you tell the police this? Did you say you think it was someone who's been stalking you –?'

'She wants to really hurt me. I know she does. If she followed me, she might have been in the pub. She might be out to get you too if she knows you're looking up her file.'

'No need to worry about me. I can take care of myself,' Rob said.

Jo was shaking with anger, 'Why can't she leave me alone?' She put her hand to her forehead. 'The police took everything down, her name and stuff, but – I'll get the insurance people to arrange to patch it up. I can't get hold of them now. I don't suppose the police will follow it up.'

'They should do. Look, I'll help you clear the glass up and make the car safe to drive. You told your bloke?'

'He's at work.' She stared at her ruined car. 'Thanks, my saviour. Thank you so much. I owe you.'

'I'm doing what any self-respecting friend would do. I'm no saviour.'

'I can't believe this is happening. Why me?' she said. 'Am I really such a bad person?'

16

When Mark got back from his shift, he looked pale, gaunt, his face creased with worry when he told her – his father, it seemed, didn't remember he owned a Classic Morgan sports car. 'It was his life,' Mark said. 'Every Sunday afternoon he'd be tinkering with it. If he can't remember that – well –'

They were in the kitchen. Between them was a pot of coffee. As if everything was normal, an average couple chatting amiably about domestic matters. He didn't believe the car was smashed by Raquel.

'That's a crazy idea. Why d'you say that? More like kids. High on something or pissed up. We get enough of them in A and E. Expect you'll lose your no claims bonus now. You should be careful where you park in town. Why were you there?'

'I was meeting a friend.' The lie slipped out easily: she was astonished at herself. 'But it was hardly my fault, was it?' she said, anxious to defend herself. 'I'm sorry if it means more expense, but I wish you'd believe me when I say I *know* it was Raquel.'

He looked at her. 'You don't know who did it.' He topped both their coffees up. 'So this friend you met. Anyone I know?'

'Someone I used to work with. Don't think you ever met her.' She got up and rinsed out the mugs, was thinking might it have been someone else who smashed her car? Was she paranoid? After all, she had no evidence it was Raquel. She thought about the night before, her meeting with Rob, the sleepless night that followed, hearing the dawn chorus, watching the yellow wall of their bedroom turning puce, wondering how she'd face Mark, whether she'd end up telling him how she'd met Rob, that she had to know, that there was no other way of tracking down Raquel.

'I was going to fetch the Morgan from my dad's.'

'I'll come with you. I'd like to see your father.' Staying at home alone wasn't an option right now, though there was still the interview to prepare.

There was no sign of Raquel in their street. She checked carefully, looking right, then left. Mark didn't seem to notice her anxiety, but why should he? A dying father was bad enough. They travelled in silence while Eric Clapton sang the blues, the iPod turned to full volume.

An hour later he pulled up outside a detached bungalow with an overgrown lawn, a large leafless tree, drooping over the broken path and a green Morgan in the car port. Mark's father had moved there before Jo met Mark, after Mark's mother had died. Mark had once shown her the house where he used to live, where Mark grew up – an old red brick house with ivy growing up the wall and fruit trees in the garden.

Now, he stayed in the driver's seat looking out at the bungalow, tapping out a rhythm on the wheel. She put her hand on his long fingers to calm them; he turned to her, smiled, said nothing about her keeping her eyes on the mirror of her sun visor. There was no way he could have not seen her. Not once did her eyes stray.

The Morgan, she had to admit, looked unreal with its head lamps perched on either side of the bonnet like a couple of cartoon eyes. Mark must have waxed it the day before; the body work gleamed, the chrome was shiny, good as new.

'Don't make them like that anymore. 1965. 1500 cc. Look at her. She's a stunner.'

'It's an it. Not a she.'

'Details, Jo.' He sighed. 'A beaut.'

Trailing his fingers along, he walked round the car, lowering his body and looking longingly inside, wiping the glass for a better view, sighing wistfully.

'Better go in,' he said at last.

The house smelt musty, of stale air. She followed Mark down the hallway, past a large living room with a round Chinese carpet set in the middle, past a spare bedroom with a single bed pushed against the wall and a powder blue candlewick bed cover. The bedroom where Mark's father lay was at the end of the bungalow. Jo stood in the doorway while Mark sat on the bed. His father, Sid, was wheezing and his face was colourless, had shrunk like his body which appeared flat beneath the heaped blankets. A large cross hung on the wall opposite the bed. Fascinated, Jo stared at it and wondered whether Mark, as a child, had been forced to kneel by his bed every night and say his prayers.

The furniture in the room was mahogany, too big and clunky for this modern square room. A convector heater was on full blast and the room was overpoweringly warm. Jo shivered, feeling claustrophobic, unable to breathe in the stifling heat, the overpowering smell of decay. She didn't recognise Sid. He didn't seem to know her, was barely aware that she was standing in the doorway, removing her coat, fiddling with her bag.

'Hello,' she said. 'It's me. Jolene.'

The man stared at her blankly. His head was turned in her direction and she saw his mouth open as if he was about to speak. The face had turned grey, death-like, the expression told her he had no idea who she was. As she half turned, intending to fetch a chair from another room, she saw his mouth twitch. She stepped nearer. Was he trying to tell her something? Did he recognise her? The twitching increased, distorting his face and she realised what was happening. The shaking spread to his arms, they were flailing, fingers digging into his palms, knuckles white. His legs were jerking violently; he was making a strange mewing sound, an animal cry. She gaped, unable to move. Saliva dribbled from his toothless mouth and his eyes rolled up into his head, showing only the white.

'What –?' she began.

Mark glanced at her while he loosened the bedclothes, but said nothing. His father was still jerking, arms thrashing, his back arched. A smell of excrement slowly filled the room. She backed away Didn't know what to do. Could still hear the strangled inhuman cry. Then it stopped. A slow wheezing was the only sound from the room. On the bed lay his shrivelled hands, nails scratching the oatmeal cover while Mark touched the man's brow as if soothing him, but still she stood there taking in the figure as he slowly recovered, his limbs slackening, the wheeze becoming more regular, the stench making her retch.

'Get some tea,' Mark said, without looking up, wiping his father's mouth with a tissue. 'Lots of sugar and a bowl of hot water, a clean cloth.'

'Right.'

The kitchen was tidy, with washed dishes stacked neatly on the drainer, but the room itself was grimy. The units were worn, the laminate peeling and the floor a yellowing beige lino. She stared at it all, unaware of what she was seeing. Why hadn't she realised Sid was so ill?

A bowl for the water was under the sink. She found the tea, sugar and milk.

Her mobile rang.

'It's me.'

'Hi.' She moved across to the open window. It looked out on a back yard. Weeds sprouted in between the flagstones. There was a broken bench at the boundary wall. She couldn't be long. Mark needed her.

'Got the file.'

She knew Rob was standing out the back at work having a smoke, could hear the articulated lorries that parked nearby, delivering their goods and a memory snagged how the overflowing bins would stink and one summer during a bin strike they couldn't tolerate it out there, had had to dart across the road and stand in a café doorway. And she thought how simple her life had been then.

'It was filed under Raquel Bannister, but the name on the notes is Rosalind Bow.'

There were raised voices coming from the bedroom. Mark's father was wailing. Was he having another fit? She moved across the kitchen to the back door. Her heart was thumping, her ears rang. Were those footsteps in the hall? 'I'll phone you later,' she said.

'Thought you were desperate for it. Thought you'd like to know I'd found it. Came to work early specially.'

'Thanks for getting it, but I can't talk now. Sorry. Speak later.' Putting her phone back into her bag she carried the tray into the bedroom where Sid was sitting in a chair next to the bed. His face was translucent, lips white. She put the bowl of hot water on the table.

'I'll get the tea. Is there anything else I can do?'

'Who were you talking to?' Mark asked.

Was he spying on her? She paused for a half a second. 'Spam.'

It was no good. She was a hopeless liar. When they got home she'd tell him.

'Is he all right? I mean –'

'Yeah. You're all right now. Aren't you, dad?'

It felt as if she was intruding. After she'd taken in the tea, she returned to the kitchen, and once more stared out at the garden, at a shed with a rusty lock, a white plastic chair, one leg broken, giving it a drunken look. A thought was beating at her temple: who was Rosalind Bow? The doorbell rang. Jo went to answer it.

'Cooey.' A nurse was bustling down the hall, followed by a woman wearing jeans carrying a holdall with a large bunch of keys hanging from her belt.

'Hi. I'm Jo, Mark's partner.'

They both nodded to Jo then went into the room where Mark's father lay. Jo followed them in. 'Is there anything else I can do?' she asked.

'We'd better go. Leave them to it,' Mark said.

'I'll just say goodbye to your dad.'

In his bedroom, the nurse was attending to a wound on Sid's leg. Diabetes, Mark had told her, ulcers on the leg as well as the rest. Taking a step towards the bed, she smiled at Sid, reached out to touch his hand.

Pupils enlarged in hatred, he snatched his hand away. 'Who is she?' Sid's eyes bored into her. She retreated. 'You're not Kathleen. What are you doing in my house?' Starting to get up from his chair, pushing the blanket off, lips trembling with fury, he lurched towards her. The nurse ushered him back.

'Jo. Let's go,' said Mark.

'He didn't mean it,' Mark said after they'd closed the door to the bungalow.

'Does he have many fits?'

'Now and again,' he said. 'He's clinging on.'

She stared at him as he walked on ahead down the drive.

Mark drove the Morgan back to their house. She followed him slowly in his car.

Back at their house, he parked the green Morgan in front of her and came round to her window. She checked up and down their road. Was that Raquel crossing the road ahead, making her way towards Jo?

'Have to put the drum kit in the other bedroom, so the Morgan can go in the garage,' he said. 'Stands out a mile, parked here. Don't want her windows smashed in. Could you give me a hand packing it up?' Looking in the direction where she was gazing, he turned her round to face him. 'Hey, did you hear me?'

'Look.' Pointing along the street, she said: 'Is that her? Is that Raquel Bannister?'

'Not *now*. What's the matter with you?'

'Can't you see?' The woman who was there: black coat, a flash of pink, a sweater or a scarf, turned into another road.

'What am I supposed to be looking at?'

'She's gone.'

'For God sake, Jo. I can't believe you're still going on about that woman. After what's happened. What's the matter with you? There's no one there. No one's following you now. It's all in your imagination.'

'It's not. I am not crazy. I know what I'm seeing. She was in Zino's. It was her.'

A baby in a pram was screaming, coming towards them while the mother tried to calm it. Louder and louder until they reached their house and crossed the road.

'But that *isn't* her. She's someone who you think is Raquel. Right now I'm going to get my drum kit out of the garage. Up to you if you want to help, though I never have any fucking time to play them. Do I?' The look he gave said he'd had enough. He'd never looked at her that way before. Feelings of guilt swamped her. Was she pushing him too far? He'd given her so much. Without him where would she live? How would she have supported herself without a job?

'Sorry. Of course I'll give you a hand.'

'Right. Let's get started.'

Then he was setting up the drum kit in the extension where his wife used to work writing for magazines. She helped him push the swivel desk chair out of the way, guided him as he shoved the desk into a corner. He showed no emotion.

'What was your wife like?'

'She wrote for magazines –'

'I know that. But what was she *like*? You never told me. Where did you meet for example? Why didn't you have children?'

He was examining a drum stick. He turned to face her. 'She had shoulder length brown hair – '

'I know, I've seen a photo. But you never said what sort of a person she was.'

'Why are you asking? Does it matter? I never pry into your past, do I?'

She said nothing, was staring at an enormous filing cabinet. Had he ever cleared it out? Or was this room just as it used to be when she was alive?

'We met through a friend. Children? They never happened. Why are you interrogating me about her? She's dead. I spent two years nursing her. That's all. Can I get on with this now?'

'Sure. No need to get so pissed off. I was only asking.'

Jo sat at the dining room table, unfolded the letter about the job interview, read through the job description and wrote on a blank piece of paper: <u>PRESENTATION.</u> From the other room she heard a cymbal crash to the floor. Now she blamed herself for querying him about his wife. His father's sickness might be bringing back unpleasant memories of his wife's illness.

Number 1, she wrote: *Experience.* With the end of her pen, she tapped her teeth. She couldn't concentrate. Her mind flitted around: Raquel. Pink umbrella. That stupid blue nose stud. Rob. Seeing him the night before. er smashed car and the file. Was Rosalind Bow Raquel Bannister?

The phone rang and she noticed there were four messages on their new answerphone. She picked up the phone, 'Hello,' she said. There was silence. 'Hello?' A voice whispered down the line. 'Pardon?' she said. The person whispered again and Jo tried to make out the words, she tried to separate each sound to make the sentence comprehensible. The phone went dead. She played the answerphone. No messages. Number withheld on the last call. She shivered, heard a door close and Mark's feet coming along the hall towards the living room.

'I'll finish setting it up when I come back.'

'Someone just rang. They were whispering down the phone at me. I get really scared when things like that happen.' She looked out towards the garden. A late afternoon sun was glinting through the branches of the beech and she thought of Mark's father, his face grey as ash. 'I wish,' she began, then stopped.

How could she tell him what she really wished? That she'd never gone away without him, that she could barely think straight and how was she supposed to prepare for an interview with all this going on? And now she felt as if she and Mark were strangers living under the same roof.

He was moving round the room at lightning speed, picking up his keys, work bag, phone. 'Sorry I snapped,' he said. 'It was probably kids on the phone anyway.'

'Where you off to now?'

'An emergency at the hospital.'

'But you've just done a killer shift.'

'I know. Staff off sick again. I've just been bleeped.'

She looked up at him and thought how he never let the hospital down. 'You've just visited your dad who –'

'You can practise your interview on me, when I get back.' He was nodding at the table, at the paper on which she'd just written: *Number 2. Aptitude.* He came across the room to her and kissed her on the top of her head, his anger vanished like ether.

'You OK?'

'Yes,' she said. 'Just emotionally fraught. See you later.'

'If you get any more strange phone calls, disconnect the phone.'

'What?'

'Or tell them to fuck off.'

Then he was gone, slamming the door behind him. The house was deadly quiet. There was no one lurking on the street. She sat at the table, doodled on the paper, and for five minutes considered the job interview, pushing from her mind all other concerns. But five minutes was all she could deal with. She picked up her bag and dug out her mobile, switched it on. No messages. No missed calls. She slung it back on the sofa, wandered through to the room at the back where Mark's drum kit lay abandoned, his cymbals stacked neatly in their boxes, wires and headphones and drum sticks scattered untidily around the room and she saw as she stared at his unaccustomed mess, how much this room was imprinted with memories of Mark's wife. There, against the wall was her old desk and the red chair on which she'd sat while she wrote and looked out at the view of the garden from the window. From the floor, where it lay at an angle, discarded, she picked up one of his drumsticks and tapped out a rhythm on the window sill, remembering the first time she'd seen him in the Lion and Lobster on the drums looking so cool and sexy playing a solo, transfixing the crowd with his skill. Now that evening felt like a daydream that never happened.

From the living room, she phoned Rob.

'You took your time.' It was so good to hear his voice.

'I'm sorry Rob. I couldn't speak before –'

'Never mind that. I've finished work. You can come round if you want. To see the file I mean.'

'To your flat?'

'You think I'm going to tie you up and have my wicked way. Joke.'

'Ha ha.'

'You said you wanted me to find the file and I've found the file. Do you want to see it or not?'

'Of course I do. But I can't come right now, I haven't got a car. Some mix up with a courtesy car. But they said mine would be ready tomorrow so I'll get there about six. Is that OK?'

They finished the phone call and she took a look outside. There was a black car parked in the space she usually used. Was someone in the passenger seat? She leaned in further. It was too far from the house to see if there was anyone there. She drew the curtains and locked all the doors and windows, went through to the kitchen.

Something wasn't right. Someone was watching the house. The feeling in Jo's gut was unmistakable. But should she leave it? If it was Raquel outside, what would she do? The phone rang. She picked it up. There was hissing – the sound someone makes when they are imitating a snake.

Unable to bear the not-knowing any longer, she grabbed her phone, unbolted the front door and made her way down the steps. The black car was still there. She approached it carefully. Her heart was beating fast. There in the passenger seat sat Raquel. A lime green ball hung from the rear view mirror. So it *had* been Raquel who'd run her off the road. Rage boiled in Jo's veins as she neared the driver's window.

Raquel was filing her nails. Jo stood at the driver's window waiting for Raquel to look up. It was obvious that Raquel was perfectly aware of her presence.

'What are you doing outside my house?' Jo said, surprising herself at how calm she sounded.

Raquel looked at her, mock astonishment on her face, then turned to the sound system and switched it on lowering the window a fraction. Hard rock. Full volume. *Thump, thump, thump.*

Jo knocked on the window.

'Hey. Listen. Nicking my passport was bad enough.' She moved closer to the glass. 'Don't pretend you can't hear me.' The music pounded. Raquel was texting. 'You can go down for fraud. I'm warning you. Keep away.' She felt fury rising, was ready to explode. Her texting finished, Raquel sat in the car looking straight ahead.

Jo crouched at the window so her face was close to Raquel's. She felt completely fearless.

'I'm warning you. If you don't stay away from me, I'll get you arrested and make sure you go down for a very long time.' She was shouting, trying to make her voice heard above the din.

A tough looking guy walking a mountain bike along the pavement stopped. 'Everything all right?' He switched his look from Jo to Raquel.

Raquel smiled sweetly at him, sped away, the tyres screeching on the tarmac.

17

She parked outside Rob's flat, looking about her at the street she knew so well. She was thinking about what she was about to do. It was wrong, this stepping back into her old life. It was unwise; the outcome might be worse than she imagined. Her mother told her to always trust her instincts, that if her heart said yes – but how much of what her mother said did she trust? But she had to do something about Raquel. She had to find out who she was.

The street was lined with plane trees where Victorian mansions now divided into smaller residences had acquired a shabbiness that the original owners would have thought better suited to the other side of the railway track. She'd always liked this area of the city – good pubs and shops that sold Indian, Turkish, Iranian and Moroccan foodstuffs which smelt of spices and freshly baked unleavened bread. The aromas took her back to the temple visit she'd attempted, when she'd climbed the steps, her leg throbbing, while she cursed Raquel. Was there more to Senaka's relationship with Raquel than he let on? Perhaps they worked together, picking out the most gullible looking tourists.

She climbed up the well-trodden frontage, her feet recalling the dip in the third step, rang Rob's doorbell, waited, dispelling all thoughts of Mark working overtime in the hospital.

There he stood, the light from the hall creating a halo effect. Like always, he put his hand to the top of his head as if this action would encourage hair to regrow. She remembered him looking in a mirror, mourning the gradual loss, searching for signs of re-growth. She'd laughed at his vanity.

'You're looking good. I always liked your hair pinned up. Shows off your magnificent bone structure.' He hesitated and she thanked him for his compliment. 'Didn't think you'd come,' he said.

'You said that before.' She followed him down the shared hall, into the door which opened into his flat and heard music. It was probably a new band. Rob had eclectic taste in music, he always kept up with new bands arriving on the scene. She followed him past the bedroom on the right, the door was ajar so she could make out the unmade double bed, socks scattered on the floor; he shut off the scene, nudging the door closed with his foot and opened the one immediately opposite which led into his living room. He'd lit a fire. Was that for her? Taking a look round, she saw the table in the bay piled high with newspapers – the table where they'd often sat eating one of his fork bending curries. Three walls were filled with collectable LPs and CDs he hadn't yet got round to putting on his iPod. The other wall, where he used to pin up posters with notifications of bands, political meetings, newspaper clippings, photos, was blank, apart from the bluetac stuck irregularly to the wall like ghostly thumbprints. She knew that he was observing her, expecting her to ask what had happened to the stuff that used to adorn the wall, but she preferred to pretend she'd not noticed.

'This is for you. A thank you.' She handed him the plastic bag she'd been carrying.

As he extracted a bottle of wine from the bag, he grinned. 'My favourite. Thanks. Go down a treat.' He put the bottle on the table. 'Take a pew.'

There was one armchair and a sofa. She went for the red armchair. He sat cross- legged on the floor, on a raggedy Persian carpet that he'd bought at a car boot sale.

'Someone just phoned me at home. She was hissing down the phone at me. And –' She hadn't intended to tell him – but Mark hadn't exactly been supportive. In fact he'd been quite annoyed that it should have happened, checking and re-checking what she told him and what the police had said until she accused him of not believing her. Did he think she'd make it all up? He'd disappeared into the back room and bashed his drums. After half an hour he'd come out and apologised, taken her in his arms – but the damage had been done. So why not tell Rob? 'She was sitting outside the house yesterday in her car. In the space I usually put my car. I didn't realise it was her at first, though I knew someone was in the driver's seat – I could see that much from the house. But then I got this feeling I was being watched, that something wasn't quite right. I'd already locked all the doors – anyway I decided to take a look outside and to see who was in the car – I didn't really expect –'

'So it was this Raquel?'

'Yeah. I told her that if she didn't stop following me, I'd tell the police, I was quite matter of fact at that point.' Jo recalled the loathing on Raquel's face, the fear she'd managed to control, the question she'd asked herself: why did this woman revile her to such an extent? 'She turned this bloody hard rock music up high to rile me and it worked. I began to shout. I said harassment was unlawful – I actually used that word. I told her she was already pushing it, nicking my passport. She smiled at me. She *actually* smiled. I lost my rag then even though she couldn't have heard me with that racket and really yelled at her – I saw red. I said if she didn't stop harassing me, I'd make sure she went down. Then some bloke who was passing intervened, asked if everything was OK. And she drove off. Then before I left to come here, there it was again, the black car parked opposite the house. With her at the driver's seat. It drove away as soon as I approached it.'

'Have you told the police?'

'Yes, I have. They told me to keep a diary of everything.' She paused. 'I don't know anyone else that hisses down the phone either. It has to be her.' Where was the file? She scanned the room.

'You should leave it to the police to deal with.' He began to skin up. 'I hope you haven't got any crazy ideas.'

'What do you mean crazy ideas? It's her that's crazy – I've written everything down like the police said. But she's still around – out there waiting. I'm terrified, Rob. Who is she and how's a diary going to keep her away?'

'Doesn't the doctor protect you from the bogey man?' He put another log on the fire, messed it around with the poker.

'Can't you be serious for once?'

'Oh, but I am. Deadly serious.' He got up and lifted up a newspaper on the table. Underneath was a file and he pulled it out, laid it on the table. 'What did he say about your smashed car? Did you tell him about her threatening you?'

'Kids he reckoned. Same as everyone else thinks. And yeah I told him about yesterday. Let me see the file. Please.'

'Just a minute. Before you read it.'

'Why?'

'Thought I'd make a coffee, or maybe –' he put on a Marlow accent, 'the lady would prefer something stronger.'

'You never could take me seriously.'

'Untrue. That's your doctor you're thinking of. Not me.'

'Stop it Rob. You're making yourself sound pathetically jealous.'

He didn't reply but went through to the kitchen. While he was there, and the kettle boiled – it always took forever – she picked up the file. In an instant, he was there behind her.

'Ah, ah,' his hand was on the top of her arm. 'I said wait.'

'This isn't a game.' She followed him into the kitchen, stood in the doorway looking on, sniffed the coffee as he spooned it into his percolator.

'Bit of a mess in here. I'll bring it through.'

'Right.' But she'd seen the pile of dirty dishes in the sink, the cooker caked with dried tomato sauce. It had never bothered her before, the chaos of his life, the pile of unwashed

189

clothes that grew and multiplied on a daily basis, in the corner of his bedroom.

'I'll help you clear up if you like.' She felt she owed him one, even though she wished he wouldn't play games with her.

'No way, Jose.' He handed her a mug. 'All that can wait.'

Back in the living room, he went across to the iPod and skipped the track that had just started and the next one swung in with a guitar riff. The music had a '90s feel to it. She sat back in the red armchair, stared at the file, a feeling of dread rising from her gut.

'You read it?'

'Oh yes. I read it. My perk. Not much to read. Help yourself.' He nodded towards it and continued preparing the joint.

She'd imagined a big fat file, held together with a rubber band, like one of the files that piled up on her desk when she was manager, one of the files that used to lie scattered on the floor when her desk space could take no more.

There was a scantily completed form in the file: name, Rosalind Bow and date of birth, a brief note and a letter with her signature at the bottom. Jo's signature agreeing to discharge all duty to Rosalind Bow and agreeing that no further assistance should be given to her.

'So this was under Raquel Bannister?'

'Uh-huh.'

'You don't think it could have been filed incorrectly?'

'Unlikely. There were other files there all referenced to Raquel Bannister, but this was the most recent. Anyway, it's got your name there. That's why I picked it out from the rest.'

'Couldn't you have brought the whole lot here?'

'And if someone saw me, what would have been my excuse? They've got worse about confidentiality since you left.'

The date was eleven months previously. *Homeless due to fire*, she read and felt Rob's eyes on her, felt her face redden and her hand begin to shake. She looked up at Rob. The table tidying had been abandoned. He was holding the skinny looking spliff, just holding it, not lighting it, he was waiting for her. The music touched her soul. He must have picked it with that in mind. She lowered her eyes again to continue reading the file. The notes were scanty, interview conducted by a C. George. A name she couldn't recall – she began to feel she was losing her grip. A few scrawled lines took up the page. Rosalind Bow had been picked up by the emergency team at 3am after a fire had broken out in her flat. They'd placed her in emergency accommodation and this C. George had interviewed her in the morning. If only she had a date of birth for Raquel Bannister.

'C. George?' she said. 'What was his first name? On the tip of my –'

'Colin George.'

'Colin George?'

'Yup. That's the one.'

C. George, it appeared from the notes, hadn't been able to track down any of the other files for the client despite there being a note that she went by different names, and had been told by a police officer that the fire was suspected arson. This was enough for C. George to consider Rosalind Bow a convicted arsonist especially as he so aptly put: *R.B. was very aggressive when I interviewed her and the police* (no name, Jo noted) *told me she was under suspicion.*

A saxophone, sweet and melodic filled the room. Rob lit up, inhaled, watching her. From outside she heard the sound of a man's voice, raised in anger. He sounded drunk. He passed by, his voice fading, vanishing into a rumble from a passing train. There was an address on the file, the place which was allegedly set fire to by Raquel Bannister, but she couldn't picture Colin George, couldn't place the name. But there at the bottom of the file was her name agreeing with C.

George's decision. The buck, as they say, stopped there. Was this the same woman?

She stared at the wall where the bluetac was scattered, a couple of larger blobs had been half peeled, had scraps of paint visible. There was a pain in her right temple. In circular movements she rubbed the spot. The fire that Rob had lit appeared to have gone out.

'Remind me who Colin George was.'

'You were his manager.'

'It's a while ago.'

He was holding in the smoke from the joint, making sure it got as deep down as possible into his lungs, like he always used to. Exhaling, he offered it. She shook her head.

'Don't these days.' She glanced down at the paper, turned it over, saw a yellow post-it stuck to the other side, hanging on by its corner.

'Beats me why you can't remember your own staff. Guess that's what happens when you –'

'Don't start.'

'He was a temp. Agency. Against union policy.'

She was reading the yellow post-it. *Bow phoned. Jolene Carr was busy, but passed message on, that decision was final.* Had she said that? She felt her body go rigid.

'You should have assisted her. Right? You should have instructed Colin George to make more enquiries before and put her in temporary accommodation if she was homeless because of a fire.'

'Since when were you an expert on Housing Legislation?'

'I'm right though, aren't I?'

She wanted a cigarette, a drink, something strong. She sipped her coffee. Scalding hot, delicious. He always did make good coffee. She was copying down the address from the file into a psychedelic diary her mother had given her for Christmas, then slipping it back in her bag, her eyes fixedly staring at the floor. The carpet, she noticed, had been vacuumed, the imprints of wheels still visible in the pile. Was that specially for her too?

'Did you know Colin George then?'

'He smoked.'

'So you shared the bin area with him in your nicotine breaks?'

'There speaks an ex-smoker. You really don't know who he was?'

'Wouldn't be asking if –'

'No one much liked him. To be honest I could never get why he worked, you know in a job where he was supposed to be helping people. Came up from London. Moved with his wife. Some super-duper executive in advertising got a job up here. That's as far as I can remember. Think he said his job was in some central borough in London, you know one of those that don't give a monkey's, the policies of indifference. More like help as few as you can.' He took another drag, keeping it in while she re-read the file feeling about the same size as an ant. 'In fact –' he changed his expression to mock surprise, '– a bit like how you became a manager.'

'You're really having a go at me.'

'Not you. Not the real you. Anyway he was only there about ten days. That's why you probably don't remember him.' He offered Jo the joint again. 'Sure you don't want a toke?'

She shook her head. With his fingers, he pinched the end, got up off the floor pretending to groan with the effort and slipped the spliff into a caddy with a purple hibiscus design, one she'd found in the market and given to him. It was supposed to be for tea.

'I wish I had all the information. I mean how many names has the bloody woman got?'

He was blowing on his coffee. She glanced at her watch and thought that she'd have to go soon, that Mark would be back wondering where she was. The track came to an end. The room shrank in its silence before the next, a bluesy number.

'I don't understand, Jo. Maybe it's me being extra stupid. I mean, maybe I'm smoking too much of this stuff and my brain is addled. But I just don't get it.' He paused, obviously expecting her to ask what, but she pretended she was reading the file.

'I mean there's this woman, Zara, Raquel, Rosalind whoever she is – whatever her name is, who you wrongly didn't assist and she somehow ends up on the same *spa* holiday – never thought I'd see the day when you'd take a package holiday –'

'Don't you start –'

'Anyway, this woman who happens to be there does a runner with your passport and money and then she follows you home and stalks you, threatens you, smashes your car up – oh yeah, I forgot – she knows you from school, but you don't remember her.'

'It's not that simple.'

'No?'

'If she's an arsonist, she's probably unbalanced – and I was always being taken out of school by my mother, so it's hardly surprising if I don't remember her. Not only did I contact the schools, but I also tracked down someone I knew in the one I spent the longest time. Nothing. She'd never heard of any one by any of the names.'

'So dead end there.'

'The Raquel woman had heard from my mother who was in the next bed to her a few months back in hospital, that I was looking for a holiday and she recommended this spa place, you know where I could get good massages. I still get quite a lot of pain from my leg.'

'Jo.'

'And before you say anything, no I didn't recognise her. I can't remember seeing her. All I remember is that the woman next to my mum had been really badly beaten up. The curtains were always round the bed when I was there. She saw me, though, and my mother told her who I was - in fact I think she even told me about this woman in the bed next to her and

194

how she'd been turned down by the authorities and what did I think she should do. And, now you'll really despise me for this – I remember saying to my mother "give me a break, I'm not at work now" and please can you find the rest of the file and give me a cigarette.' She was gripping the chair arms, stopping the tears holding up behind her eyes, making her nose itch and her mouth turn down, the muscles of her face preparing for the onslaught. She got up, began to pace the floor, stopping at the table, picking up a *Private Eye*, looking at the illustration on the cover, hearing Rob behind her turning the page of the file, as if *he* were able to make any sense of her story by reading it again. He hadn't noticed she was about to cry and she'd managed to adjust her emotions. Was it possible that Raquel had stayed with a violent man after she'd been refused assistance by *her,* the manager? Did that make Jo inadvertently responsible for the beatings she'd obviously suffered? Was that why all this was happening? Some kind of Karma for being so indifferent to someone else's plight? So did she deserve it all? Taking the *Private Eye* back with her, playing out the pretence, she sat with it on her knee.

'No.' he said in between inhalations of dope.

'No, what?'

'I'm not giving you a cigarette if you've given up – and I'm really sorry you get so much jip from that leg. And I hate to see you cry.'

Across the room, their eyes met for a fraction of a second and, they exchanged a look that belonged to their past, of an understanding that reverted back to a time when there was no need for words to pass between them - then she looked at her lap and turned over the front page of the magazine. 'So that's it. Now she's following me round –and I think –'

Rob was waiting expectantly.

'I reckon she wants to kill me,' she finally said.

'What the hell are you going to do? I hope not anything stupid.'

She paused, wriggling in her chair.

'What would you do?'

'Me? I'm just an IT man who wears a union hat sometimes. I don't know Jo. I don't know what I'd do.' He paused, also staring at the fire, poking at the glowing embers, while the ashes fell into the pan. 'I expect I'd leave it alone. Hope she'd get tired of it – I dunno, Jo. It all sounds so incredible, but if you really want my opinion – she doesn't sound like a nice person, don't do anything that would aggravate her.'

'I feel I have to get to the bottom of it. And –' she was going to tell him about Senaka, about those words of his, but it was all too much.

'You working?'

She shook her head. 'Got an interview next week.'

He put his fist to his mouth. 'You said before. Forgot.' He was looking at her strangely – she could read his expression, it was like he wanted to say something – something of importance, but had lost his nerve. 'I could've helped you get redeployed. If you hadn't been sniffing after that other union rep –'

'What's this got to do with Raquel Bannister?' she snapped.

He began to blow on his coffee again, though it must have been cold. 'Maybe you wouldn't be bothering with all this if we were still –'

'You implying things would be different if I'd stayed with you –'

'You got me wrong.'

'What then?'

'Doesn't matter,' he said.

'Tell me.'

'You know. If you hadn't changed so much –'

'I haven't changed,' she said knowing that she should leave soon. The conversation was getting too close, too personal. Already she'd been here too long. The curtains were undrawn – he never drew them – one of their disagreements which mushroomed out of proportion. The familiar orangey street lamp was shining its faint and measly beam on the road below and she watched a dog do its business across the road before it was tugged away by a lead belonging to an owner, invisible in the shadows.

Someone texted her. She took a look. Amy. 'I have to go.'

'What will you do, then? About this woman?'

'Haven't decided yet. You'll get me the rest of the files?'

He was standing now, wiping his scalp with an open palm and splayed fingers as if he were pushing back strands of hair. 'I'll have to go in really early one morning, you know.'

'Please.'

'Stay and share some pasta with me. We could open that bottle of wine –'

'Honestly, Rob. It's a nice idea but I have to get home.'

'Cooking the doctor's dinner? You ask me, he doesn't deserve it.'

Hesitating, she decided to ignore this comment. 'You'll get the rest of the file for me?' She was reaching for her coat, shrugging her body into it, picking up her bag, searching for her car keys. He was following her out along the shared hall, thanking her for the wine, opening the front door. When she reached the bottom of the steps, she turned and waved. He waved back and she stepped towards her car where she sat in the driver seat, trying to calm her pulse. Sweat broke out on her brow and the keys dropped from her hand twice. She tried to control the tremors that were running through her torso as she realised how well she'd hidden the crawling fear that was running up and down her spine as she read and re-read the single page about Rosalind Bow.

18

Jo drove to the other side of the city, a long way from where she used to work, miles from anywhere she recognised. Here, the houses were Victorian terraces, not like the grand mansions where Rob lived, but back to backs originally built for factory workers. Across the road from where she parked she saw a Mosque set in a modern two-storey building and a newsagent's with a board nailed across the left-hand window, a mangy dog tied to a gate with some string. Two young women in burkas walked along the pavement. So this was Raquel's stomping ground. Was she making a mistake coming here? But she *had* to walk the street that Raquel Bannister had trodden, to trace her footsteps, shop where she'd shopped. Wouldn't she then understand the woman? And she might discover more about her.

She left her car and turned into the busy road where traffic was creeping along, stopping, starting; and road works, drilling, a line of cones. She watched people hurrying, intent on their business.

The pneumatic drill was getting louder as she looked for number 22a. She passed two off-licences with grills over their windows and three pubs – all red brick with woodwork painted in different shades of brown. The light was greyer here, as if this street had its own weather system. It was raining and somehow it felt as if it never did anything else in this place, that it was rare for sunshine to dry out the paving slabs, or crack the tarmac on the road. No trees here. No flowers. Nothing. Had Mark believed her when she told him she was going to look again for an outfit for the interview next week? So many lies. But why wouldn't he? And why was the black car never outside the house when he was at home? If it had been they could have approached the woman together. Did she *know* Mark?

She wished she'd been able to take a copy of the file. Or better, that Rob had handed it over. His look of surprise when she rang his bell for the second time that evening had quickly switched to an expression of disappointment when she asked if she could borrow the file. And she wasn't surprised when he told her no. Could she trust him to keep his word and find the rest of the notes?

A bicycle, its rider wearing a pink and black helmet, was coming towards her, weaving in and out of groups of elderly women making their way carefully along the pavement. The symmetrical patterns on the helmet stood out against the grey hard street. Shouldn't she get out of its path? But she was rooted to the spot. Head down the cyclist was making for her, front wheel aimed at her legs, the markings on the helmet, pink and black like narrowed eyes. A woman in a blue coat loped off the pavement. A horn blared. She heard herself scream. Somewhere in her head a bell rang. The bicycle swerved round her, steering onto the road, cutting in front of the bus. The bus skidded. Rain pelted down. She saw the woman in the blue coat stepping back onto the pavement, her face as white as the sky was grey.

From somewhere, Jo heard herself say: 'Are you all right?'

'Didn't you see it?' someone said to her.

She was gulping air as if she was drowning. Then the real rain began. Torrents. She looked through it at the road where traffic was stopping at the lights and saw the tail end of the bicycle with the rider standing on the pedals.

She was getting wet to the bone. Wouldn't it be good to sit in the comfort of her car and head home away from this ridiculous idea? Instead she went into a café that smelled of chips, ordered, sat in the window. A waitress with dyed red hair stood over her while she warmed her hands round a cup of cappuccino. She'd watched the bus nearly knock down the woman in the blue coat, the waitress told Jo, had seen the daredevil cyclist cut so dangerously across the route of the bus. Jo didn't want to talk to this woman. Through the smeared window, she watched puddles form where the pavement sagged and the kerb was broken. Of course the cyclist wasn't Raquel Bannister. Wasn't her imagination running away with her? The waitress, returning to Jo's table with the bill, continued with her tirade about the narrowness of the pavement, the junction at the traffic lights. This was the second near miss she'd seen in a week. The council didn't care about broken roads. Jo phoned Amy.

'Get my text?' Amy asked.

'Yeah, thanks. Sorry it's taken me so long. Only I met Rob. Twice in fact. It kind of preoccupied me. I haven't told Mark.'

'Jeez. Why didn't you tell *me*?'

'Sorry.' She explained about the file, about going to Rob's flat, but said nothing about where she was now. That could wait till she'd found out more. 'So you said you'd been thinking. What about?'

'So she's an ex-client. That's really scary. I was hoping it wasn't–'

'It made me feel sick when I saw the name. I told the police.'

'Are they going to arrest her?'

'They told me to keep a diary.'

'Have you?'

'Dead right I have.'

'I was thinking maybe you should contact that driver guy and ask him what he knows about her now she's turned up here as well. I mean he can do that surely?'

'But he already said he didn't know any more.'

'Everyone there was lying to you. She was supposed to have checked out. Right? But she was in the country. You kept seeing her even before she was in the airport. She was obviously behaving like that to freak you out.'

'It worked. She did freak me out, is still freaking me out.'

'That guy owes you an explanation.'

'You are right about that.'

'Where are you now?'

Jo paused, looked at a cigarette burn on the table. 'It's complicated. I'll explain when we next meet.'

'Be careful.'

'Of course.'

The waitress was hovering. There was only one other table taken in the café. Trade was quiet. No one had spare cash, the waitress said. Things could only get better. Nothing else for it than to look on the bright side. That was her motto. She told Jo all this as she wiped the already clean table next to Jo.

'I'm looking for number 22a,' Jo said.

The waitress stood, hand on hip, a blue dishcloth clasped in her hand. 'Only worked here for three months and never given the number a thought. Hang on, I'll ask Tony. He's in the back. Lived round here for years, he has.'

She slid past Jo, lifted the counter and disappeared into the kitchen.

The curled bill had been slipped under the vinegar bottle. She took it out and spent some time straightening out the paper and checking outside for a break in the rain, noticing when at last, drivers' windscreen wipers were at rest, seeing that the cloud burst had finally come to an end.

The waitress returned. 'He says this is number 303. He reckons number 22 is on the other side of the road, along a bit, where that fire was. I remember it now. Was working at The Red Lion. Some woman they reckon. A bit.' And she jabbed at her temple with a finger. 'What is it you're after? Anyway, it's a bit of a walk. Take about fifteen minutes. Bit longer for you, maybe. Got a bad leg, haven't you? Don't mind me saying?'

Jo did mind. So she paid and left. Didn't say another word. Though she felt the blood drain from her face while the waitress chattered on about the fire. Raquel Bannister was infamous by her actions. Fire caused by an unbalanced woman, Jo thought. A nice bit of tittle tattle for the locals. But surely she wouldn't have agreed to 'no further assistance' if there'd been any doubt about Raquel Bannister's mental health. But are all arsonists insane? Maybe Raquel Bannister was bad not mad. Or was she Rosalind Bow?

She passed The Red Lion on her search. A gang of smokers loitered on the pavement, seemingly indifferent to the jaw clenching cold. She passed the pub, the smell of tobacco smoke wafting up the street alongside her. She'd been walking for more than twenty minutes. London Road seemed to go on and on. No end in sight.

Number 22 was a hardware shop. Difficult to see from that angle, craning her face upwards. She waited for a gap in the traffic, walked to the other side of the road. She stood on the kerb gazing up at a window above the shop. In parts, the brickwork was still black, though only a dribble, a smear down one side of the window frame. In her mind's eye she'd imagined a wrecked flat with a hole in the roof where the fire had burst through, and scaffolding while repairs were carried out. She'd pictured boarded up windows and signs saying *Keep Out*, or *Dangerous Structure Unsafe*. She'd thought the fire would have gutted the shop downstairs, that it too would be boarded up with fly stickers tacked onto the wood and signs of dereliction and squatters, empty vodka bottles rolling down the road. And when the waitress talked of the fire, Jo had worked on the vision she'd held, she'd magnified it until the fire had caught hold in the flat next door, had raged along the terrace. An arsonist on the loose. *No further assistance.* But the fire could have been an accident. Why would Raquel/Zara/Rosalind harass her to such an extent? What was this school friend thing about?

She opened the door to the hardware shop. There was an old-fashioned jangle and she peered in, shutting the door behind her. The shop was silent, empty. She looked around for signs of fire, smoke damage, a blackened wall. Someone to tell her what happened. It was a small narrow shop, the shelves on either side of the room stacked to the ceiling and the floor covered with pots and pans, dustbins and plastic bowls. She sniffed. Bleach and cleaning fluids, carbolic, the odd petrol aroma of new plastic, the sour stench of tomcat. From a door behind the cash desk, a man in a brown overall arrived on the scene. Two strands of white hair were combed back and greased across his head. He was sitting on a stool behind the till. She edged herself along the line of metal dustbins and compost containers and leaning across them began to browse along a shelf laden with tinned cat food, packets of dried catnip, the odd fluffy mouse squeezed in between the anti-worming tablets, all the time feeling the man's eyes burrowing into her. She picked up a packet of mixed flower seeds from a stand. Took them to the man. He rang the prices up on the till. No eye contact. She had to say something. No point in coming all this way if she left without answered questions.

'One pound and ninety eight pence,' he said.

'I was wondering –'

With his sky-blue eyes he observed her.

'Did Rosalind Bow live upstairs?'

'Never heard of her.'

'Oh. Right.' Her mind went into overdrive. 'She sometimes goes by Raquel Bannister.'

He squinted at her. 'Aye. That's the one. Who's asking?'

'I'm a friend. That's how I know she uses those two names.' Was she digging herself into a hole? 'Any idea where she's living now?'

'Nope.'

'That's a shame.'

'That why you here?' Those blue eyes taking another look at her.

'No. No. I came –'

'Nothing but trouble she was. Landlord's cleaned up the place after that fire and the mess she left.'

'Was there a fire?' She tried to look incredulous and again he stared at her. He didn't ever seem to blink.

'Aye, a right old to do. Three fire engines. Police everywhere. No damage in here. Just as well.'

'Must have been a relief.'

'That'll be one pound and ninety eight pence,' he said again.

She gave him two coins and her mind whirled. 'She owed me some money, you see. I had hoped –'

'Three months' rent she owed. That sort –' He shook his head. 'You might find her down the market. Saturdays.' He popped the seed packet into a white plastic bag.

'Right. Thanks. Keep the change.'

She turned away from those eyes. Couldn't wait to leave.

'Just a tic,' he said. 'You a friend, you say?'

'Yes, but –'

'Wait there. Got something you can give her.'

He opened the door behind him and bellowed: 'Sandra.'

She took a step back. 'It's OK.' She really wanted to get out of this shop with its smell of cat piss.

A woman appeared. Bulges of fat drooped over the waistband of her stretchy trousers. She sat on the stool. The man went out through the door; she heard him climbing a staircase.

'Do you think he'll be long?' Jo asked after five minutes.

The woman glanced at her and shrugged. She had the same shivery blue eyes of the man. A clock on the wall with a price tag of £15 clicked on every minute that passed. The man emerged again, a bulging plastic bag in his hand.

'You can give her these. Don't know why I'm doing her a favour. Nothing but trouble that one. And you can tell her that from me if you like. Landlord's got a new tenant.

204

Nice lady. Moved in a couple of months ago and he left this with me. Asked me to deal with the bills, tell them she's moved out. I act as caretaker, you see.' He puffed his chest out slightly, as if proud of this role. 'Just as well you came in today, I was going to chuck them out.' He sat back down on the stool. 'Anything else you need? Got some sacks of compost in the back. Two for the price of one. I'll get them –'

'No. No. Thank you.'

The parking voucher had expired when she got back to the car. No time to investigate the contents of the bag. She flung it on the passenger seat and drove towards Meresbridge. Was she any clearer about who Raquel was?

At the top of her road, she stopped by the park with the empty swings and slide. There was a wind here and the swings rode gently on the breeze as if occupied by ghost children. A man was taking his dog for a walk, whistling at it when he threw a stick. She thought how complicated her life had become. Leaning across the seat, she emptied out the contents of the bag onto the seat. Two chipped mugs, one black, one red, three teaspoons, final reminders, telephone, gas, electric. The dog was playing a game, crouching in the grass, waiting for the stick to land. Above her, clouds scuttled across the sky and branches of the winter trees trembled. She heard the man's mobile phone go. He answered it and the dog ran round and round the park, its large ears flapping. A crumpled and stained letter with a familiar letter heading. She opened it out. It was the top copy of the letter she'd found in the file. Across it were the words FUCKING BITCH in red biro. The letter was signed by Jo. Like the one she'd seen in Rob's flat. It confirmed no assistance could be given to Raquel Bannister as it was deemed that she had made herself intentionally homeless through the action of arson.

The man had finished his phone call and was calling to the dog to come home. Jo licked her lips, feeling the dryness. She drove slowly past the park where the empty swings twitched in the wind and turned into her road, spotting Mark's car parked outside their house. He was home from his shift. A tremor of relief briefly swept over her, was replaced by trepidation. How could she tell him about the letter without also explaining the visit to Rob's flat?

There was someone on the steps to their house. A woman wearing a black coat, a leopard print bag slung over her shoulder. She turned and darted a look at Jo. The woman had short blonde hair. Was that a glint? Did the woman have a nose stud, or was her mind playing tricks again? She went to open her car door. Dizzy with fear. Couldn't think. Couldn't breathe. Calm, she told herself. Move.

She opened her car door. 'Hey. You. What the hell are you doing?'

The other woman ran down the steps, up the road and was gone.

19

How could she unlock the door with her fingers trembling? She banged, rang the bell.

'It's me.' She hammered; saw the door opening a crack then wide when Mark saw it was her.

'Haven't you got your key?'

'I saw her here on the steps. Her, Raquel Bannister –'

He drew her in, closed the door. 'What are you talking about? No one's been here. No one. You have to stop this. You'll make yourself ill.'

'That woman is everywhere.'

Holding her by the shoulders, he pointed to the mosaic tiled floor where several strewn leaflets lay.

'Takeaway pizza. Genuine Chinese. No monosodium glutamate. We should try that.' He was holding each one up for her to see: 'Curry house, real English Fare. Take your pick. I think we've solved the identity of the mystery woman.' He put his arm round her, pulled her to him.

'Don't laugh at me, Mark.'

'I'm not. These were pushed through the letter box. I heard –'

'Why didn't you answer the door when I rang the bell?'

'I just did.' He slipped a lock of her hair behind an ear, kissed her on the lips.

Wandering into the living room, as if she wanted to make sure everything was as it should be, she went round checking, not really knowing what she was doing. Table, yes.

Four chairs, yes. Studio pottery. Yes. She swung round to Mark who'd been watching her. 'I think she's an ex-client.' She pushed her hair away from her face. 'I'm sure in fact. There's something going on. It scares the living daylight out of me.'

'What are you talking about?'

Hesitating, she took a quick look into the street, drew the curtains. 'I got in touch with someone who still works at the office and they found her name –'

'Who? That's absurd Jo. That's mad.'

Tracing the curve of a blue bowl with her forefinger, she said nothing for a while, wondering whether she should tell Mark about the ironmonger's shop.

'I thought they'd closed your department down –'

'They did. I worked there for a long time. I got to know a lot of people,' she said.

He left the room and she heard him opening the fridge. Was he opening a bottle of wine?

'So what did you find out about her?' he called out.

When she went through to the kitchen, Mark was sitting at the table. He was staring into space, a glass of white wine in front of him. It was unlike him not to fill his time with activity.

'She might have been involved in starting a fire in her flat. That's all I know. God, Mark. I'm so tired of thinking about her. You OK?' she asked. 'Not like you to drink during the day.'

'Arsonist? What else does your ex-colleague say? Are you sure it's the same woman, I mean, it does sound extraordinary –'

'*Did* you find anything out about her from the hospital?'

'Just medical stuff. Nothing else.' He put his head in his hands. 'You know I was looking forward to you getting back. I've got some time off. I was thinking we could go for a spin in Dad's old Morgan. Go to Morecombe Bay. It's not far. Maybe we should go anyway. A walk will help us think straight. Fresh sea air. Come on babe. You and me walking along the beach –'

'Bit late. It's nearly two. It's dark by four.'

'It gets dark later than that now. It'll do us good. We've not spent any time together since you got back.'

'Not sure I'm in the mood. Can't you understand that?'

'She won't be bothering you any more now you've told her the police know – and I'll support you. I'll be there for you. I know I've been bad tempered – well I'm sorry. From now on it'll be different. Come on,' he said. 'I've got some free time for once.'

She sighed. 'OK.' What harm could it do? For the rest of the day, she'd force herself to forget about Raquel Bannister, get away from the house. 'I think I might call the police again tomorrow, see if they've done anything.'

'You could do.' Wiping his forehead, he glanced at her. 'Yeah, that's a good idea.'

Out in the street he opened the passenger door with an exaggerated bow and she stepped on board, daintily taking his proffered hand.

He'd donned his father's driving gloves and they spoke in clipped Queen's English, saying, 'What-ho' after each statement. She called him Jeeves and laughed in an effort to put Raquel out of her mind, and they took to waving to people at bus stops and at traffic lights, at other car drivers. The road ran alongside a lake, and a pleasure boat left a white trail in the water. When the shore came into view, she saw sheep munching grass on the fells. With her leather clad hand she ran her fingers up his thigh touching the worn, polished leather of the seat in between his legs. He smiled at her. This is how it used to be. In her mirror she painted her lips and deliberately snapped the sun shade back. She would not be tempted to look.

His mobile rang and replacing her hand on her own lap, she listened, hoping it wasn't the hospital. 'No,' he said. 'No.' He put the phone back in his pocket.

'Who was that?'

'Spam. Double glazing.'

In an hour they were parked on the Bay. It would be dark quite soon.

'Shall we go? What-ho?' he said. 'Time for a stroll along the sands?'

'OK, Jeeves,' she said for the hell of it.

They stepped across rushes, walked along the hard wet sand. Above them seabirds cackled and spun in ever increasing circles, over their heads, out across the sea. The tide was right out and the beach wide with undulations where the waves had receded. There were puddles of seawater left behind by the tide and dark strings of seaweed were strewn across the dark, damp sand. Further up along the bay, quicksand could suck you under in minutes and she couldn't stop herself thinking about that, imagining the sensation of drowning in sand. The wind caught her hood and blew it back down. Bareheaded, the squall shrieked in her ears, she watched the clouds multiply in density. No sun here. She looked out to sea. It was a long way off, an opal sheen, but still she could see the huge rollers fighting with the wind. Ahead of them, in the distance there was another couple walking, like them, with the sea on their right. Mark's strides were narrower, to keep up with her smaller steps.

'I fancy some chocolate. There's a shop over there. D'you want some?'

'Nothing for me. I'll keep going. You'll soon catch me up.'

He strode off over the road then shouted something which the wind snatched away. He pointed along the row of shops, hurrying in the same direction.

She turned to face the wind coming from the direction of the latte coloured rollers. She'd walk for a while across the beach and watch the waves. The tide was far out. Ahead of her were some scattered shells. Their whiteness showed up against the dun coloured sand. And she remembered walking along an Indian beach with her mother, watching hermit crabs struggle along dunes inside their badly fitting houses. Together they'd crouched in the sand and in Jo's memory, she thought they'd stayed there for hours. Then of course as she knew it would eventually, her mind turned to the time she'd limped painfully across the burning sand pursuing Raquel Bannister. Then she was back on the Bay, icy blasts whipping her face.

She reached a collection of shells. A ribbon of blue mist lay like a blanket along the horizon. The waves seemed far off. Time enough for her not to worry. Hands to knees, she studied the shells and watched as minute crabs popped down their tiny holes. She followed their trails, picked up a couple of large shells, put them to her ear. Later, she couldn't recall how long she watched, her attention absorbed by the crabs and their battle for survival, but when she straightened, the ocean was hidden by an encroaching sea mist. And the mist was rolling in. Thick, covering the sky, the sea, the beach – a greyish mist, with shapes that disappeared and became other shapes. She yelled for Mark but felt her words sink dead, flattened. As fast as she could, she ran in the direction of the car, in the direction of the town that bordered the coast. She ran and ran. The car had to be near. The outline of vehicles appeared, then vanished. Was the mist making her see things that weren't there? The light was fast fading, turning indigo. Her hip jarred against the shorter leg, but still she pelted across the sand, aware of the great roll of sea mist chasing her up the beach. It seemed that the sound of the sea was getting nearer, that the waves were crashing just beyond where she stood, that she was facing the sea. Or was she? Everywhere was shrouded in fog. She shouted for Mark again. She screamed for help. How had this happened? The sound of the sea seemed to be all around her. She ran. Didn't know which way. 'Help,' she shouted again. No reply. A pulse was throbbing at every point in her body. She was shivering and sweating, felt like she was running round in circles, water splashing her face, her hands. She was heading towards the sea. She turned, flung her arms out in front of her. She called, hearing the sound vanish into the fog, turned and ran again. Someone was following her, panting, the breath hard. Her heart was raging. A dog barked and barked again. She felt it rub against her leg, heard a whistle.

'Stay with the dog. Don't run off.'

The dog continued to bark. Out of the fog a figure appeared. 'Stick with me and the dog. Let's move. It'll be dark soon.' He whistled. 'Here girl.' The dog was there trotting beside them. 'Can't you walk faster? It gets dark out here quick.' His voice was gruff.

'Can't walk that fast.'

'I'll carry you then, lass.'

He lifted her up and carried her, his wellington boots squelching in the muddy sand. She smelt the oil of his jacket, saw the fog all around, heard the dog at the man's feet, panting and barking while the man kept on repeating. 'Good girl. Show us the way back.'

Then they were at the line of parked cars and she saw Mark pacing. He leapt across the grass bank. 'What were you thinking of, going off like that? You could've walked into the sea in that mist. You've been forty bloody minutes, Jo. Why didn't you wait for me?'

'I'll be getting along,' the man interjected while beside him his dog panted.

'Thank you so much,' she said.

'Yes, thanks mate. We owe you.'

'As long as the girl's all right.'

He shook their hands and wandered off, whistling after his dog. Across the street, the door to a pub opened and for a minute, the street was engulfed in a flood of light and laughter.

She looked out at the violet sky, heard the waves coming in and felt her anger and frustration bubble to the surface. 'I want to go home,' she said.

Close behind, she followed him to the car.

'I could do with a drink,' he called out to her. 'And I'm hungry too.'

'Yeah, I am too.'

He walked ahead of her, tramping across the road and she thought how she'd longed to sit in a cosy country pub while she was sweltering in the sun without him. Why couldn't it have been like her daydream? At the door of the pub, he stood, hands in pockets, waiting. Inside, it was warm and yeasty with a fire burning in an inglenook. They sat in the corner, away from the fire, where a crowd of drinkers were sitting at a long table.

'I'll get you a brandy,' Mark said. 'Warm you up.'

He had a half of bitter. They ordered a basket of scampi and chips each.

'Look,' he said. 'I'm sorry I was angry. You were out so long. I was beside myself.'

'I thought I was going to die.'

'I was pretty scared too.'

The scampi and chips arrived. The brandy was warming her brain. From the long table by the fire, the man with the dog walked towards them. They all shook hands but he refused a seat and stood close to the table while the dog lay at his feet. The man didn't want a drink either, said he had a pint back there with his mates, that he just wanted to say hello.

'You all right now, lass?'

'Thanks to you. Yes. Thank you.'

'Thanks to Lucy. Not me. She heard you calling out. Started barking. That's what she does.' He bent and ruffled the thick black fur on the dog's back. 'Be careful if you go out on the bay again. Gets dark quick and those sea mists – well you saw –'

'Yes, I saw.'

'Then there's the tide. Looks all nice and faraway, then it turns like an angry woman.'

'Thank you for helping me,' she said, thinking how he heard her shouting, an angry woman like the turning tide.

'Long as you're all right. That's all that matters.' He shook their hands again, returned to his drink, his friends, their murmuring chatter. She and Mark watched the table, listened to the rise and fall of their voices.

'Can't let him go without a drink. Hang on,' Mark said suddenly.

She watched him at the bar. She watched him stoop towards the man with the dog and put a drink in front of him. More people came through the door, bringing traces of sea mist on their clothes, hanging like cobwebs, rubbing their hands. She looked around. Copper warming pans and sepia pictures of fishermen from another era hung from the walls. It was a local pub, a family pub, friendly, safe.

Smiling, broadly, Mark was standing. He walked back to Jo.

'Nice bloke,' he said.

She smiled and nodded.

'Feeling better?'

Again, she nodded. 'I was really scared – I thought – never mind.' What would have happened to her if Lucy the dog hadn't found her? She toyed with a chip. 'When I was a child I was in, I don't know which country, probably Morocco – yes I think it was. I lost my mother in a souk. I thought I was going to die then. I remember that. I kept running round and round looking for her. It all looked the same. Smelt the same too. I was crying, couldn't stop – standing outside this tannery, crying for my mother. Do you know what a tannery smells like?'

He shook his head, put his hand over hers.

'Shit. They smell of shit.' She removed her hand and tucked a loose strand of hair behind one ear.

'Your mother found you though?'

She smiled, shrugged. 'Eventually.'

They both finished their scampi and chips. 'What if this woman is really out to get me?'

214

'As soon as we get back we'll phone the police, ask them what enquiries they've made.' They clinked glasses and despite the warning, the sense of unease she felt in her gut, she said no more about Raquel and left the pub with Mark. It'd been a long day – her head lolled on the leather car seat and she slept, dreamt of a thick black fog and the orange eyes of a dog coming at her. She woke quickly. Saw Mark, hunched over the wheel, one eye flicking to the rear view mirror. She lowered her sunshade and looked in her mirror. The light dazzled her. The car behind appeared inches away. The headlights were full on and they were travelling down an unlit narrow country road. Mark accelerated. Behind them, the car accelerated too.

'Turn off,' she said knowing there were no turnings off this road.

He said nothing.

'How long's it been like this?'

'A few miles. Since we passed the lake. Can't shake the bugger off. And the Morgan's losing power. Rattling. Can you hear it?' His tone uneasy.

Light from the other car's headlamps flooded the car. 'Why doesn't it overtake?'

He didn't reply. His knuckles glowed white on the steering wheel. She looked in her mirror again, had to put her hand up to shield her eyes. Ahead of her was the winding country lane ahead, with trees and bushes rushing past, the odd farmhouse, a terrace of cottages by the side of the road. There was no moon. The road went on and on, winding through valleys, cutting through tiny hamlets where the lights from the houses glimmered softly. The occasional car drove past them going the other way, their tyres swishing on the wet road, blinking their headlights at the car behind them. The light from the car behind seemed to get brighter and closer at every bend in the road.

'You'll have to turn off into someone's drive, or a lane, or a farm track. They'll be bumping us in a minute – it's *her,* she wants to kill –'

The impact came without warning, jolting them forward. She felt her head being forced backwards; she put one hand up to cover the crown of her head while the other one was gripping the seat belt. 'She's trying to kill us.' Her voice was a thin shrill, swallowed by the cold air flooding her lungs.

'You OK?' he yelled.

'No. I'm not.'

The Morgan moved faster, the engine grinding. The car behind crashed into them again. Jo screamed. Up ahead, she saw traffic lights. Green. She clenched her fists and beseeched the lights to change. At red, Mark stopped and opened his door.

'Where you going?'

'Wait here.'

'Mark –'

The driver of the car behind was continually revving. What was Mark doing? Jo leant across the driver's seat, tried to see what was going on. Couldn't see a thing. She waited. Should she get out too? The lights were changing. She called out to Mark, saw him striding back towards their car.

'That's sorted,' he said when he was back in the car and changing gear, starting up the car again.

'I'm calling the police.' She got out her mobile.

'No need.' He put his hand on her arm. 'It was an accident. They're in a hurry. Emergency. Let's get home.'

'What do you mean, an accident? It was deliberate. I'm going to call the police.'

'No. Leave it. I've told you it's sorted.'

She looked at Mark. She looked in the mirror of her sunshade. The car had gone. Too tired to argue, she said no more and he drove as fast as the Classic Car allowed. He drove with his fingers tapping the wheel at every traffic light or junction and she saw him lick his lips in the biting wind.

While Mark put the Morgan in the garage, she phoned the police, was still waiting for someone to answer when Mark came in.

'What are you going to say?' he asked.

'Did you get the number plate?'

'I told you it's sorted. They apologised and said they'd pay for any damage – don't fuss, Jo. Not after the day we've had.'

A man answered the phone and Mark went through to the kitchen and switched the radio on. A comedy. Canned laughter.

She gave the crime reference number she'd been given the other day then waited as he looked her up. 'She tried to run into us, push us off the road.'

'Did you get a number plate?'

'No. But she's always in a car outside our house. Drives off when I approach her.'

The man coughed. 'Were you driving?'

'No, my partner was.'

'Did he get a number plate?'

'No.'

'Any witnesses?'

'No.' She stopped realising how stupid she must sound.

'Have there been any actual threats?'

'Only what I've told you.'

He paused. 'I've added this to the notes. Someone will look into it and get back to you. If you get any more incidents please continue to inform us,' he said.

There was a sinking sensation in her stomach. No movement from the kitchen.

'Going to have a sleep,' she said, putting her head round the door of the kitchen. Mark was working on his laptop.

'What did they say?'

'Said I've got to note down any events that crop up that I think might be linked to her. Was it a woman driver?'

'No,' he said, glancing at her. 'Some guy. Young. Recently passed his test, he said. Shall I hire a film?'

'OK. I'll be back down in an hour.'

In their bedroom, she listened to the silence coming up from the street below, broken only by a dog barking, or the swish of a car driving past; couldn't stop her mind whirring. She looked up at the moonless night through the velux window. Had they been followed to Morecambe Bay? Why hadn't she checked the promenade for a black car? She wished she'd not let her vigilance slip. She wouldn't do that again. Her head was aching. She got up. No painkillers in the en-suite. She went down to the first floor bathroom and was standing at the door, hand on the door knob about to go in. Mark's voice. Who was he shouting at? More to the point, why didn't she trust him? Or was she becoming so paranoid everything seemed suspicious? She silently breathed, listened to his raised voice coming from the living room, tried to catch what he was saying. The boom of his voice carried through the thick walls and up the stairs, but the words were impossible to distinguish. Then he was finished and she heard him coming up the stairs towards where she was standing rigid.

'You coming down to watch that film?' he called from the hall, looking up at her. Did his eyes appear cold?

'Who was that you were talking to?'

He hesitated. 'Work. Why?'

'You were shouting.'

'They wanted me to go in again.'

'Are you?'

'No. Come on. Do you want a beer?'

Everything was as it should be – a couple about to watch a film, sitting close together on the sofa together, a glass of beer, a bowl of crisps. What was it? What was wrong? Why was Mark lying – and she knew he was.

20

The alarm went off at six the next morning. Jo woke dreading the day ahead, alone in the house with the prospect of Raquel Bannister haunting her. Mark was getting ready for his early shift.

In the kitchen, Jo made some coffee, hugged herself to keep warm. While the central heating creaked into action, she watched the steam rise from her cup of coffee on the table

'I'll grab some breakfast at work,' Mark said.

'See you later,' she said. 'I hate being here alone. I wish I had a job.'

'You'll get one soon – I'm sorry. I'd stay here with you, but you'll be fine.'

There were plates piled in the sink from the night before. She loaded the dishwasher and switched it on. What was Mark hiding from her? Why was he protecting a woman who could've run them off the road and killed them, or at least harmed them seriously? Or was it all in her head? Was the driver a young guy as he maintained?

While she cleaned up the kitchen, she heard a letter landing on the mosaic tiles. She buttered her toast then went to see what it was. A jiffy envelope with a neat typed label addressed to her. She tore it open. Three photographs slipped onto the floor, but she saw the figures on them, knew immediately who they were.

Calm, she told herself and took a deep breath. She stooped to pick them up, spread them out on the table. Mouth dry. Couldn't breathe. She gripped the table and the room spun. Get to the phone. Mark's phone was on voicemail and she could hear the tremor in her voice as she pleaded with him to return home. Slow. Calm. Water. She drank a glass and paced the kitchen, the slate cold beneath her bare feet. While a pulse throbbed at her temple, she stared at the photographs, turned them over. *'I'm watching you.'* The words were typed on the back of one photo. Jo gasped. Was Raquel outside again, waiting for her? Images of raised bloody knives, Raquel's face full of loathing flitted across her mind. Had she seen Mark leave, was she planning the attack while Jo was alone? *Why* couldn't Mark be there for her? She snatched the front door open. No one there. No black car. She stood at the top of the steps. 'Where are you? Come on, show your face.'

Back in the house she grabbed the phone and called the police, gave the reference number, waited an age to be put through to another department.

'Good morning,' a tired sounding man said. 'Can I help you?'

'I have more evidence about the woman who is following me,' she blurted out. 'She's sent me three photographs that must have been taken yesterday. They're all of me and my boyfriend at Morecombe bay – we went there yesterday. And there's a note, it's typed, on the back, says she's watching me.' She was garbling, words getting mixed up.

He sniffed, blew his nose. 'Excuse me.'

'Raquel Bannister, sometimes goes by Zara.' She thought quickly, remembering what Rob had told her. 'She may well have other names. The woman I reported before. The woman who's been following me. I told you all this –'

'Hold on one minute. I'm reading the notes.' He sneezed. 'Apologies.'

She half collapsed on the sofa, felt the pulse in her temple, looked out of the window, saw a woman hurry past. Woolly hat. Duffle coat. Not Raquel.

She took a deep breath. This man would help her. Raquel would be arrested and charged with harassment. But taking photographs wasn't a crime. She began to panic. 'Please do something. I know something bad will happen. She tried to run us off the road on the way back from Morecambe Bay. There could have been a serious accident. I didn't see the number plate, but I reported it last night and Mark.' she stopped. What really went on between Mark and the driver? 'So she must have been following us. I mean it makes sense. Doesn't it? She's stalking –'

'Is there any indication of who sent the photographs?'

'No. But who else could it be?'

He said nothing for a few seconds and she heard him tapping on a keyboard. 'Can you bring them to the police station?' he said.

'What will you do?' The letterbox. Another letter dropped to the floor.

'I can't say at this stage, Miss Carr.'

'Can I have an alarm? Have you tracked her down? Have you done anything?'

'I understand that it is stressful for you, but you need to bring them in and make a statement.'

Slowly she breathed out making her body relax. 'OK. I'll do that. I'll do it today.'

She went picked up the post, a letter addressed to Mark: FINAL DEMAND Electricity. What was *that* about? Didn't Mark pay the bills with direct debit? And wasn't it about time they had joint bank accounts with shared domestic bills? Hadn't they been together two years? But that would have to wait.

At the police station she waited for half an hour in a queue. She was numb with anxiety. What would the police do? With everything else she'd reported would the photos be enough evidence for them take out an injunction against Raquel? At last it was her turn to go to the counter. She gave the reference number and breathed slowly while the officer searched on his computer.

221

'I phoned earlier. These were dropped in to where I live. She must have followed us. She's stalking me. *Please* can you do something?'

'Just a minute,' he said kindly – or was he being patronizing – and spoke into his phone, repeating what she'd just told him, silently nodding as he listened.

Jo started to sweat. What was the other officer saying? Why was it taking so long?

'What are you going to do?' she said when he had finished the phone call. 'This is really serious. Please I can't go on like this.'

'We are taking it seriously Miss Carr. An officer will be in touch with you very soon.'

Jo looked around at the crowded room. People coughed, shuffled their feet and sighed.

'Do you know when?' she asked, her face close to the glass.

'I can't say exactly. Miss Carr, but not too long I hope.'

'So that's it?'

'As I said –'

'Can you give me an alarm? What if she wants to kill me?'

He sighed. 'We realise how unsettling this is for you. But as I said, we will be in touch with you very soon –'

'But she could attack me anytime –'

'We are looking into these allegations, Miss Carr.'

There was nothing for it but to leave. And hope. Was she just a statistic? How long would the police take to act? She felt so alone.

She would go to the market as intended. She wanted to see why Raquel was there. Would finding out more about her give her a better idea of who she was and what she wanted? Besides, she had to take some kind of action.

Stalls spilled out onto the road and crowds of people jay-walked. The traffic was stop – go – stop. In fifteen minutes she barely moved an inch. She may as well take a look. Find Raquel, maybe watch her from afar. She was curious. Wanted to know what her stalker did here. What could happen to her surrounded by so many people?

After she'd parked, she dodged squashed oranges chucked in the dirt alongside remnants of leaflets, rotting apples and shreds of plastic bags. It was mucky in that part of the market, the cheap end where stalls sold second-hand clothes; piles of sweaters and nylon blouses. The sun was still shining with a bitter wind. She'd been to markets in northern India, Thailand and Morocco with her mother, exotic markets where the sun boiled your flesh, and she remembered a Bangkok market, where a woman selling bamboo baskets had looked after her for an afternoon. The woman had taught her how to weave a basket while they sat together on a rush mat and Jo had wanted her to be her mother; she'd cried when her real mother arrived to collect her.

Now she passed a wizened stallholder selling used shoes. He was sniffing and rubbing his Fagin-gloved hands together. A pair of yellow high heels looked bright amongst the other shoes. They reminded her of a similar pair at the foot of the steps to the temple she'd visited with Senaka. Would she ever discover what his connection was with Raquel?

Most of the stallholders were men, faded men with a longer past than a future. There was a woman with a nose stud drinking from a blue and white striped mug. Was that Raquel? Jo edged closer, waiting to get a better look, and pretended to study a 1960's black and white basket chair. The woman looked up. Her face was long with thin red cheeks, staring tired eyes. Not Raquel.

Even more people now were taking their time, picking up this and that, blocking the way with their stooped bodies and their wailing bored children. She pushed past. Everywhere was the musty smell of damp clothes. Knowing how big the market was, Jo walked faster, following the aroma of coffee to a mobile café, bought a coffee and warmed her hands round the polystyrene, looked up the street of stalls, thinking of the photos. Was Raquel following her now? She spun round. No sign of the woman.

She approached the ethnic clothing section. Billowing out in the light breeze, she could see multi-coloured skirts and pantaloons. Could Raquel be here? She slowed and stopped at a stall where silks hung from hangers. Over-priced hand-painted blouses lay neatly folded on the table. The woman sitting behind the table looked half-starved. Jo hesitated, fingered one of the silk scarves, feigning interest. The woman stood and smiled. There would have to be a conversation or at least some pretence of one.

In intricate detail, the woman described how she took her ideas from dreams and brought them to life on a sketch pad.

'They're really nice.' Better not be brutally honest. Jo wondered how many she'd sold.

The woman spent some time straightening neat piles of silk handkerchiefs.

'I heard.' No. that wasn't right. Jo started again. 'Do you know someone called Raquel Bannister – sometimes she calls herself Zara, or Rosalind Bow. I heard she has a stall at the market.' That sounded completely mad, she thought.

'Haven't been here that long, you know.' The woman, apparently unfazed was closing her eyes, concentrating.

'I'd be really grateful,' Jo said tentatively.

The woman opened her eyes wide. 'Does she sell jewellery?'

'I'm not actually sure what she sells –'

'You could try up there,' she said. 'She might sell jewellery.' She stopped fiddling with the ridiculous silk handkerchief and turned her big sad eyes to Jo. 'I can give you ten per cent.'

Jo glanced at the carefully laid out fabrics.

'I think that's right. If it's who I'm thinking of I haven't seen her for a while. Twenty per cent for two. Can't do more than that.'

Jo hesitated, thinking how she really didn't want one. She picked out a silk square that reminded her of the headscarf her mother used to tie round her head, gypsy-style with colours like strawberry and vanilla ice cream. She handed over the money, took the small packet. She walked away, her stomach turning somersaults, thinking *this is it.*

Was she half-crazy doing this?

Jo moved on, feeling her mouth dry, her skin cold with sweat. But it was too late to turn back now, not when she was so close to finding out more about Raquel. The crowd was pushing, gathering pace. A gap formed and she slipped in, took a look at another woman with long straggly hair who was behind a large table covered with a black cloth. Jo's stomach was still lurching. She'd ask. From a little distance, she observed, watching the woman take money while she put items in small packets, chewed on gum, chatting the whole time. South American flute music poured out from a stall nearby. Jo cast her eyes up to the end of the market. There were a few more stalls. Jewellery, all of them. She watched the stallholder behind the black covered table chewing gum and wondered, remembering Raquel's fast movements as she selected food for her breakfast on the first day in the hotel when she met her.

Jo stood in front of the stall and picked up a pendant. A silver one with a stone set in the centre.

'You won't find anything like that in the high street,' the woman said. 'Solid silver. Got a hallmark and that –' she touched the stone, ' – is a moonstone. Got all the paperwork.'

Carefully, Jo returned the pendant to the black velvet cloth, thinking she was no good at this; detective work wasn't her. The woman's long mousy hair was parted in the middle and hung in rat-tails to her shoulders. Her eyes were red rimmed and when she wasn't talking, she stared into the distance vacantly, chewing and fiddling with a nearly empty packet of cigarettes, turning back the carton.

'I'm looking for someone –'

'Oh, yeah. Who's that?' The woman's eyes snapped to Jo's face. She picked up the smouldering cigarette from where it was balanced on the edge of the table.

'Someone called Raquel Bannister.'

'Raquel Bannister?' The woman gaped. 'You mean Rowena Bannister?'

Thinking fast, Jo nodded. 'Blue stud?' she pointed to her nose and was relieved when the woman smiled just a little.

'This is her stall. Her gear. Do you know her then?'

Jo felt her heart miss a beat. 'Sort of –'

'Fancy that.'

A lightning thought flitted across Jo's mind: Raquel might appear any minute; she'd have to think of something to say. 'So – ' Her voice sounded clogged and she cleared her throat while the other woman sniffed and fiddled with the jewellery, straightening chains and turning earrings so the stones lay flat on the cloth. 'So, will she be here, today – later on I mean?' She was trying to remain calm; to keep her voice flat and even.

'She's not here this week. Or last week. And the week before she was away.'

'So do you often work her stall?'

'You like that pendant then? Got a square one, here too. Bigger moonstone.' She stooped and looked through a box on a chair next to the one she'd been sitting on. 'Here. It's a good price, you know. Yeah, I'm here most Saturdays – this one really suits you.' The woman chatted on and on, the words coming out in torrents, in between the frantic masticating. 'My dad had a jewellers' in London. Not a lot I don't know about precious stones and metals and those two pendants are the last ones like it. I've already sold the other four.' She inhaled on her cigarette and spluttered and snorted, coughed and coughed and coughed again.

'You OK?'

'Couldn't get me a cup of coffee from over there?' Still hacking, she burrowed in her bag. 'Got some money. Hang on.'

'Don't worry. I'll get it,' said Jo. 'Back in a minute.'

'Cheers. Three sugars. I'll give you the money.'

There was a mobile café opposite with a few people queuing. She stood at the end and turned to face the stall. There was a good collection: jewellery with gemstones that resembled turquoises, garnets and quite a few moonstones. Now she knew how her stalker made a living and she guessed that's why she was in Sri Lanka.

Jo edged her way up the queue towards the man selling coffee and tea, watched the woman at Raquel Bannister's stall. There was that vacant hungry look in her stare. She knew that look. Was it cocaine, speed, or crack that was whizzing round the woman's brain? She saw her puffing on her cigarette, the nose red and blotchy, the greyish flesh taut across her cheeks: speed. She watched as the woman laid down the cigarette and zoned in on a potential customer, chatting, chewing, chatting. She turned and gazed directly at Jo, then resumed selling. The woman was an expert, sure enough. Knew how to sell. She watched, mesmerised, exhausted and cold, still waiting in the queue for coffee. A woman wearing a pink sparkly scarf wrapped round her neck was approaching the stall and Jo felt her breathing quicken.

'You going to be here all day?' someone from behind her said.

Jo earthed herself, bought two coffees and wandered back to the stall. Up and down the market, her eyes roved, searching for the woman with the pink scarf. There was no sign of her. She put the coffee on the table, stood a little to the left, waiting for the woman to finish the sale of a silver ring, trying to calculate her next move, trying to work out what to say next, without making the woman suspicious. 'Thanks a million,' the woman said when she'd closed the deal, sold a ring and there was no one waiting. 'Hasn't stopped today. You still interested in that pendant? There's a ring that matches it. Just sold one. They're going really well today. Well, they're an excellent price.' She took a sip of her coffee. 'Needed that.' She dug in a bag. 'Here you are.'

'No. Honestly. Anyway I haven't got change.'

Thoughts jumbled in her head. What to say? But speed woman was chatting on, telling Jo how she'd learnt everything she knew about jewellery about watches and diamonds, about gold from her father.

'Was that her just then? Was that Ra – Rowena? I thought I saw her just then?'

'Think I'd have noticed.' She took a gulp of her coffee.

'Where does she buy all this?' Too late, the words were out. She hadn't meant to blurt out the question like that. Speed woman stopped suddenly and looked at Jo, studying her as if she were prey. 'India, Sri Lanka, Thailand, mostly. She knows all the places to go –. How do you know her?'

'I've known her for ages.'

'So why you get her name wrong?' Speed woman extracted a bar of chocolate from her bag and broke off a piece. She pulled the chewing gum out from her mouth, dropped it to the floor, popped the chocolate in to replace it and chomped. She was looking up and down the market, her eyes piercing the crowds.

'She always preferred Raquel. You know, when I knew her. I haven't seen her for a while,' Jo said feeling her face burn. 'You know how it is. We lost touch and a mutual friend said I'd find her down here. She's moved from where she used to live. You know over that ironmonger's. Do you know where she's living now?'

Speed woman broke off some more chocolate. 'How did you say you knew her?'

Jo baulked. Had she gone too far? 'These are really good quality. She knows her stuff, doesn't she? I mean she knows what'll sell here. She's got an eye for it.'

'Do you want me to pass on a message? I don't know when I'll see her, but if you want I can tell her you – what

228

was your name again – that you were asking after her –. I don't know where she lives. I didn't know she used to live over a – what did you say?'

'Ironmongers.'

'Whatever. We have a business relationship. Pure business. So I've never been to where she lives –. Here's 50p for the coffee. Thanks.' She picked up a bracelet and began burnishing the silver metal.

It was time to go. But for a bit, Jo remained, watching the woman polish and chew. She knew she should stand aside. She also knew that the woman was getting suspicious. Was she any better off for coming here?

A man halted at the stall and Jo left speed woman hurling her spiel at the prospective customer. She hurried away, walking past the stall where she'd bought the over-priced scarf, past the ancient chairs with the stuffing falling out, past the piles of crockery picked up from house clearances. She walked, feeling her face grow hotter, knowing she'd come close to something best left alone. Reaching her car, she opened the door. Her phone rang. It was Rob.

'I found the rest of the file,' he said. 'Needed a forklift truck to get the thing out of the building – bloody weighs a ton.'

'Can I come over now?'

She heard the uncertain pause.

'I'm not far,' she said.

'Right now?'

'If that's all right.'

'Yeah, sure,' he said.

'You don't sound too sure –'

'You got me wrong, but –'

'What?' she asked.

'It's complicated. I'll explain when you get here.'

His tone of voice alerted her. 'Twenty minutes.' She started her car and swung out into the road.

21

Rob took a while to get to the door and when he finally opened it, he let Jo in, keeping his head down. He turned away from her and made his way down the shared hallway leaving her to close both doors behind her.

'What's up? What happened to your face?'

'Don't fuss. I'm all right.'

'You look terrible. Why've you got a black eye? That cut on your cheek looks really nasty. Shouldn't it be covered?'

'I'll get the coffee on,' he said and began to make his way towards the kitchen. She followed him into the long narrow room. This time he didn't tell her to go and wait in the living room.

'Two visits from you in the same week,' he said. 'Must be Christmas.'

'Are you going to tell me what happened?' She began to pace the kitchen 'I'm sorry. No wine this time.'

'Don't worry about it.' He paused, head to one side, examining her, coffee scoop poised in one hand as if trying to think of the right phrase. 'You look strained. Has that bloody woman been threatening you again?' He rinsed out a cafeteria, glanced at her. 'Or is it Mark?'

'Of course not.' She shook her head to emphasise the denial and because she wanted to gather her thoughts. 'You been in a boxing ring, or what?' She thought about the photos in her car. Should she tell Rob about them or simply take them straight to the police on the way home?

'I had an argument with a lamp post.' He was leaning against the work top, waiting for the kettle to boil, watching her fill the washing up bowl with steaming hot water, and squirt washing up liquid in. Her body was itching with pent up energy. She wanted to be active. Doing his chores was a sort of 'thank you' too.

'Obviously, I don't believe you.'

He shrugged and stirred the coffee into the cafeteria, filling the kitchen with a delicious aroma. 'It's the truth.'

'Rob. Stop it.'

'Stop what?

'You know.'

He sighed. 'Leave the dishes and I'll bring the coffee in. You want some toast?'

'Are you going to tell me?'

'I want to know what's going down with you. You were as white as a sheet when you got here. Bit more colour now. Must be the effect I have on you. Now go.' He turned her round so she was facing the hall.

She went back into the living room and slung her coat on the red chair, noticing how cold it was in the room, seeing Rob's work bag on the table and next to it a fat file held together with an elastic band. She'd seen files like this before. Turnstile files they used to call them.

'Strawberry or honey?' Rob was standing in the doorway.

'God. You look terrible.'

'Well?'

'Honey, please, Honey,' and despite everything, she giggled, then stopped abruptly. Now was not the time for merriment. She thought of speed-woman eying her suspiciously. Had she made the situation worse by going to the market? She stared out of the window at the familiar view. At least she was safe here.

'Hands off that file until you've had your toast. Don't want sticky finger marks all over it,' he called out from the kitchen.

'Can't you be serious for once?'

'I am. Deadly.'

The homely smell of toast and coffee made her realise how hungry she was. Rob cleared a space, folding today's *Guardian* and put a mug and plate piled high with toast on the table.

'Not sure I can get through a quarter of that.' While she spoke, she glanced round the room. It was tidy. Newspaper put into neat piles. CDs in their covers. New wooden blinds replaced the off-white curtains she'd never really liked. His coat was hung up behind the door while hers was slung over the back of the red chair. Her mind was still buzzing.

'Fatten you up. Take a pew.'

She sat at the table, one eye on the enormous file and one eye on the street outside. A train rumbled along the nearby line. She liked that sound, always had. She glanced out at the sky, it was already getting dark.

'Right.' Rob sat opposite her and bit into a slice of toast. 'Tuck in.'

'So this lamp post,' she said with her mouth full. 'Why did you have an argument with it and why did it give you a black eye and a cut on your cheek?'

He took a sip of coffee, sat back in his chair. 'You're not going to let this one go, are you?'

'Nope.'

'I got into a fight, that's all. No big deal.'

'With?'

'If you must know –' he sighed, put his hand to the top of his head in that familiar way. 'OK. The guy I used to buy my gear from.'

'Dope?'

'Of course. What d'you think? Silk underpants?'

'Sorry. Stop making me laugh. This is serious.'

'I fully apologise for my inconsideration,' he said in a droll voice. 'What happened was, if you must know, is that my old dealer did a spell in prison, so while he was inside, I found another one. Well I had to, didn't I?'

'No.'

'D'you want me to tell you or not?'

'Course.'

'Then he came out of prison. So I went back to him and the guy I'd been buying off, Baz, didn't like it, so.' He pointed to his black eye.

Jo felt her mouth fall open. 'Which one's Baz?' She felt suddenly doubly frightened. 'Big guy. Pony tail?'

'Yeah, that's the one.' He flicked a glance at her.

She said nothing for a while remembering the private club and her mother fawning over Baz. 'Does he own a club, this Baz?'

Hesitating, he took in a deep breath and massaged his head. 'Some place with pole dancers. He's got his fingers in all sorts of pies. A mate told me about him. Some mate. Nasty piece of work. I never felt happy buying stuff off him. Bastard. In fact the entire incident got me thinking.'

'If it's the same guy, my mother's seeing him. I met him at his horrible club. God, what a creep. And I thought I'd met him before. I felt like I'd been in that God awful place too. And my mother's hooked up with him –'

'Your mum?' He paused, searching her face. 'Actually, you *have* been there before.'

'What?'

He'd been cutting the toast into quarters and he put the knife down, looked at her 'I never told you. I didn't see the point. I mean you didn't remember anything about that night before that wretched party. And you were recovering from that bloody injury. It didn't seem important. You had enough to put up with. All those operations. And then, well you know the rest.'

'What are you saying?'

'You were at his club before you went to the party. That's where you and me. We met Baz. You went a bit wild there, dancing and stuff. You were off your head.'

'Oh my God.' She was thinking of the dancers on their cramped stages, her mother telling her Baz was in business, a kind man, she'd said, a teddy bear.

'You better warn her. He's not a man to be messed with. He's a cunning bastard, Jo.' He pushed the plate nearer to her.

She rang her mother. The phone switched to voice mail. She left a message. Urgent, she said. Please ring me.

'Wouldn't have put her with Baz. More the beatnik isn't she? I really hope she's OK though it wasn't actually Baz who got me. He watched while one of his small time guys walloped me. So what's going on with you? '

She told him about the photos but decided not to say anything about the car trying to run her and Mark off the road. 'The police have got them now. I really hope they do something.'

'They probably know her anyway. And it's evidence.'

'Christ, I'm bloody tired of it all.'

Outside the house a baby began to howl and Jo looked out at it, knowing that Rob was searching her face. She watched a youth slam a front door across the road and thought back to the day on Morecambe Bay. Why had she allowed her vigilance to drop?

'There's more to this, isn't there? Don't forget I know you, Jo.'

'Can I see the file now?' She reached across the table for it.

'Ah, ah. Sticky fingers.'

'For God's sake.'

'Want me to get the sack?'

'You're being absurd now.'

She went into the bathroom. There were no towels heaped on the floor and the basin and toilet positively sparkled with cleanliness. While she washed her hands, she looked round her. Was this Rob's doing or did he have a new woman in his life? A pang of envy hit the pit of her stomach which she immediately quelled.

234

'Right,' she said when she returned with hands that smelt of vanilla. She sat down opposite him and grabbed the file. 'Shouldn't you go to the hospital about your face? I mean it looks awful.'

'Gravity,' he said. 'That's why it looks bad. Tapping the stitches on his cheek, he said. 'A nurse did this. A nice female nurse.'

Ignoring him, she unwound the rubber band from the file and turned over the beige cover.

'Thanks for getting this.'

'Personally, I think you're mad trying to handle her on your own. But who am I to comment?'

The first few pages were handwritten reports about a man called Alan Banner and she thought how coincidental this was that his surname was similar to Raquel Bannister. She glanced at Rob – not a muscle moved in his bruised and blackened face; she was watching him for signs as he got up and switched his iPod on, jumping tracks as he always did, until he found one to match his mood, taking his tobacco pouch from the mantelpiece. She turned the page over and saw more reports on Alan Banner. Thumbing through more sheets, she searched for any sign of Raquel Banister or Rosalind Bow, Rowena or even Zara. The sound of old Blues filled the room. 'This is the wrong file.' She slapped it shut, shoved it across the table, watched his face carefully again. Eyebrows raised, he was flicking through the loose leafs of the file, slow at first, then faster. He put his hand up to his head and pulled the non-existent hair back from his scalp.

'I was wearing shades. Must have pulled out the one next to hers. I only took it out of my work bag five minutes before you arrived and I didn't think to check the name. Fucking stupid I know, but –'

'You were wearing sun glasses in that poky room?'

Pointing to his black eye, he said. 'I didn't want people to see this. You know how funny they are about files. Especially as I am, as you know, just a humble IT man. I mean how would I have explained myself –'

'But this is really important, Rob. Why didn't you double check? Why didn't you take your sunglasses off while you were in there? One minute more that's all it would have taken. I can't believe you got the *wrong* file –'

'OK. I'm sorry. But why don't you get the police involved rather than fucking around with files? This is so like you –'

She put her head in her hands. Why was everything becoming increasingly complicated? 'I'm sorry I yelled just now. The last thing I want is for you to get into trouble. I'm just so – I don't know – what a bloody mess.'

'I'll get it Monday.'

She sighed. 'Thanks, Rob. You're a star.' She stopped herself saying more. Watching him roll a cigarette, she had a sudden urge to move closer to him. 'I saw you cleaned the bathroom. Quite impressive.'

Leaning across her, he closed the curtains. 'That's just the start. You won't recognise this place once I've finished –'

'You got a girlfriend, then? Not that it's anything to do with me .'

'No.' He looked away from her, so she could see his profile, the regular features, the high cheekbones and their slight sheen. He'd always had good skin. Living on the edge never seemed to take its toll on his health. 'I might just give it all up, all the drugs and stuff. You know, get back to base. This eye got me thinking – I'll get the proper file for you, if you want. Suppose you're going to be off now you've got no further use for –'

'Rob. Stop it.'

He lit the cigarette. 'Feeling sorry for myself.'

Getting up, she paced the room, noticing for the first time a framed Rothko print on one of the walls, thinking she must be in a state not to have seen it when she came into the room, all the time working out what to tell Rob, thinking that she should really get home. Removing her coat from where she'd flung it first, she sat in the red chair and swivelled herself round to face Rob, told him about the flat over the ironmongers and her visit to the market.

'Unbelievable. You should have been a private detective.'

'I wanted to know who she was, try and understand where she was coming from.'

'And are you any wiser?

'Not particularly. No. Now I think I shouldn't have tried to track her down. Do you think I've made the situation worse?'

He said nothing while he blew a smoke ring. Then with great ceremony he pinched the cigarette out and drew his chair nearer to her.

'You might irritate the hell out of me sometimes, Jo. With your uppity holier than thou attitude when you used to get more out of your head than I've ever done – but I still care about you and – and – Fuck, Jo, I think you should stop trying to find this woman you say is stalking you.'

'I *cannot* let her get me.' All this stress was making a drum beat in her temple. She darted a look round the room as if seeking an escape route. 'I have to be cleverer than her. I have to be prepared for her. To be honest, I reckon the police probably think it's some jealous thing between me and another woman . But unless she wanted to kill me, why would she be behaving like this.'

'Jo.'

'And there's another thing. I'm sure Mark knows who she is.'

She really hadn't meant to tell Rob this and now she had, she felt as if she was being disloyal to Mark. Again that sensation of guilt and shame rushed through her. But Mark should come clean. Her mind shifted from one point to the other, from protecting Mark to betraying him. Meanwhile, Rob was returning the file to his bag while a Blues piano crushed her mood to an even lower state.

'What makes you think that?' Rob asked eventually.

237

There was still time to defend Mark. She wasn't ready yet to take sides. 'I'm just being paranoid, I expect,' she said, though she knew the damage was done.

He rubbed his head; his thinking position. She pointed at the wall adjacent to the Rothko print where there were streaks of tester paint. 'So you decided on a colour?' It was an opportunity to steer the conversation away from Mark. Then she'd go.

'You tell me, no – you yell at me that you think this woman is out to murder you. Then you mention that the man you live with is in on it. And you want to discuss my choice of colour for the flat?'

'He isn't in on it.'

He picked up a piece of cold toast and layered honey on the butter. Watching his dextrous fingers carefully manoeuvre the knife across the toast, she began to feel sorry that she'd involved him in her quest. She was facing away from him, staring at the empty grate, listening to the music. Difficult to think straight with all these emotions laid bare by the Blues. 'He isn't,' she repeated for emphasis. Rob seemed to be concentrating on his toast, taking several bites at a time. The track came to an end and without the music the room seemed colder, Rob sadder.

'I'll wash these up. Then I must go.'

'I'll find it on Monday. First thing.'

'Thanks.' Though she wasn't sure it was a good idea to come to Rob's flat again. Or see him another time. All that history. It was no good.

But for history's sake, she washed every dirty plate and mug and the frying pan and one baked bean encrusted saucepan. They worked together like they used to, with him drying and stacking and her scrubbing while from the living room a woman sang about lost love.

Then at the door she avoided his offered mouth and kissed him on the cheek. They hugged each other. She kissed his other cheek, then lightly on his lips. 'Shouldn't you put a cold compress or something on that eye? Isn't that what you're supposed to do?' she said as she went down the steps.

'I'll give it a go and I'll buzz you on Monday when I've got the file.'

By then she was at the bottom of the steps. Too late to say more. From the car, she waved and watched as his hall was plunged into darkness.

It was gone six. She was later than she said she would be. As she drove, she thought about the file. She tried to remember Rob's expression when she told him it was the wrong one. She couldn't quite remember, though she knew she'd studied his reaction. Surely he'd have realised before, that the file was nothing to do with Raquel Bannister. The thought that he'd done it deliberately, so he'd see her again seemed absurd. It wasn't him. Being desperate, playing mind games. No, not Rob. Her brain ached with thinking. The road was jammed full of traffic. She drove carefully, always with one eye on her rear view mirror. But no one followed her. Not even on the motorway which was fairly clear. As she stopped at the traffic lights, she entertained the notion that eventually Raquel would become bored with following her, though that intuition inherited from her mother told her that this was wishful thinking, nothing more.

She drove round the park. It was lit up and had turned a ghastly orange from the street lamps. In front of her, a car did a three point turn and as she waited, she looked towards the swings, thought she saw a figure gently moving to and fro, rocking in the pool of orange. Briefly, she screwed her eyes up tight before staring at the swings again. The figure had gone. With her foot hard on the accelerator, she drove past the park, turned into the road which led into hers.

All the lights were on in their house, but there was no sign of Mark's car or the black car which she'd dreaded seeing again. Burglars, she thought and raced up the steps, to the front door. Options crowded her mind. Mark at knifepoint bound to a kitchen chair. A burglar with a gun. Mark being dragged to the cash point. That would explain the absence of his car. Or was Raquel in their house? But surely she wasn't able to pick locks as well as everything else she was capable of. Jo entered the hall. There was not a sound. No moaning. No pleading.

'Hello,' she called out.

She stood in the kitchen doorway, then turned into the lounge. Both rooms were empty and she went into the extension where she stood by Mark's drum kit shivering, suddenly very cold. In the quiet, she was aware of her heart pounding. Had she left the door open when she left earlier in the day? About to phone Mark, she heard footsteps running down the stairs. The steps were light, much lighter than Mark's. Was that *her*? Edging towards the lounge door, her breath staying locked in her lungs, tongue moving round her lips, moistening them, she froze. She *would* get this woman. *Move*, she told herself. But her feet remained obstinately rooted to the floor.

The front door slammed. For some minutes she remained where she was, breathing silently, listening to the sounds from within the house. She crept up the stairs, pausing on each floor, her hearing tuned to any movement on the other levels until she was at their bedroom door at the top of the house. It seemed a long way down to the safety of the street and she peered down the stairwell, not knowing whether or not she wanted to enter the room where they slept. She swung the door open. Screamed. Blood sprayed on the walls, on the bed, splatters solidifying on the floor. She saw blood smeared across the mirror. Red everywhere. She began to shake, her limbs trembling uncontrollably. Blood, blood, blood.

22

Her scream was a trail of sound that streamed out through the open bedroom, spiralled down the stairs and out onto the street. Jo heard steps coming up towards her, two at a time, then someone was at their bedroom door. Mark. He looked at her, stunned, then stepped across the room, walked round then back to her.

'What's going on? What happened? Who the hell did this?'

'I thought she'd killed you. I thought this was your blood.' She was shaking and he drew her to him. 'When I first saw it I thought there'd been a massacre. She wants to kill me. I know she does. She wants me dead.'

'It's red paint. Not blood. Jo. It's red paint.' He was kissing her wet face.

Sobbing on his shoulder, her body trembling, she felt Mark's arms round her pulling her to him. He was making soothing sounds, as if she were a child. She'd never screamed like that before. Not since she *was* a child. Not since a creep in one of the hostels she stayed in with her mother had put his hand down her knickers after he'd shoved her into a dark damp corner.

'She was here when I got home. I heard her running down the stairs. What does she want? Why is she doing this?' She pulled away. Did Raquel want her to crack up? Was that her motivation?

'You don't know for sure who did this. Did you see her?'

'Why are you protecting her?' Pulling away from him, she pointed to the opened drawers, underwear scattered around, the red paint drying on the wooden floor. 'Why else would Raquel do this if she didn't want me dead. She sent me some photos of us at Morecambe Bay. She's been watching us, Mark. Watching me.' She started to shake out her knickers and put them in the laundry basket. She had to do something to undo the invaded sensation that swamped her, making her feel sick.

'You didn't say anything about photos.' The expression on his face was changing. He looked worried, haunted. 'And why do you think I'm involved in this? My own house?' He strode to the window and looked out. 'It's probably best if you don't touch anything, Jo. The police will want to take fingerprints. What photos?' He frowned.

She dropped a sock, watching it land alongside a smear of red. Paint was daubed on the walls and floor. Trails of red extended outwards from the bed. 'The police have the photos now. I took them to the station.'

'I'm calling them right now,' he said. 'Let's get out of this room.'

At last, she thought, as she watched him go down the stairs in front of her. He was taking her seriously. Finally. But why had he not believed her before? As he went into the living room to phone, she remembered the headlights flooding their car on that narrow windy lane, Mark's knuckles, white, gripping the steering wheel, how she'd been jolted forward when the other car had run into them. Why hadn't Mark wanted to involve the police then? But did it really matter now? Fingerprints would be all over the house. The police would match them to their records.

She made a pot of tea, got out two mugs and sat at the table. She was feeling calmer. Everything would be all right. Again and again, she told herself this, repeating the words like a nursery rhyme. She stood at the kitchen sink waiting for Mark to finish the call, staring out at the moonless night. The police would find Raquel, arrest her for unlawfully breaking into their house and for harassment, threats to kill. Everything would be fine. What about Rob? If there was no reason to see him, no file to find, did that mean there was no need for contact? Was it better this way?

'The police will be here soon.' He was behind her, smoothing her hair, slipping his fingers between the locks. 'They'll get whoever it was.'

'It was her. I'm telling you. It was Raquel Bannister.'

'What did the police say when you showed them the photos?'

'Not a lot.'

'I'm going back to our room. Make sure my camera's still there.'

Then the police arrived. One man, one woman. Mark raced back down the stairs.

'We have a report of vandalism,' the man said while they waited on the doorstep and removed their hats.

'Come in. I'll show you,' said Mark.

'She's been stalking me. I reported it before and now she's broken in.' A calmness had entered Jo's voice. 'It's not random.'

'Let's take a look then,' the man said and they all began to go upstairs.

At the second floor, Jo hesitated. She leant against the wall, beside the blue and white vase. Tracing the outline of the pattern with her eyes, she breathed slowly, puffing out air.

'I can deal with this. You don't have to come upstairs.' Mark was already leading the two police officers up the next flight.

'I need to be there too. It was me who found it.'

'Why don't you wait downstairs?' he called out from the top floor. 'No need for you to be up here.'

What harm could it do her, to see the mess again? When she got to there, the two police officers were treading carefully in between the splashes of red paint, taking photos.

'It looks like blood, doesn't it?' she said.

The policeman turned to her. 'Were all these clothes pulled out from the drawers by the perpetrator too?'

'Yes,' she said, staring round at the red paint. It was meant to scare her. A warning of what was to come.

'We'll take some photos. You don't have to stay up here, if you don't want to,' the policeman was saying.

'Shall we leave them to it?' Mark said.

'We'll be down in a minute,' the woman said and Jo noticed a lock of blonde hair that had slipped out from her chignon.

After a while, the police joined Jo in the living room. She explained to them about Raquel Bannister tormenting her with her phone calls, following her, taking her passport, her money, her smashed car, the threats. An ex-client, she explained. It was her, she told them. Mark put his arm round her. She told them about the envelope containing Mark's torn photo and about the photos she'd received in the post.

They looked up from their scribbling and scrutinized Mark and she felt like a fool. Raising their eyebrows, they exchanged looks and told her they knew all about the threats and the smashed car and the photos.

'So you're going to do something, then? Can you arrest her?' While she spoke, she saw Mark peering into the silent dark garden. The police took the photos and slipped them into a folder.

'We're taking it seriously. Yes, Miss Carr. Was there anything stolen? Jewellery, money, anything?'

'No,' Mark said. 'I had a look round.'

'Any idea how the perpetrator got in to the house?'

There was no sign of forced entry. No windows broken. The male officer took a look round the house. There was no sign of a break–in.

'How did she get in, then?' she asked.

'Maybe they picked the lock,' Mark said.

The two police wanted to take fingerprints. They put on latex gloves and went round the house brushing white powder onto door jambs and handles.

'Do you think they'll put her away,' Jo said as she and Mark drank hot sweet tea.

'I'm sorry I wasn't here when you found it. I honestly don't know what they'll do,' he said as he stirred more sugar into his tea.

'Should we offer them tea?' she said. 'Isn't that what we're supposed to do? Sip tea in an orderly manner? Tea from hand painted bone china while they, the police, solve crimes.' He kept his head bowed and she thought of the floral cups and saucers that had belonged to his wife. Then she remembered the final demand and nodded to where it lay on a pile of other letters. 'Did you see that?'

He glanced at the bill and replaced it on the pile of other letters. 'I'll deal with it.'

'Are we short of money? I don't understand, there's no mortgage to pay and –'

'It was an oversight. I'll pay it today.'

'But –'

He put his hand on hers. 'Please. Drop it.'

Neither of the police officers wanted tea. Nearly finished, they told them. In any case they'd just had one at another house. And she wondered whether the previous break-in was less complicated than theirs.

Mark put his hand on her shoulder. 'You OK?' he asked.

'I feel like screaming again.'

He looked at her.

'There's something you're not telling me, isn't there?' she said.

He sighed and nodded. He reached for her hand. 'Wait till they've gone, then we'll go out.'

'So there is something?'

With his fingers he drummed the table. 'We'll go to the pub down the road. Have something to eat. Since you got back two weeks ago, we haven't spent that much time –'

'Now. Tell me now.'

'There's not a lot. But I do remember this Raquel woman in the bed next to your mother – and well, yes – I do remember it was her telling your mum about the spa holiday.' He paused. 'I talked to a colleague. He jogged my memory.'

'*I* didn't?'

'There was only medical stuff on the file.'

Then the police were at the door telling them that they'd finished and that if they did find anything was missing to contact them immediately. Fingerprints would be checked against their records they told them.

'Someone from CID will be in touch,' the man said before they left.

As Mark was showing them the door, she heard his bleeper go off, listened to him pick up the phone in the living room and call the hospital where he worked.

Waiting for him to return to the kitchen, she held her cup of tea tightly, her firm grip nearly breaking the fine porcelain. She wouldn't let him go to the hospital. He had to go to the pub with her as he'd promised and tell her everything. There was more than he'd let on. But how could he know such a woman? What could be his connection? Back in the kitchen, he stood in front of her, his head just about hanging in shame. 'I'm sorry. I have to go in.'

'Why you? No. Not now.'

'There's been a road traffic accident on the M6. There are still a lot of staff off sick. I'm so sorry Jo.' But already he had left the room, was darting round the living room, collecting all his stuff, taking his coat from the hook in the hall. 'Be back as soon as I can.'

Grabbing his arm, she said: 'Can't someone else go in your place? Isn't there a bank of nurses or something? This is an emergency here after all. We've just been broken into. I'm frightened to be here alone.'

In the same instant, her mobile went off, the ring startling her. It was her mother. Mark had heard the salutation; 'Hi Mum.' He put his phone back in his pocket and kissed her on the top of her head. 'Be back soon,' he said in her ear. 'No more than a couple of hours. You'll be OK.' What else could she do? Compared to a heap of mangled bodies lying on the motorway, didn't her plight diminish? With one hand, she waved to him, while the other held her mobile. While she spoke to her mother, she went round the house, checked all the locks on the windows and double locked both doors, her leg aching inexplicably, more than ever.

'You said it was urgent,' her mother said. 'So here I am.'

Jo told her mother their house had just been vandalised, that Mark had had to go to the hospital to deal with an emergency.

'Darling. How terrible. I can pop round if you like. Keep you company.'

What was this? Her mother offering to come to her in her hour of need? Jo hated herself for thinking this, thought what an embittered person she must have become, even to consider it, but was there an ulterior motive to her mother's offer?

'I'll be all right,' she said. Knew that she couldn't tolerate her mother fussing. 'Are you still seeing Baz?'

There was silence and she allowed her mother to take her time lighting a cigarette, heard her blow smoke in a sigh.

'We're having a break from our little romance.'

'You mean you're not seeing him?'

'To be honest, sweet, I didn't think you liked him.'

'I never actually said that, did I? But I am relieved you've split up.'

'He wasn't right for me darling. Are you busy on Monday?'

'No, but I've an interview on Tuesday.' She thought how she still had to prepare for the presentation.

Someone was talking to her mother, a woman's voice murmuring gently and music too; a sitar. Jo knelt on the sofa, took a look through the curtains at the street outside. All seemed quiet.

'Shall we meet up at *The Enclave* then, darling? One-ish? I'll buy you lunch?'

'Christ. This is new. We usually only see each other once every blue moon and I have this interview to –'

'Is that all right then? One. On Monday. Plenty of time for you to get yourself ready. They'll snap you up, darling. With all your experience. Such a clever girl. Not like your mum.'

What else but to agree to meet? As she said, there was time enough for the interview planning. No need to query her mother about Baz. Events had taken their course.

Jo looked about her, at the laptop on the table and the garden lit up by the outside light showing green through the window. Outside a car revved and two people passed chatting to each other, ordinary people with ordinary lives. Free of fear. All around her the house creaked. Raquel's words came back to her as if she were standing right next to her. *Fancy leaving a clever guy like that behind.* Why hadn't she wondered then whether Raquel knew Mark?

She sat at the laptop to prepare for the interview. She had to at least give this interview her best shot. Jobs were few, the competition tough. She stared at the screen, tried to concentrate. Her efforts were fruitless. How could she possibly think about this job now?

Something creaked. Were they footsteps coming down the stairs? Had Raquel been hiding somewhere in the house all this time? She swung round. There was nothing. Only the click of the radiators. Only the creak of the wood on the stairs. She concentrated on the presentation, checking her skills against the job description. Her mother was right. With all her experience, she should walk into this job. Except for the time she'd messed up. Except for the time she'd overlooked a wrong decision made by a temporary member of staff with mean-street leanings. But in the end what did Raquel want? She thought of her mother telling her she worried too much. She thought of Senaka telling her Raquel was a good girl. And then of Mark about to tell her what he knew of Raquel.

248

She put down her pen and began to pace. She remembered Senaka saying *'She say she see you in England.'* Didn't Raquel Bannister have a good enough life buying and selling jewellery? Had she suffered that much by being turned down by a non-thinking manager?

Jo could no longer think straight. Lying back down on the sofa, she forced her eyes to stay open, determined not to sleep, needing to stay alert. In the end, she woke to the sound of a milk float chugging up the street. Mark wasn't home. She opened the curtains. It was still dark. There was a jagged line of pink over the distant mountains where dawn was breaking. She shivered and reached for the phone. Something must have happened. Two hours, Mark had said. It was five 'o clock. She called his mobile and he answered immediately.

'Sorry,' he said. 'I didn't want to wake you. That's why I didn't phone.' He sounded worn out, his tone flat. 'I'll be back in half an hour.'

The half hour ran into an hour.

In the bathroom on the first floor, she took a shower and as she dried herself, she heard a key in the door. She fled down the stairs, her heart just about breaking through her rib cage. Mark.

'My dad's taken a turn for the worse.' His face was creased in a frown. 'I have to get back there. He might not last much longer. He's developed pneumonia. I came back to check you were OK. Then I'll be off again, Sorry.' Absentmindedly, he kissed her. He wandered into the kitchen, put the kettle on. 'Just have some black coffee first,' he said.

'Shall I come with you?'

'Yeah, OK. That would be good.'

Rapidly, she dressed. She thought about Mark's father, how sick he'd looked after the fit. She remembered how she'd thought it would've been nice to have had a father – that at least Mark had enjoyed an uncomplicated childhood. Or had he? How had a madly religious mother affected him? Why would he never talk about it? In the back of her mind one thought rumbled continuously: now she'd have to wait for

Mark to tell her about Raquel. She despised herself for thinking this while he endured the last days of his father's life. But at least she knew she was not going crazy. At least she knew some of the truth. But that didn't stop the fear that gripped her.

23

Jo's fear played on her imagination: she was continually haunted by images of Raquel splattering the red paint in their room. The memory of light footsteps she'd heard coming down their stairs, sent shivers down her spine. It would be a long time before she would be able to sleep in the top bedroom again even after the paint had been removed. Or was the entire house now stained with fear? Would she ever feel comfortable sleeping there?

At least she had an appointment to see a CID inspector. That was her only hope. But so much could happen before then.

Sunday morning passed as if in a dream, as if this thing with Raquel Bannister belonged to another part of her life while Mark's father lay near to death. It was like an interlude before some new kind of hellishness became her reality. The news that Mark's father had deteriorated even more made everything else seem unimportant. She needed to somehow stop this Raquel woman from consuming her life. It was that or go crazy and last night as she tried to sleep in the unfamiliar bedroom on the first floor, she thought she was already approaching insanity.

In the afternoon she drove to Sid's house as arranged. She'd spent the morning preparing the presentation for Tuesday. She drove, always alert to the possibility of being rammed by the car behind.

Other families spent their Sunday eating roast dinners, watching football or getting drunk in the pub. Wasting their lives away, her mother had always said. So much to see in the world, so much to experience. Why watch it all fly past on a screen?

She turned into the housing estate where Sid lived, passing row after row of similar bungalows and a few men washing their cars.

At some traffic lights she watched in horror as a black car draw up beside her in the right lane. The woman driver was wearing a scarf round her head tied at the back, bandana fashion, a multi coloured scarf, the sort you can buy all over Asia. Jo stared, her face growing cold. The traffic lights changed but Jo was transfixed. As if taunting her, the woman began to turn her head towards her. Jo suddenly became aware of car horns blaring behind her, of a man shouting at her, telling her to get moving. Releasing the clutch, she tried to accelerate but her car had stalled. Restarting it, she lurched forward and sped away feeling the pull of insanity taking her under again.

Sid's house was quiet but the door was ajar. She stepped into the hall and called out to Mark. The house smelt worse than before, of urine, faeces and cleaning fluid. She called out again and heard a cough from the bedroom at the end of the bungalow. There was another and a nurse appeared from there.

'Mark?'

The nurse looked flustered. 'Who are you?'

'I'm Mark's partner.'

Without saying more, she left Jo standing in the hall and walked back to Sid's bedroom leaving the door wide open for her.

Mark was sitting on the chair beside the bed, holding his father's hand while the nurse stood by. The stench was more powerful and, instinctively, Jo put her hand to her mouth. Apart from the bundled bodies she'd witnessed on the banks of the Ganges when she was six, apart from the starving children with mutilated limbs she'd seen in other parts of India, she'd had no experience of anyone close to her dying and despite her yearnings for a dad, she and Sid hadn't spent much time together – he'd never really approved of her, though Mark always denied this.

Sid was dead. It seemed it had just happened. His eyes were still wide open, as though he were staring at something terrible and the expression on his face was like nothing she'd ever seen before – as if in the minute before he died he'd seen a premonition of what lay beyond the grave. There was a stain spreading on the sheet he lay on and she could see his hands were still clenched as though he'd been trying to grasp something. Jo began to shiver as Mark closed his father's eyes and mouth then drew the sheet over the body.

In the kitchen, the same one where not five days ago she'd carefully prepared tea on a tray, she waited for Mark. When he appeared, she saw how his long lean body was sagging.

She hugged him. 'I'm so sorry,' she said, knowing the sorrow she felt was for more than his father's death. She kissed his pale dry cheek. 'I'm really sorry.'

'There's nothing after death. That's it. Finish. My mother was wrong.'

'Don't say things like that. He's only just gone,' she said.

An hour later the ambulance had been, taken Sid's body away, and finally gone. 'Let's go', Mark said. 'I'll come back another day. Sort a few things.'

She followed him in her car as he drove slowly back to their house. He drove as if he was already preparing for the funeral or perhaps he was being extra careful, his mind full of grief but when they got home he kissed her hard on the lips pressing her against the hall wall.

'No. I'm not in the mood,' she said, and pulled away.

He went to the kitchen and she heard him open the fridge. 'Want a glass?' he asked and she took the offered red wine.

'That's that then.' He turned from her. 'I guess I'm an orphan now.'

How could she reach out and comfort him with all these unanswered questions? When would it *not* be insensitive of her to ask again? 'I'm sorry,' she said, uselessly.

Brushing against her as he passed, he left the kitchen and went down the hall into the room where his drum kit was laid out. Jo drank her wine, then went upstairs to the first floor bathroom. How much worse could it get?

An undefinable atmosphere had replaced the absolute terror of the day before. Grief? Anger? She couldn't quite identify it. She lingered in the shower, while he clattered and banged downstairs. Half an hour later, she heard the sound of him playing the drums. Why should he worry about disturbing the neighbours when his father had just died? She went downstairs and watched, tapping her foot in time. As he played he turned towards her and his head jerked rhythmically with the beat of the drum. This was the Mark she'd first fallen for. She thought back to their very first encounter. Lisa had known a guitarist in the band, so she, Amy and Jo had got free admittance into the club. Jo had stopped doing drugs and drinking excessively by then. As everyone else grew rowdier, she'd simply watched the drummer and thought how gorgeous he was and couldn't believe her eyes when he joined them at their table during the interval. They had talked incessantly while the noise of the pub became a distant hum. He told her she was amazing. She was flattered. He took her seriously too. Such a nice change from Rob's constant jokey manner, she'd thought.

During their first meal out at a Chinese she'd told him about the fall from the window, the two operations, the pain she'd endured that she'd thought would never go.

'You should change your job. Go for management. Front line work will burn you out. Eleven years is too long. No wonder you're getting pissed all the time. Not good for you –'

'Never thought of myself as management material.'

'You can change. You're clever enough. Beautiful *and* clever.'

She'd felt the fire in her cheeks.

Now as she leant against the doorjamb, listening to the drum beat she thought how odd it was you could live with someone for two years and still not entirely know them. He stared at her for a second while a lock of hair slipped over his brow. Then he turned away, focusing his mind on the beat.

From the other room, she heard her phone. She let it ring, in no mood to talk to anyone, but watched Mark work out his grief through his drums. The phone rang again. And this time she went through and took the call. It was Rob.

'I came in today and got the file,' he said. 'Sunday too'.

'It's been hell here,' she said.

She told him about the red paint and the police, how they'd taken the photos as evidence. 'I've got an appointment with some guy from CID.'

'When for?'

'Tuesday afternoon. Got that interview at 10 –. Mark's father died this morning as well as everything else.'

He paused. 'I don't know Mark, but that's terrible for anyone.'

'Yes,' she said. From the other end of the phone she heard a guitar riff, a male singer and closer to her ear, she heard Rob blow out smoke. 'How's your eye?' she asked.

'As I said I came in early to get the file. Seven o'clock to be precise, so's no one would be around the office and now it's sitting in my bag. And the eye is coming on nicely. Turning a pleasant yellowish colour. Thanks for asking. So when d'you want to see this file?'

From the other room there was silence, the drumming had ceased.

'Thank you Rob. You're a trooper.'

'No. I'm bloody daft.'

She could hear Mark making his way through to the room where she was.

'I – I must go now. I'll – I'll phone you back later and fix a time to come to yours.' She was going to say more, tell him how she'd been thinking about him, but Mark was looking at her from the doorway.

She heard him sigh. 'Make sure you do.'

In the morning, she woke at six, while birds sang and car engines faltered in the icy air. From the bathroom, Mark told her he was going to work, his shift began at nine thirty and he wouldn't consider cancelling.

'Are you sure you should?'

'I'll be fine,' he said.

She was meeting her mother at eleven. But she left as soon as Mark went to work, even though she'd be early. The black car was there again. Had Mark seen it? Surely he would have warned her. Jo walked nearer. Raquel was staring at her; her eyes seemed to pierce Jo's soul. She shivered and began to approach the woman. Raquel stared at Jo while she got out her phone, ready to take a photo as evidence. Raquel started the car and sped away.

Shaken, Jo sat in her car for a while. She looked at the space where Raquel had been. She drove away too fast, clutching the wheel, and when she reached the motorway was overtaking without using her mirrors, zipping across lanes. She ignored all the horns and curses of the other drivers. She felt like she was running for her life. By the time she came off the motorway she'd calmed herself. Didn't she have an appointment with the police? She would tell them. It was more evidence.

She'd arranged to meet her mother in her old haunt, The Enclave, and she felt, as she careered round the old part of the city, that she was, in a way, returning to the womb. How many times had she met her mother here? What would her mother's reaction be when she told her about Raquel? She parked in her usual spot, outside a bakery with crusty-looking loaves and baskets of freshly baked scones in the window, thinking now would be a good time to phone Rob. As she burrowed in her bag for her phone and switched it on, it rang.

'I'm doing this for you, Jo. I don't understand you. First you're desperate for me to get that woman's file. I've been trying to get hold of you. Why's your phone switched off?'

'Sorry. I couldn't talk last night. Things were difficult. I told you about Mark's dad –'

'And I said I was sorry. Leave your phone on. Right?'

'I'm really grateful you're putting your neck on the line for me – and – it's so good to hear your voice again.'

He paused. 'Yeah, likewise. Can't talk for long.' She heard the sound of a dustbin cart unloading and knew he was standing outside the office, having a smoke. 'I took the file home and I was going to have a nosey.' He paused and she pressed the phone to her ear. 'But I was meeting a mate so I didn't have time. It's a big file. Stop chasing after her. Especially now.'

'She was there again. Outside the house. Waiting for me.'

'Fuck.' He paused. 'Did she say anything?'

'Nothing. Stared. Drove off. It's she who's chasing me. You've no idea how scared I am.'

'She's bad news. Keep away from her. Don't go digging anymore.' He paused. 'Got to go now. Meeting. Tedious, but there you go. You should have called last night. Would've had more time to talk. Come round at six. OK?'

'Rob – yes of course. See you later.'

Outside the car, people were entering the bakery while others left clutching paper bags. An assistant with her hair bundled into a net cap was picking out some baps from the selection in the window. Jo moved like a robot, barely conscious of her actions; stepping onto the pavement, locking the car, turning left and walking round the corner, before turning right. Only then did she swing round. Only then did she become aware of footsteps behind her. She walked faster and faster towards The Enclave sign which seemed to be static instead of getting closer. She turned round. The woman following her was wearing a black coat and swung an umbrella like a baton, to and fro, to and fro. Rooted to the spot, Jo watched as the woman drew nearer and nearer coming towards her at speed, flicking her blonde hair from her face. She stopped in her tracks. Froze. Anger flowing through her gut.

'Stay away from me,' Jo said.

Without turning to look at Jo, the woman turned into a pub and, as the door opened, for a few seconds, music disturbed the quiet.

Jo came to her senses and ran along the street.

24

It was a relief to be in The Enclave. There were so many memories to distract her here, and despite her fraught nerves, the warm air and herbal smells made her feel marginally better.

She fetched a coffee and croissant from the man behind the counter who recognised her and gave her a larger coffee than the one she'd ordered. Small cushions were dotted round a platform that ran along one wall of the café and these as well as the squashy sofas were all occupied. A table looking out onto the street was available and she selected a chair which faced outwards to where a shop opposite sold South American imports. From here, she'd be able to watch for her mother and sightings of Raquel. *Back to Black* by Amy Winehouse was playing. She sank into the vocals and remembered the many times she'd met her mother here before.

Dope used to be smoked freely in The Enclave, so her mother told her. Clients used to lounge around on oversized pillows as if they were in a Kasbah. The air was perpetually filled with Patchouli which the women saturated themselves in or Sandalwood from the incense sticks they used to burn to conceal the smoke of chillum pipes…

She visualised the red paint, heard again Raquel's footsteps running lightly down the stairs.

No.

…the music was mystical: sitars to get stoned by and *Pink Floyd* for contemplation. Then, her mother would say with a faraway look in her eyes, there were the police raids. The Enclave would go clean for a few months before the giant pillows would once again be occupied by the regular clientele.

She looked at the painting of a sunset on the wall opposite and tried to absorb herself in the reds and yellows, the purple sea and the rush of orange.

The images were there again – Raquel sitting in the bar on the beach. Raquel appearing on the road, staring at her, motionless. Raquel in Senaka's house.

She would not allow herself to think of Raquel.

Suddenly she heard low laughter and felt hands tight round her head, covering her eyes with their fingers. She jerked round.

'Darling, whatever's wrong?' her mother said. 'You expecting Jack the Ripper or something?'

'Why did you creep up on me like that, Mum?'

Her mother kissed Jo on the cheek. 'You know coffee's bad for stress, darling.' She laid her hand on Jo's and leant across the table. 'Hello, Simon,' she called out. 'You know my daughter, don't you? Peppermint tea for me. You want the same darling? It helps the digestion. Jesus, you look pale. Simon, bring the teas over, there's a lovey. Some nuts and carrot cake too, please.' She removed her hand from Jo's, fidgeted with her hennaed hair, chattering on as if the club and Baz had never existed; as if it wasn't her that had worn that tiny, tight top. It was always the same. Like a chameleon, changing her look to suit a man and then in between returning to the original mum in long jewelled skirts and beads. A great loneliness suddenly shook Jo to the core and she realised how much she wanted to see Rob. Why had she made such a mess of her life?

She began to cry. The tears were lavish and extravagant and very soon uncontrollable.

Her mother took hold of her hand again.

'My darling,' she called out above the music and fetched a tissue from Simon. Then, making Jo even more embarrassed than she already was, her mother pulled Jo to her bosom, patting her head. Sniffing, covering her face, Jo pulled away. But she couldn't stop. She began to hiccup and sniffle, knowing she had an audience in the couple who'd just entered The Enclave and pretended they hadn't seen. Her mother said nothing but supplied the tissues and virtually force-fed her peppermint tea. Eventually Jo's eyes stopped leaking tears.

'What's happened?'

'Nothing. I'm all right now.' She blew her nose.

'Is it Mark? Has he done something? Has he asked you to leave – I always wondered whether it was a rebound thing. Wasn't it only a year after his wife died that you two met?'

'Christ, Mum.'

'Well, is it him?'

'You won't believe me.'

'Now, darling. Why would your mother not believe her own daughter?'

Jo finished her tea and began to nibble at the cashew nuts her mother had bought for her. Thankfully the tears had subsided, but she felt awful, as if she was coming to from a heavy drug. 'I'm OK, honestly.' Her mother was wearing kohl and had the look of the mother of her childhood, but with additional lines which the black eye makeup couldn't entirely hide. This strangely alarmed Jo as she realised her mother was aging rapidly. Why had she never noticed before? She sighed, wondering whether she should have seen her more often. 'So you got rid of Baz, then?'

While glancing at the door, her mother put her cup to her lips and sipped. It was always she that finished with the men. Never the other way round. At an early age, Jo had learnt this well.

'I'm not going to let this go, darling. I've a good mind to phone Mark now and ask –'

'Christ, mum.'

'Well? And why wouldn't I believe you?'

Jo rubbed her eyes. Her mother took her hand and Jo felt the roughened palm caressing her. But she wasn't going to break this firm promise she'd made to herself never to confide in her mother about relationships and never to tell her what was really going on. Even if she kind of believed Jo, she wouldn't be able to understand the idea of a woman pursuing her daughter with such vengeance. According to her, only men pursued women. And a part of Jo blamed her mother for befriending Raquel in the hospital, for allowing her into her confidence. She knew this was irrational. If she said this, her mother would look hurt and tell Jo it was unfair to blame her for making friends while she stayed in hospital, especially while Jo had been too busy to make daily visits.

She couldn't face an argument. Not now. Not with Raquel so much on her mind. Not while she no longer trusted Mark. Ideas flashed through her head: Raquel as a serial killer bent on destroying any woman who got in her way. Or was she a serial arsonist who had managed to escape conviction? Whatever it was, why was she so hell-bent on revenge?

Jo wiped her eyes and tried to conjure up an excuse for the tears, knowing her mother wouldn't let her go without a believable explanation. Her mind raced as images of Raquel with a knife held at her throat flashed before her.

'Mark bought me a kitten and she's gone missing,' she blurted out while staring out at the South American shop opposite. A man had emerged swinging a carrier bag.

The lie had slipped out. No going back. But what did it matter if her mother didn't believe her? She was desperately trying to block out the awful image of Raquel's leering face, the sharpened knife glinting.

Her mother chewed on a nut and regarded Jo with shrewd eyes. 'I'm sorry to hear that, darling.'

'Blossom was my first pet.' She saw her mother nod to a man she obviously knew, then Jo felt her stroking her fingers.

'One can get very attached to pets. How awful for you. Are you sure there's nothing else? It's not like you to get into such a state about a pet Don't get me wrong, darling.'

'Yes, that's it. But I feel a bit better,' she said, fully composed now. 'Anyway, you didn't tell me about Baz.'

Her mother touched the mole under her left eye, a habit which told Jo she was nervous. 'He just wasn't my type, darling – he had to go.' She moved her face closer to Jo's. 'But I've got some amazing news –'

'He beat up a friend of mine, you know?' said Jo. 'Sounds like a right bastard.'

'What are you talking about? That's ridiculous.'

'Your Baz, sorry your ex-Baz. He gave Rob, you remember Rob? He gave him a black eye.'

'Rob? Really? Not my Baz, darling. He was a brute but it must have been someone else. He's not the violent type. How is Rob? Make sure you pass on my good wishes to him. I always liked him and he simply adored you.' She smiled at another man who'd just come in, then turned back to Jo. 'I have some wonderful news. I must tell you.'

Jo sulked like the truculent teenager of old; she chewed on the nuts, flicked open the pages of a newspaper on the table, refused to meet her mother's eyes. News from her mother was frequently about another new man. She picked up her peppermint tea, moved her chair back with a scraping sound, creating more space between them. She stretched her legs out and crossed her ankles, sipped the beverage and nodded at her mother. 'What news?' Because someone turned the music right up, she had to repeat. 'What news is this, mum?' And she pulled her chair back to its old position opposite her mother so she could hear her answer. 'Hang on,' she said. 'I need to go to the loo.' She knew she was playing games with her mother but she also dreaded hearing about another man her mother had taken up with.

'You'll really like Harry,' her mother called after her. 'When I first met him, he reminded me of your father.' But Jo was already half way to the toilet, pretending she hadn't heard her mother. The memory of Jo's father was faint, like an old sepia photograph. Jo looked back and saw her mother staring fixedly at her daughter's bag while her hand moved across the table as if she intended to look inside. Then she turned to Jo, smiled and withdrew her hand.

There was a queue for the solitary Ladies and it seemed to take an age for Jo to get back to the table.

'Let me buy you lunch, sweetie. I have so much to tell you. Harry said he might be able to pop in today.'

'Is that why you keep looking at who's coming in?'

'He's an artist.' Her mother said, proudly. 'Abstracts.'

Jo's phone rang and she saw her mother pushing her bag across the table towards her while she nodded. 'Better take it,' her mother said.

There was no name on the screen, but Jo noted she'd missed several calls from Mark.

'I'm phoning on behalf of Mark Cartwright.'

'What? Mark? What's happened to him?'

Her mother coloured a little and with her finger pressed cake crumbs from her plate and popped them into her mouth. Jo looked away.

'Nothing. Nothing. He's fine. I'm a receptionist at the hospital, Carol's my name and he told me he's been trying to call you.'

'Can I speak to him?'

'Unfortunately, he's had to attend to an emergency …which is why he asked me to phone you. He says can you please go home. *Now*. He said it was urgent and he'd be there as soon as he can.'

'What? Why? I'm not going home if he's not there. Did he tell you what happened? Why did he say I had to go home?'

'An emergency. Something serious, he said. He told me a neighbour contacted him. Mr Cartwright said please get home as soon as you can, as he can't right now. That's the only information I have.'

'I'll call him.'

'As I said, he's in theatre. There was an emergency. Otherwise, he said he'd be there too. He asked me to pass this message on to you and say he's sorry.'

'I'll call him.'

'Mrs Cartwright.'

'I'm not Mrs Cartwright. Mark and I are *not* married.'

'I didn't mean to offend –'

'No offence taken. But *his* getting to our house *is* urgent. Tell him that when you see him, Carol. Please tell him.'

Jo cut her off and called Mark. His mobile went to voice mail and she began to sweat. Her voice was hoarse as she turned to her mother. 'I – I've got to go – something –' Her breath came out in short sharp pants; she couldn't get herself into gear. The Enclave was shrinking, crowding her out, the colours so bright they dazzled her. Her mother's voice sounded distant. Someone changed the music and the café vibrated with electronic whines. She had to leave, had to get back, and in a daze she somehow made it to the door. Her mother called out to her, followed her and grabbed her arm. Jo shrugged it off and pulled away, couldn't hear what her mother was saying. Her senses were focused on getting home.

25

The car was miles away, or so it seemed as Jo went quickly down the street and turned the corner ignoring the jar in her leg which felt worse than ever. She broke into a run, then her fingers were searching in her bag; wallet, phone, curled receipts. She found the keys.

She drove fast. Through the back streets pushing forward at roundabouts, accelerating at amber traffic lights until the motorway sign loomed ahead. It'd take her forty minutes to get home, thirty if she put her foot down. She stopped at a red light and tried Mark again. No reply. She phoned home and listened to the phone ringing. Was there time to call the police? She dialled the number. The lights turned green. With one hand, she steered the car over the crossroads.

'Can I help you?' a woman said on the phone.

'There's a woman who's been stalking me. She's an arsonist and –'

'Can you slow down? I can't understand what you're saying. Can we start with your name?'

'Please can you get a car to 14 Lowcroft Way, Meresbridge?'

'Are you driving a vehicle, madam? Please can you pull over so we can continue this conversation in safety?'

'No. Because I'm freaked out and asking for your help. My name's Jolene Carr. If you look me up you'll see. Please get there as soon as possible.'

Ahead of her was a dual-carriageway where heavy traffic flowed. She threw the phone onto the passenger seat, from where it slipped onto the floor. It rang, but now she couldn't reach it, couldn't see the name on the screen. She knew what she was returning home to. She swallowed, ridding her mind of the image of flames reaching high, of the house a burnt out ruin.

The road changed to motorway. She kept to the speed limit not wanting to alert the traffic police. The traffic got heavy. Soon she was at a standstill. Beads of sweat trickled down her face. How much longer would this take? After twenty minutes, the traffic loosened and she was free to move.

Since she'd stopped the weather had changed. The clouds were closing in and a murky fog was forming. The rain turned to a thick mist. The windscreen wipers did nothing to clear the glass. Already it was an hour since she'd left The Enclave.

At the bottom of her road the park was shrouded in a swirling mist. It rose from the grass and seeped into the trees, their branches naked and clawing in the gloom. It was difficult to see through the fog. She slowed, looking for the turning that led to her street. A large shape appeared ahead of her and she braked. Her fingers were numb. She squinted through the fogged up glass, saw a dog with red eyes, snout in a muzzle. Her thoughts were jumbled together in a tangle of images: Raquel on the beach, Raquel outside her house, Raquel driving a black car, Raquel with an Alsatian. The dog was pulled away by its lead and she saw the owner, a man with a shaved head, glance at her, before he dragged the dog across the dripping park.

She turned her car round, driving as fast as the speed bumps allowed, past other small slate cottages and neat box hedges. She drove up the quiet residential street, a strange smell becoming more potent on the prevailing wind.

She imagined their street blocked by fire engines. An ambulance standing by and a police car, its lights flashing, all of its doors open wide, waiting for the culprit to emerge from the burning building. Choking smoke, neighbours standing at their doorsteps, unable to stop themselves watching, scarves, tea towels, handkerchiefs held across their faces to keep the fumes at bay. Raquel would be led away in handcuffs from the slate cottage. It'd be blackened by the fire, a yellow marker tape around their home marking off the scene of the crime.

But there were no police cars or ambulances or fire engines. She drove past their neighbours, a mixture of traditional slate cottages and new bungalows, aware of an eerie silence hovering over the area. Now the only smell was of her own fear. She parked in front of the house, ran her eyes along the parked cars. No sign of Raquel's.

Jo went up the steps, unlocked the front door, thinking that at least the lights weren't on. The house seemed quiet. Had it been a false alarm?

'Hello?'

There was no reply.

She passed through the hall, looked inside the kitchen and saw a cafeteria on the table and two mugs. A plastic bottle of milk stood on the worktop next to the sink. The fridge was open and she saw the screw top of a wine bottle on the floor. She listened. A tap dripped. No other sound. She retreated into the hall. The house creaked. Stop. Look around. In the living room she stared at the pine sideboard, the painted green fireplace, the mahogany dining room table with its four matching chairs and the floral armchair she'd always disliked. This wasn't her home. It was the home Mark had shared with his wife. Fire would have been a way out –an opportunity for them to use the insurance to start again. Was that what she wanted? A new life with Mark? A door slammed. She jumped. Put her hand in her bag. Where was her phone? Then she remembered it was on the floor of her car. She swore and listened again, then went into the room where Mark's drum kit stood against the far wall. The window was closed. The red rose-patterned curtains hung motionless.

Someone else was in the house. She sensed it. Should leave. But she had to know.

She crept up the stairs, calling out as she did so. In a trance, led on by a strange instinct, a curiosity to see what lay beyond, she climbed each step. She opened the bathroom door on the half-landing. Her body tingled with goose bumps. Next floor. Two bedrooms. She kicked open the bedroom where she and Mark had been sleeping since Saturday. The blue room she'd laughingly called it when she first moved in. Clothes scattered on the bed, sweater and jeans she wore yesterday, blue T-shirt, green and white duvet pulled back. She stopped. Why was she doing this? What did she have to prove to herself, to anyone? The other bedroom was cold and draughty, a single bed shoved against the wall, a pink and brown striped rug on the floor. She turned and looked down the steep staircase. She wished Rob were here. He'd know what to do. She began to retreat back down the stairs.

'You took your time.'

She didn't stir an inch, recognising the voice. She looked up and met Raquel Bannister's eyes.

'You coming up?' The blue nose stud looked larger, brighter, than Jo remembered. 'Been here a fucking age.'

'What are you doing in my house? How dare you.'

'I took the liberty of helping myself to a bottle of wine. I've drunk the whole fucking bottle waiting for you.'

Jo turned and ran back down the stairs. She should never have come in. She should never have tried to go upstairs. Raquel was behind her. Jo felt a hand on her shoulder, dragging her back. She was shoved against the wall.

'Thought you could get away? And there's me, being all fucking polite waiting for you. Could've smashed the place up by now.' She moved in closer. 'Giving me the once over this morning. Looking at me like that. As if I was a piece of shit. That's you all over. Little Miss fucking pig-face.'

For a second, Raquel's hold slipped as she turned to look where a leaflet had just been dropped through the front door.

'Help. Get the police. *Help.*'

Jo made a dash for it, squirming from beneath Raquel's hold. Then she was at the front door. But her fingers wouldn't move fast enough. As they touched the latch, she heard Raquel coming down the stairs close behind. Intending to open the door she lifted her hand. There was a slap on her shoulder and her hair was grabbed, forcing her head back.

'You're very rude. After all this time, Jolene Carr. And you a manager telling everyone what to do. You have no fucking manners.'

She struggled. She tried to free herself but Raquel's grip was strong.

'You'd better come upstairs, hadn't you, Jolene Carr?'

Raquel had tight hold of her – Jo tried to wrench herself free. It was no good. Not with a bad leg. She made one more attempt, throwing the full weight of herself against Raquel. But her hair was being pulled so hard she couldn't resist. Raquel was shoving her back up the stairs, forcing her up at every step, kneeing open the top bedroom door, dragging her over towards the bed.

'Get your hands off me.'

But Raquel was pummelling her in the small of her back, pushing her onto the bed. Jo felt her skull crack on the wall, saw Raquel sneering as she backed away, banging the bedroom door shut; she leaned against it and stared, her mouth forming a smile – though her eyes were narrowed and emotionless. Her hair was mucky, tousled, the peroxide growing out. She was wearing high-heeled black knee length boots, a short black skirt and pink skinny top. The colour looked so incongruous against Raquel's snarling features. She smelt of stale sweat. Raquel couldn't have washed for days and now the room was filling with her stench and hatred.

'What do you want?' She sat on the edge of the bed and faced Raquel trying to hide her fear.

'You like the décor?' Raquel said, smiling. 'I went to a lot of fucking trouble picking this colour. Had a bit of help from my old mate at the shop, but you'd know about that, wouldn't you? A measly packet of seeds you bought. Fucking stingy cow. Mark said you were a useless bitch.'

'Mark?'

'Trouble with you, honey. You trust everyone.'

'What are you talking about?'

'Stupid cow.'

'The torn photo –'

'Fucking slow too.'

'You haven't told me –' She had to draw attention to her plight. She dashed to the window, the back of her head sore from where it had hit the wall, and leant out. She filled her lungs with air. Screamed. Banged on the window. Saw two skateboarders careering down the road. Nothing. She swirled round and saw Raquel flicking her gas lighter on and off, the flame reaching higher each time.

'Dear Jo, so fucking melodramatic.'

'Why've you been following me?' She kept her eyes on the flame, scanning the room for inflammables. How much time would she have to get out before the house went up? Her mouth was dry with a metallic taste like tarnished silver. Was this how it was all going to end? She was sweating hard, heart knocking against her chest, dizzy. All the signs of an imminent panic attack.

No, not now.

'You think I don't know about you going to where I used to live, you reckon that bloody man in the shop wouldn't tell me, huh? You think I didn't hear about you fucking nosing round the market, pretending you're a friend? You think I'm stupid? And you have the nerve to ask me why I'm following you. Cunt.' She turned her head and scowled. 'You were the same at school. Stuck up fucking cow.'

'What school?'

She lit a cigarette. The flame on her lighter soared higher. 'Pretty huh?' She glared at Jo. 'Jessica Atherton at your service.' She took an exaggerated bow. 'You thought you were something else, something fucking special. You thought the bloody sun shone out of your arse.'

A vague memory infiltrated Jo's mind. Rich kid. No one liked her. Smelt bad. Always hanging around the peripheral of the school yard. Light-fingered. Stole from everyone. She remembered now.

'You snitched on me.'

'You can't be Jessica.'

'Don't call me a liar, fuck-face.' She took a step nearer. She was getting too close. 'You're a squealer.'

Jo dragged her memory back to her time in that school … Jessica nicking her school bag. Her treasured silver trinket box gone … the only thing she possessed that belonged to her father She'd carried the box round with her everywhere.

'D'you know what my dad did when the fucking school told him?'

Jo stared at her, took a step back. 'You punched me. You probably deserved whatever he did. You stole something that I could never replace –'

'He had a belt. A leather belt. I had welts for bloody days. It was *your* fault.'

'No.'

'I was going to teach you a lesson, but that bloody mother took you away. Then there was your signature on that fucking letter. Jolene Carr. I'll never forget that name. Stupid fucking cow.'

Her knees trembled. She backed across the room and gripped the sill to steady herself, gulping air, willing the police to arrive. Why hadn't she insisted? Would they come here anyway, alerted by her panic? Would they look up the address and read the notes? She looked out at the iron grey sky, at the cars lined up below, military style. How could this be happening? She darted across the room, picked up the phone and saw the cord to the phone had been pulled from its socket

'Had to do something while I waited for you to get here, didn't I, fuckwit?'

Jo watched as the woman sucked on her cigarette, clicking the lighter on, then off. The rain was starting up again, tapping on the skylight. 'What are you going to do?' Her voice sounded assertive, she made sure of that – didn't want the woman to see how terrified she was.

'What am I going to do, she asks?' She cocked her head again as if she was talking to someone else in the room. Every word was pronounced with derision. 'What do you think?' The flame on her lighter rose higher and Jo instinctively backed away.

'Look,' Jo said in a reasonable voice. 'We can walk out of here together –'

'Fucking walk out of here together, d'you hear that –'

'Can you please stop yelling –'

'Don't interrupt me, bitch.'

'Please.'

'Shut the fuck up,' she snarled while she sucked and blew on her cigarette. 'Mark and me are an item. We're going away together when I've finished with you. Got frigging bored with you. You and your pathetic leg. "Oh wait for me," she mimicked. Sex with him is great.'

'How do you know Mark?' She was shivering. What was the woman talking about?

'He picked me up, you stupid fucking cow. Dying for it, he was.'

Jo was at the window, hammering on the glass. 'Help,' she screamed. She watched a couple of fell walkers pass below the window, their rucksacks bulging with provisions. They didn't react to her screaming. How could they possibly hear her from up there? Why had she trusted Mark? How much did she know him? 'What do you want?' Her voice was shaky. Stay solid, she told herself. Don't let her get you.

'You gonna pay.' She aimed the flame at Jo.

'No.' Jo crouched, gathering strength, breathing deeply. Self-defence for women. Taught in a gymnasium. Women pretending to wrestle each other, using their bodies as missiles, shouting war cries to frighten off their opponents, glad of the afternoon off work, thinking they'd never have to use it, that nothing would ever happen to them, gathering round the coffee maker at break time chatting – no, they'd never remember what they'd been taught. And why would they need it? Violence at work was such a rare event –

She took a deep breath, picked the phone up and aimed it at Raquel's head. 'WAAAAAAAAA.' She hurled herself at her assailant and snatched the lighter from her grip. 'NOOOOOOO.' She grabbed her under the chin, smelling her bad breath again, wanting to gag, forced Raquel's chin up and kneed her in the groin, punched her hard in the chest, smelling her own singed hair. Her strength was astonishing, her injured leg forgotten. She grasped Raquel's wrist, twisted it and heard her howl, told herself to get out. For a minute she couldn't shift herself, was frightened of what she'd just done. Raquel was recovering, slowly standing, glowering at Jo. There wouldn't be another chance; she got down the stairs in record speed. She opened the front door, leapt down the steps onto the pavement, got into her car, put her key into the ignition, locked the doors. Her heart was beating double time and prickles of sweat ran down her face. Raquel was at the bottom of the steps, then at Jo's car door, shouting, her contorted face at the window, hammering on the glass, trying the door. 'Fucking bitch.'

She fumbled with her key, couldn't get it in the ignition. Then – at last. Foot hard on the accelerator, Jo drove off while her heart thumped and sweat poured down her face. She veered round the park. Raquel was behind her. Where the hell had she parked her car? Why hadn't Jo seen it before? She drove faster. Had to call the police, call Mark, speak to Rob. She took deep breaths. Turned left, then right, through puddles, with trees and little houses whizzing by, the whole time knowing that Raquel was close behind. She drove past the church and graveyard, sheep happily nibbling the grass, saw a man walking, a bouquet of blue and yellow flowers in his arms. Then up ahead there was an elderly woman bundled in a maroon coat on a zebra crossing; she took her time, waving at Jo to thank her for stopping, while behind her, Raquel revved her engine, until Jo started off again pushing her car to its limit, watching the black car in her rear view mirror getting closer and closer. A truck was parked a little way ahead. She propelled her car past it, then sped past a skip and a house standing on its own with scaffolding erected round it like a cage until she felt the car behind shunt into the back of hers, straining her neck. She glanced in the rear view mirror. There was another shunt. The wheel slipped from her hands. She was losing control of her car.

It swung into the verge.

No. *No.*

Using all her strength she got her car back onto the road and keeping her foot hard down on the accelerator drove down the isolated road. At the end of the houses was a row of shops, newsagent, post office, a hairdressers. She saw traffic lights ahead. Amber . Felt the engine rebel, lurching like a wild horse as she worked it harder. There in front were the traffic lights, now red, but she had to get across. A bus was coming the other way. She bit her lip hard and went straight over the lights, the bus's horn blaring, its brakes grinding as she made it to the other side of the crossroads. She took a quick look in the rear view mirror. No Raquel. It was tempting to slow down. But she mustn't, though she breathed more easily, turning into a country lane, driving past the hedgerows and more grazing sheep, the lake she and Mark had passed before, taking another look behind her. Tyres screeching she turned right down a lane. Surely she'd lose her now. In the distance she saw Raquel there again. *No.* Then she was driving faster and faster, forcing the gap between her and Raquel to get bigger. She was looking for a large white house on the right, a dentist she'd once visited. Ancient stone walls swept by, mountains rising in the distance and she started to moan. Was this the wrong lane? There was a bend coming up. Then it was there on the right, the long stone wall she remembered and just ahead the dentist's house. A lorry was coming up on the other side of the road. If she put her foot down, she'd just make it. Without indicating, Jo swung in front of the lorry into the gravel drive of the large white house skidding into a corner of the garden under a spreading oak tree, hidden by its branches, and stopped parallel to the road while the lorry's horn blared and she watched and waited for the black car, hoping, praying, that Raquel hadn't seen her swerve into the drive. The engine ticked over and heat seeped through the vents. Through intertwining branches she saw Raquel's car speed past. Was she safe for the moment? There was her mobile on the floor. She reached across, picked it up, saw three missed calls from Rob, one from her mother. From the direction she'd been heading somewhere further along the road there was the sound of metal crashing into metal, an enormous bang and a car horn blasting incessantly. Jo felt her body tingle and freeze. She would stay here a little while and wait till the coast was truly clear, wait till she'd calmed herself. She opened the car door. On the edge of the fresh country air, was the smell of burning rubber.

She was still shaking when Rob called again.

'Why don't you answer your phone?'

'I think she's dead – she was in the house – got out – she was going to kill me – I was so frightened – she was this girl at school – it was *her* – she said – oh God.'

'You're garbling, Jo. Slow down. Breathe.' He waited a second. 'Where are you?'

'In the dentist's drive.'

'Which dentist? Why are you in a dentist's drive?'

'Is it all my fault, Rob?'

'No. Listen to me. Are you listening Jo?'

She said nothing.

'I got the file here. She's got a lot of aliases. But her real name is Raquel Bannister. She's dangerous –'

'Yeah, I found that out. She's crazy.'

'I'll come and get you.'

'I'm going to find out what's happened. There was a crash up ahead. It – it might have been her.'

'Jo. This is insane. Listen to me.'

'I'm fine. I have to know. I'll call you in a bit.'

She ended the call, remembering the pure hatred on Raquel's face. The memory still frightened her. How could you sustain a hatred for so many years?

She phoned her mother and told her everything.

'My poor darling. I'm so sorry. Why didn't I believe you? I've been such a terrible mother. My little girl.'

The stench of burning rubber and petrol still hung in the air. She eventually emerged, the innocent bystander leaving the drive of the large white house. At the end of the road the police were there and the road was partially closed. The ambulance and fire engine she'd seen go by before were gone. The smashed and burnt car was still there. She knew it was Raquel's and the certain knowledge made her feel ill. Though she slowed to take a proper look, not wanting to arouse suspicion from the police she didn't hang around too long. But she saw that the passenger side was almost untouched, while the driver's side was a wreck. A shiver passed through her as she drove by the scene. So Raquel was dead. What did that make her? Was she responsible?

26

Raquel had been sedated. There were lesions on the only section of her nose that was visible and they each glistened with pus. The blue stud had been removed. Without it, she looked odd, as if her entire personality had been that stud. Her eyelashes and eyebrows were charred and blistered; her mouth was distorted, swollen. One eye was closed, the other stared unseeing at Jo. Apart from her chest rising and falling, she could have been dead.

After Jo had seen the wreck she'd driven home, knocked back a large brandy, and packed a small case. Enough for a couple of nights. She would come back later for more, when she could face returning to the blood coloured room. She couldn't have been more than twenty minutes. Couldn't wait to leave. She was about to phone Rob again. Mark got in first. He told her Raquel was in Critical Care suffering from severe burns. After she'd told him everything that had happened that afternoon, she threw up. She vomited until her throat was dry and sore.

There was a tube in Raquel's mouth and another coming out from under the foil that covered her torso. There were intravenous lines and monitors beeping and her limbs were encased in plastic. The foil sheet across her body rose and fell rhythmically, in time to the bleeps and clicks of the machines. Jo studied the face. It was grotesque. Was that eye watching her, was Raquel still scheming? She moved in closer. The face was still. No movement; her heart kept going by machines. Her every vital organ measured for change. How had it come to this? Did it all start with Jo 'grassing her up' about thieving? Or was it later when she was refused assistance? Why hadn't she been a more competent manager?

One nurse was gazing at a monitor. The other had her back turned and was on the phone. Jo wanted to hate this woman, but now Raquel was lying there, helpless, she felt hatred – yes, but mixed with a measure of guilt. The door opened and there was Mark.

'What are you doing?' he whispered.

'Why do you think I'm here?' She frowned at him, not wanting to say more with the nurses there. Then the nurse who had been looking at the monitor left.

'How did you get in?' He was watching the other nurse who was still on the phone.

'Easy. I followed a visitor,' she said softly, turning to look at Mark full-on.

'You shouldn't be in here. They're strict about that sort of thing.'

'So what are you doing here, then? You don't work in Critical Care.'

He went to the door. 'Come and have a coffee.'

'Why would I have a coffee with you?'

'Come on. We can't argue here.'

She'd been in the hospital cafeteria once before. It was a long way from Critical Care, and she was barely aware of her surroundings even when she had to stop and keep close to a wall to allow more space for two porters hurrying past them. Neither of them said anything to each other as they traipsed along the lino clad floors. It was as if they were strangers.

The café was empty. They sat near the window with a view over the city. Mountains rose on the distant horizon. The two women behind the counter giggled uncontrollably at a private joke.

'Will she live?' Jo asked.

'Who knows? Why do you care?'

'Bored with me, she said you were –'

'What are you talking about?' He leaned nearer to her.

'What's the point in denying it, Mark? She said she picked you up. Or was it you picked her up? I can't quite remember.'

He was toying with a toothpick, rolling it between finger and thumb. 'She told me her name was Jessie. I'm sorry Jo. I am really sorry. When I realised it was she who was harassing you, I told her it was over. I told her to stop.'

'Is that all you're going to say?'

'No, of course not. Listen to me –'

'She chased me in her car. I thought I was going to die. She was going to burn the house down with me in it.' She stopped, realising the truth of it.

A black guy wearing a smart suit and buttercup yellow tie sat at a table nearby and sausage roll smells drifted across. Jo showed Mark her mobile phone. 'Five calls you made to me. When you knew how freaked out I was about what's been happening. Then you get a receptionist to call me instead of you going. I am struggling to understand what you did. She wanted to kill me. Why did you leave it to me to deal with?'

He ran his fingers through his hair; those long dexterous fingers she used to love so much. 'She said she was Helen, our neighbour. A burst pipe. I was in such a hurry – why would I think it was Raquel? God knows how she got our neighbour's name.'

'Then why didn't you go home and find out what was happening? Why the hell did you leave it to me? The whole time you'd been messing around with this woman.'

'I tried to stop her. She's nothing to me.'

'Bit late for emotional confessions.'

'You have to believe me.'

'Do I?' She tugged at her singed lock of hair and examined it. 'How can I possibly stay with you?' Roughly, she tucked her hair behind her ears. 'First you cheat on me. Then you do nothing when Raquel, or Jessie or whoever she is tries to kill me. Your –'

'The drive from here takes an hour. I would have been too late by then, love, wouldn't I?'

'You've not been listening to anything I've said and don't call me love. I'm not your love.' She stared through the window at the traffic going silently round the roundabout below. 'I'm leaving you. We're finished.'

Mark gripped Jo's hand. 'No. Let me explain.'

'Don't.' she said, pulling her hand from under his.

He swallowed and she noticed how tired he looked. No matter. Not her fault that his father had just died. He'd lied to her.

'I'll get some more coffee.'

'I want to know everything.'

He breathed deeply as if he carried a great weight. This only served to irritate her more.

While the table took up his full attention, she waited. 'It was when you lost your job. You changed. You weren't –'

'So it was my fault –'

'Can you listen?'

For a minute the nurses behind their table stopped chattering.

'I didn't know who she was. I didn't recognise her, you know, she looked completely different. I didn't realise she was the same woman who'd told your mother about that bloody spa holiday. Then Christ I couldn't believe it – it was uncanny – you wanted to go where Jessie had been, then she told me she'd be there too. Wouldn't it be nice, the three of us – then my father got sick.'

'How long were you fucking her – this Jessie?'

With his forefinger he crushed one of the biscuits.

'Jesus, Mark.' She glared at him.

'I tried to stop her bothering you. She agreed to. Look you have to believe me I told her repeatedly –'

'Ahh, did you? That was generous of you. Where did you first meet her?'

'Does it matter?'

'A pub.'

'Which pub?'

'The Horse and Groom. Where all the staff here go.' He pointed back down the street outside with his thumb, eyes still downcast. 'I need another coffee. Please Jo.'

'How long? You still haven't said.'

'Don't you think I wish I'd never met her?'

'Poor you.'

'Do you want a coffee?'

'Yeah. Black.'

Her body had begun to shake again. She called Rob.

'She's in hospital. Critical Care,' she said.

'Fuck.'

'I've just seen her. Tubes everywhere. She's badly burned.'

'What about you?'

'Yeah, well, you know. Could be better.'

'I read more of the file. She was abused by her father. She changed her name from Jessica Atherton to Raquel Bannister when she came out of prison. Changed her looks too.' His voice trailed. 'Had surgery. That's what it says. She'd set fire to her father's house. Mother dead. Social services involved etcetera.'

Jo took a sharp intake of breath.

'There's only a short summary about that. But I read the parents were wealthy. Kept horses or something. She was sectioned after another arson attack.'

'I remember her from school. She was –' There was the emotion again, the remorse, the feeling that the whole episode was her fault. 'She looks so different. Christ.'

'What happened?'

'I'll tell you tomorrow. It's too much to explain on the phone.'

'I'm really sorry I didn't get the right file. If I had –'

'Doesn't matter now.'

'You still coming round for that curry tomorrow then?' he said.

'Actually I can't think of anything better I'd rather do. Tomorrow, right? I'll have got myself more together by then.'

Mark put a coffee in front of her. Folding his long body, he sat in the seat opposite. 'Who were you talking to?'

'Rob.'

'Rob?'

'Yes, that's right, Rob.'

'You been seeing him then?'

'Not in the same way you've been seeing Raquel.'

He was blinking rapidly. 'Suppose I deserved that.' He put two sugars into his coffee, stirred it, looked back at Jo.

'It was her outside our house when you made out I was imagining things. It was *her* in that car, wasn't it? After we'd been to Morecambe Bay. You went and talked to her. What did you say?'

He put his hand to his forehead. 'I told her to leave us alone.'

'Did you give her money?'

'I felt sorry for her. She of said she needed a deposit for a flat.'

'Looks like she got a lot of money out of us. One way or another.' She laughed wryly.

He wouldn't look at her. Instead he spooned out the remainder of his coffee from the inside of his cup. 'She's known to us as well – not me, to the psychiatric services –' he said. 'I found out when she was admitted today. She's got a personality disorder. She uses different aliases. God, I should have known. It appears she'd stopped taking her medication. They'd had no contact for several months. Something must have set her off. No one thought to go and check her records when she was in the ward, you know, in the bed next to your mother,' he hesitated, glancing out of the window. 'I am so sorry. I didn't know, I thought she'd get tired of harassing us. I completely misjudged her, there was so much –' He failed to finish the sentence but watched the progress of the nurses shunting the chairs about. Then they'd gone, and the canteen returned to its hushed tone, an elderly couple in the corner, the woman wiping her eyes. 'I never thought she was capable of threatening you like she did. I'm so sorry, Jo.'

'So you said.' she said. 'Incidentally, she wasn't harassing *us*. It was *me* she was after.' She drank some coffee. No point in telling him what else she knew about the woman. Let him wallow.

She and Mark faced each other across their table strewn with cellophane, crumbs, spilt coffee and watched the cafeteria workers collect stuff from tables.

'I could have been killed.' She paused. 'Did you give her a key to our house? Is that how she got in?'

He put his head in his hands. 'She took a key and copied it. I was furious when I found out.'

'Idiot.'

'How can I get you to forgive me?'

'You can't.'

Another male nurse was making his way across the canteen towards them. 'Excuse me,' he said. He glanced at Jo. She'd only met one other colleague before, a Registrar who used to play the guitar. Looking at Mark, he said, 'I think you should come.'

'Can't it wait?' she said.

'It would be better if you came now,' the other nurse said directly to Mark.

'I'll be back shortly,' Mark said.

She watched them thread their way through the tables and chairs, Mark's long lean legs striding to the door. He turned at the doorway, as if to take one final look at Jo.

Hands shaking, she drank her coffee. Outside the hospital the stream of traffic looked unreal, quietly making its way through the city. The only sound was the wail of sirens. She thought of Rob. Why had she always denied her feelings for him? It was strange how meeting Raquel had led her to realise this.

She watched a lorry being unloaded by two men in orange jackets. Fatigue was turning her brain. Everything had a fuzzy look to it, as if she were watching one of her dreams being acted out. A cafeteria worker with a clear jolly face and pert blonde curls beneath a white frilly cap appeared with a damp cloth and proceeded to gather the biscuit crumbs and wrappers into one cupped hand before wiping the table clean.

Jo got herself another coffee. Mark had been gone a while, fifteen minutes at least. She stood and gazed out of the window before wandering across the cafeteria to the door and up the corridor. A cleaner was polishing the lino, pushing the machine with a faraway look on his face. She had no idea how to get to Critical Care; she'd followed Mark in a daze up corridors, down several flights of stairs and through a long, packed waiting room when he'd led her here. She asked the cleaner but he didn't understand, and in any case Mark hadn't said he was going there. The corridor had yellow and green abstract pictures on the walls and the lino was grey and shiny from hurrying feet and constant washing. It was time to get back to the cafeteria. She sat back down at the table, thinking back to how it all started. What was it Amy had said? Senaka owed her an explanation. Why had he made out it wasn't Raquel she saw all those times?

It didn't take long to find The Green Spa Hotel's website on her phone and two minutes later she was listening to the ringing tone.

'Can I speak to Senaka?' she asked as soon as the phone was answered.

'Who is it?''

'It's Jolene Carr. I was —'

'Ah, Miss Carr. Do you return here?'

'Sorry. That's not why I phoned. I would like to speak to Senaka.'

'He working.'

'Oh, OK. Forget it.' She heard voices, a heated discussion in Singhalese. Then:

'Good morning, ma'am. This is Senaka. I am sorry for you waiting. How can I be of assistance?'

'No need to apologise.' She took a breath, remembering the vivid scar on his arm. Was she wasting his time? She had to get straight to the point. 'There's something I have to tell you. Raquel is seriously injured, in hospital. She might not survive.'

'Oh, this is sad news. I pray for her.'

'You know she was in the airport in Colombo? I saw her. This time it was definitely her.'

'Ma'am?'

'So even if she'd checked out of the Green Spa Hotel, she was still in the country. Do you know more about that?'

'Ma'am. Jo, I am good Buddhist.'

'Yes, but –'

'So I say you the truth. I pray every day. I pray for you.'

She held the phone closer to her ear, so as not to miss a word. 'The truth?'

'She pay me to stay in my house. She say me it is a secret, like the children make. She make a joke out of it. She say no one must know. I am poor. I owe money because I borrow for my son's education. I have only him. The others in my family are taken by the tsunami.'

The canteen seemed to be shrinking, the colours brighter. She sat upright on her chair.

'How much money did she pay you?'

'Two hundred pounds, English money. I am sorry ma'am. I say you because I cannot lie any longer –'

'Did she give you my passport?'

'No. You tell the police? I go to jail for long time. Prison very bad here. My son –'

'I won't tell the police.'

She heard him sigh. 'You are good person.'

'No. I'm not actually.' She was remembering his shabby house. Of course he would have taken money from a tourist if it was offered for doing little. Wouldn't she have done the same in his position?

She finished the call and texted Amy. Still no sign of Mark.

286

She waited some more. Should she go? She'd said all she needed. The canteen was filling up again. Now there was a pleasant aroma of melted cheese and she realised how hungry she was. There was nothing to read, nothing to do. By now he'd been gone forty minutes and her coffee was cold.

Her phone bleeped: *That's fine. It would be great to have you here. I've made a bed up. We'll have a drink later, Amy xx.*

Then she saw him at the door, his face ashen and tired-looking. He was winding his way past the chairs and tables, saying 'excuse me, sorry' to the nurses and visitors engrossed in conversation.

'You've been a long time,' she said.

He sat opposite her and starting folding another serviette in half then quarters, then again. 'She won't be troubling us anymore.'

'What are you talking about? ' she said.

He paused, swallowing rapidly. 'Raquel. She's gone.'

'Raquel's dead?' She felt a rush of panic.

'I thought you'd be pleased,' he said. 'I did it for you.'

She watched him He was still fiddling with the serviette while he stared out of the window. Christ. What had he done? All the time she'd been terrified of Raquel, she'd been sharing a house with a murderer.

'Why?' Her breathing was rapid. 'Why?' she said again. Had he killed his father, his wife too? She felt very cold.

'She wouldn't listen. I kept on telling her to leave us alone,' Mark said.

Goosebumps travelled the length of her body. 'Is this what you do, then? Finish people off? What sort of person are you?' She began to gather her belongings together.

He went to put his hand on hers. 'We all have to die sometime.'

'Don't touch me,' she said, putting her coat on, throwing her bag onto one shoulder.

The walk to the cafeteria door seemed to take forever.

Her mind flitted around remembering the sound of the crash, metal against metal, then the explosion, then the figure wrapped in foil, her face unrecognisable and to the beach where Raquel had taken her on the first day of her holiday, Jessica Atherton on the edge of the playground and then to Senaka fishing out leaves from the swimming pool while the scar on his arm shone pale in the sun.

Mark had *killed* Raquel.

She waited for the lift, then walked to her car. It was raining again. The mountains beyond were invisible under the blanket of cloud and the wail of a siren was growing ever closer. She sat in the driver's seat and looked out at the puddles forming on the tarmac, at the drops of rain, expanding, growing, as the downpour increased.

She shuddered and drove out of the hospital grounds.

Acknowledgements

I would like to thank the numerous people that have read various drafts of this novel of which there are many but especially Louise Hume who commented tirelessly on various stages of this novel. Also my husband Dave for his incredible patience and support. I would also like to thank Alan Hamilton, Norma Murray and Laura Wilkinson for reading early drafts and my sister Marilyn Sington for her editing.

In addition thank you to Sussex Police for providing me with crucial advice on stalking as an offence.

And last but not least, a thank you to all my friends and family who have allowed me to talk endlessly about the progress of this novel while it was in the making.

About the author

Amanda Sington-Williams grew up in Liverpool and has lived and travelled overseas extensively. She has an MA in Creative Writing and Authorship from Sussex University. Many of her short stories have been published and some of her poetry has been read out on the radio. She lives in Brighton with her artist husband David Williams.

www.amandasingtonwilliams.co.uk

More from the author.

The Eloquence of Desire

Published by Sparkling Books in 2010

ISBN: 978-1-907230-16-5
ISBN: 978-1-907230-11-0

Set in the 1950s, The Eloquence of Desire explores the conflicts in family relationships caused by obsessive love, the lost innocence of childhood and the terror of the Communist insurgency in Malaya. Richly descriptive, the story told by Amanda Sington-Williams unfolds as George is posted to the tropics in punishment for an affair with the daughter of his boss. His wife, Dorothy, constrained by social norms, begrudgingly accompanies him while their twelve year old daughter Susan is packed off to boarding school. Desire and fantasy mix with furtive visits, lies and despair to turn the family inside out with Dorothy becoming a recluse, George taking a new lover, and Susan punishing herself through self-harm. The Eloquence of Desire is written in Sington-Williams' haunting and rhythmical prose.